CW01669382

The Gibraltar Protocol

A Daniel Warren Thriller

by Pedro Avery

The past is a weapon. The future is the target.

ACKNOWLEDGEMENTS

First and foremost, to Sophie, without your unwavering support and patience during the countless hours I spent hunched over my laptop, chasing Daniel through his digital maze, this book would never have existed. Not to mention your tolerance for my writing on that sun lounger in Torreguadiaro.

My deepest gratitude to Rhiannon D'Avenc, my collaborator, who helped me finish and edit this book. Your kind words and support have been amazing, and this wouldn't have happened without our chance meeting.

Thank you to KM and Barney Dalton, who ensured the cybersecurity elements felt authentic, and to Hannah Saunders, who provided invaluable insights into continuity and story flow.

I'm also grateful to David Cadman for your 'just do it' approach, to Richard Cook for being so brutal with your feedback when it was needed, and to Jonathan Durden for also pushing me forward.

Finally, to every reader who takes this journey with Daniel through the shadows of the digital world - thank you for diving into his story.

Any errors that remain are entirely my own.

Copyright © 2025 Pedro Avery

All rights reserved. No part of this book may be reproduced, stored in a retrieval system, or transmitted in any form or by any means—electronic, mechanical, photocopying, recording, or otherwise—without the prior written permission of the publisher, except in the case of brief quotations used in reviews or critical articles.

This is a work of fiction. Names, characters, places, and incidents are the product of the author's imagination or are used fictitiously. Any resemblance to actual events, locales, or persons, living or dead, is purely coincidental.

First edition

ISBN: 978-1-0682888-3-8

Cover design by Richard Cook (Richard Cook Design)

Printed in the United Kingdom

Dedication

For Felix, Izzy, and Max, you are the greatest story I'll ever be part of.

This book is dedicated to the three of you. I want you to know that your dad has always believed in the power of trying, in the courage of taking risks, being curious and in the strength of showing up—especially when it's hard.

If you can imagine it, you can do it. That's not just a phrase, it's a way to live. With effort, belief, and a refusal to settle, anything is possible.

I hope this book reminds you to dream fiercely, act boldly, and never stop pushing yourselves.

Because the world doesn't need more perfect people. It needs people who *try*.

Love, always.

Dad

CAST OF CHARACTERS

BRITISH INTELLIGENCE & GOVERNMENT

Daniel Warren - Foreign Office operative, Sir Rory's protégé
Sir Rory Brown - Permanent Secretary, Foreign, Commonwealth & Development Office
Sir Bob White - Head of MI6
Nikita Cowling - Cybersecurity expert, seconded from National Crime Agency to Bank of England
Peter Nichols - Executive Director for Risk, Bank of England
Barney Dodd - Executive Director for Markets, Bank of England
Bernie - Sir Rory's longtime personal assistant
Hawthorne - MI6 lead investigator
Matt - Retired Naval officer, extraction specialist

TEAM LIQUID TUNDRA (GAMING TEAM)

Tonka - Support player
AranaNegra - Team leader, Midlaner
Luna - Support player, based in Tulum
Underlord - Carry player, Ukrainian hacker
Phantom (Viktor Ivanov) - Offlaner, Russian hacker

SPIDER'S NETWORK

Alberto Lopez - Founder of Cryptropolis, master hacker
Sofia Ortega - Venezuelan socialite, Spider's former partner
Rafael - Double agent, former SEBIN, turned by Spider
Xaliima - Alberto's assistant at Cryptropolis

MEXICAN CONTACTS

Maria (Luna) - Hacker and gamer, Eva's girlfriend
Eva - Daughter of Mexican telecommunications mogul, CIA informant
Jezer - CIA handler operating in Mexico

OTHER KEY FIGURES

Marisol Díaz - Gallery owner in Caracas, intelligence contact
Emilio Sanchez - Mexican cartel leader
Yolanda - Spanish police officer who arrested and then helped Yash
Paco and Nuria - Yash's foster parents in Bilbao
Hassan - Yash's deceased younger brother
Rusanganwa - Rwandan boy who befriended Yash during migration
Uncle Beson - Yash and Hassan's uncle in Somalia

Prologue:

Manipulating the Shadows

Spider had waited a long time for this.

He watched his screens with calculated glee, steepling his fingers to support his head as he took in information from all of the channels at once. It was enough to sit back and observe the glow of the moving pictures and strings of text lighting his face from one moment to the next, flicking through colour and shadow.

It had been a lifetime of putting the pieces into play, moving them across the board, always learning and plotting. Plans and schemes that had failed, put him back, left him at square one. All the while, improving, strategising, and never making the same mistake twice.

All of those moves had brought him here, to this moment, to this time.

The perfect time.

Reporters on the news channels spoke over one another, their voices overlapping in a cacophony that tested the limits of his comprehension – though never exceeded it.

" – the strong sense here in the US that this latest deal between China and Brazil signals the end for –"

" – analysts suggest that the dumping of USD reserves will continue to spiral, with more countries taking –"

" – queues stretching around the block here in New York –"

" – the Prime Minister's successful campaign relied on the promise of a collaboration with the US Treasury, a move which critics now say –"

" – remains to be seen whether the governments' proposed joint project can come quickly enough to help –"

Spider had waited a lifetime for this, and the universe had answered. This moment of catastrophe, of failure, of panic was everything he had ever hoped for.

The perfect moment for him to destroy the United States once and for all.

A smile played across his lips as he watched the urgent expressions of the newsreaders on the screens. Give them a few months, and they would see what real panic was.

The plan was a simple one, brutally so. He would let them build their project. He would watch them prepare it for launch to the world, thinking it was their saviour, never knowing until it was too late that it was to be their downfall. He would even let them use it for a while, until public confidence grew, until so much was invested that it would be impossible to recover.

Then, when he had the beating heart of the country in the palm of his hand, only then would he close his fist in the space of a heartbeat.

They would never see it coming until the lifeblood was crushed out of them.

Every last man, woman, and child. Every legislator who only legislated for their own gain. Every billionaire fat on the profits of an arms race or the exploitation of nations that could not fight back. Every politician who lived on lies, and would choke on the truth.

Even the United Kingdom – once oppressors, now boot-licking toadies to the US President, wholly in his thrall and just as complicit as he was – would feel Spider's wrath.

The time of their domination was over, and rightly so. These crumbling old empires were on their knees, and all it would take would be one swiftly-aimed kick to the head to have them on the floor. Generations of cultural genocide, of fatal meddling in international governance, of destroying a planet that could take no more: had they really thought they would get away with it forever?

Had they forgotten that the men and women whose backs were broken to make a foundation for their nation would have children who would grow strong to avenge them?

He smiled because all he had to do was bide his time. No one was coming to stop him. No one knew the terrible secret of what he had set into motion.

All of them would fall at the stroke of a button.

It would be Spider's finger to press it down.

PART ONE: WEB

Chapter 1.

An Unexpected Invitation

"Hurry up," the security guard said. "He's been hollering down the stairs for you."

Daniel cursed under his breath, adjusting his grip on the heavy wooden box as he rushed through the entrance to the Foreign, Commonwealth, and Development Office on King Charles Street. The heat of the summer was almost too much to bear, but he hadn't stopped to loosen any buttons or enjoy the shade, and now he was inside the air-conditioned building, he was glad of it. The edge of the crate bit into his fingers as he passed the rigorous security scanners, entered the regal Durbar Court, and rushed up the magnificent staircase designed by the superb British architect Mathew Digby Wyatt It was only the yowl of warning that prevented him from tripping over Palmerston, the Foreign Office cat.

Daniel finally came to a stop, panting for breath, outside the famed Locarno Suite – a place not for informal business, but to impress the most important guests with the colonial history that seeped from the very walls. He couldn't hear Sir Rory Brown calling for him now, but it was only a matter of time; he needed to get this expensive crate of port off his hands before the shout sounded again

– and preferably also before his arms gave way and he dropped the whole lot.

The doors to the suite cracked open, and Sir Rory's longtime personal assistant – Bernie – poked his greying head out. "Ah, Daniel, good man," he said. "Hand that over, will you?"

Daniel was only too happy to relinquish his burden. The box was weighty, and the unique white port it contained needed to be chilled before serving. Someone else, probably Bernie himself, could take care of that.

Unconstrained now, his arms felt empty; Daniel shook them in the air a couple of times to rid himself of the lingering feeling of the sharp edges of the crate. He'd emerged from Lancaster House with the chill of the wine cellar still clinging to his skin, a stark contrast to the warm summer evening outside, but he'd had no time to marvel over the sensation. From Green Park to King Charles Street, via the Horse Guards Parade and past the Clive of India memorial, the crate had weighted his every rushed step. The route, lined with monuments of a storied past, seemed fitting for the night's impending discussion—a conversation that could shape the future of nations.

"How is he?" Daniel asked, fearing he already knew the answer. He ran his hands back through his dark hair, hoping he'd avoided a sweaty appearance.

Bernie gave him a knowing look. "This will help," he said. The port was a rather particular choice: it was rumoured that Margaret Thatcher had been gifted twelve magnificent blue bottles of Kopke 1963 in 1985 by the then-Premier of Portugal, Mario Soares. The Iron Lady, as she was known, had turned them over to the state, who then kept them in the government's special wine cellar. Sir Rory had remembered its treasures and knew he would impress. Most ministers in the UK government didn't even know the cellar existed.

Tonight's meeting was no ordinary gathering, and it called for no ordinary beverage; it was a convergence of power and influence, underscored by the rare Kopke 1963 white port.

Daniel checked his watch; it was 5:10 pm, and soon it was time for the delegation from the US to arrive. "I'd better get going," he said, his heart jumping in his throat at the thought that he might still be late.

Bernie nodded sympathetically. "At least you had a chance to build some muscles and get some cardio in," he said.

Daniel laughed – it was a good joke. He enjoyed being Sir Rory's primary go-to person for administrative errands, and it certainly gave him more than enough opportunities to build his fitness levels. Only the week before, Sir Rory had insisted that Daniel bring up four bottles of Cheval Blanc 1990 for an impromptu dinner with Andrew Gilbert, the Governor of the Bank of England. It made Daniel feel a little special, and he knew it annoyed his colleagues, who struggled to catch Sir Rory's eye despite their best endeavours to bring Sir Rory the best of the best intel on everything. Sir Rory wasn't from Oxford, Cambridge, or the increasingly influential St Andrews. He wasn't impressed by their ilk.

But Daniel wasn't from any of those places either – and maybe it was this that truly annoyed his colleagues the most. Because Daniel had found his place here the hard way, worked his way up, and found every possible chance to interact with people like Sir Rory until he was noticed.

Daniel gave a short wave and turned to go, the doors shutting behind him – but he barely took two steps before he almost collided with the gorgeous Becky.

Becky had been Sir Rory's secretary for the past fourteen years, and her path crossed with Daniel's often. She was always immaculate, and always formidable. "Where have you been?" she demanded, without formality. "Sir Rory wants to see you immediately."

Daniel smiled ruefully, not wanting to waste the energy on explaining that he'd just carried a very heavy crate a very long way at an almost unsustainable speed. "Lead on," he said, simply, and followed Becky down the corridor.

Becky's long dark hair swayed behind her as her heels clicked smartly along the floors. She took Daniel efficiently and directly to the doors and, with a polite knock, walked straight into Sir Rory's office.

Tired and a little sweaty, Daniel entered to see Sir Rory and another impressive figure, Sir Bob White, the Head of MI6, waiting for him. Becky closed the doors behind him, leaving the three of them alone.

"Daniel, meet my good friend, Bob!" Sir Rory boomed, turning the instant the door opened. Sir Rory was a giant of a man and clearly a former rugby-playing second row from his earlier years at Cambridge. Daniel felt just how much of that strength the man had retained when a bear claw of a hand clapped his shoulder. "Bob, this is my young protégé, Daniel."

The statement sent a thrill through Daniel's veins: Sir Rory had never described him that way before.

"Good to meet you," Sir Bob said gamely, stepping closer to shake his hand. "He's the man for this, you say?"

Daniel's ears perked up, his eyes swivelling back to Sir Rory. The man for what?

"Absolutely," Sir Rory said, with full confidence. "Daniel's intelligent, a fast learner, resourceful, with a strong sense of justice, and a natural talent for blending in."

Daniel felt himself beginning to blush under the praise. Sir Bob was eyeing him appraisingly, but Sir Rory wasn't leaving him so much as a pause to get a word in edgeways.

"Is he known outside of these offices?" Sir Bob asked, narrowing his shrewd eyes.

"No," Sir Rory pronounced. "And he can be trusted fully. He's a natural Spanish speaker, and he's just come from completing a few projects for me in Venezuela. Isn't that right?"

"Oh, it was nothing," Daniel said humbly. "I was happy to help. Just had to negotiate with the Maduro government. We got their agreement to a letter of intent on energy cooperation."

Sir Rory snorted. "He says it as if the negotiations weren't like pulling teeth. He's done some fantastic work on the ground in Eritrea, Lebanon, and Sierra Leone, too. Displayed some excellent judgment on those. In short, Daniel's my man, Bob, and you can treat him as such."

Sir Bob placed a hand on Daniel's shoulder now. "Well, then it sounds like I could utilise you on this latest and most important project," he said. "Are you free to stay for the meeting with Lewis Everett at six?"

Daniel's entire focus was on trying to calm his racing heart and stop his hands from shaking. This was unprecedented, and he recognised what was happening as a massive step up in his role. Lewis Everett was the US Secretary of State, Sir Rory's counterpart on the other side of the ocean. Meeting him implied a lot of trust.

Negotiating with the leaders of developing nations or those who were seen as too difficult to bother with was one thing. Working with the US delegate was completely another. A flare of nervousness shot through him, but Daniel quelled it. There was hardly enough time to panic, which was a great thing. He needed to focus.

He started mentally racing through everything he knew about Everett, glad he hadn't neglected his knowledge of all the governments they might potentially interact with.

Daniel understood the importance of this upcoming meeting without knowing the details. There had been an air of anticipation all morning and extra chitter-chatter in the Red Lion Pub on Whitehall at lunchtime. Many secret meetings had occurred during the past twenty-four hours – an unusually high number. The PM had also been seen; he had used the back door to the Foreign Office, just across the road from Number Ten, to sneak in and also catch up with Sir Rory, though there was no sign of him now.

"I'd be happy to," Daniel said, managing not to let his voice quiver on the understatement. "But, ah…?"

He wanted to ask about what his role might be – surely his ability to speak Spanish wasn't important when dealing with the Americans? – but Sir Bob was already shaking his head. The hand on his shoulder squeezed tighter for an instant as Sir Bob pulled him in closer.

"Don't worry," he said. "Sir Rory will explain more about your specific role tomorrow – there's no time to get you fully briefed before Everett arrives. Come to Vauxhall Cross at 8 am. But remember to go via Thames House to gain your clearance and double-check your biometrics at 7 am, and make sure you take along your passport. The security team will be ready and waiting for you."

"Right," was all Daniel could manage, nodding his head to show that he had understood. He repeated the instructions in his mind, hoping he wouldn't forget any of the steps he needed to take.

"We've had to skip a bit of red tape to get you in tonight, you understand," Sir Rory said, raising an eyebrow as he leaned in towards Daniel, making sure he had his attention. "There'll be a bit of back-filling in the morning, but I trust you to prove I've made the right choice."

"Welcome to the team," Sir Bob said, reaching down to shake Daniel's hand again. Beside them, Sir Rory chuckled – the sound of a man watching his protégé reach his potential.

Daniel understood that now was the time for Sir Rory to make his moves; the Permanent Secretary to the Foreign and Commonwealth Office, a position he had now held for eight years, was nearing the end of his long and illustrious career in the civil service and was looking forward to his impending Lordship. After forty-five years of loyalty to his beloved country, he had earned the right to slip without fuss into the House of Lords.

The longest-serving civil servant in this privileged position since Thomas Sanderson in 1906, Sir Rory was right at the top of his game. Achieved in the most part by his diplomatic excellence, his brilliant and unfailing analytical mind, and his charming nature, he had been trusted by many Prime Ministers from both sides of the house to diffuse and correct many of their muck-ups in foreign policy or often just their use of wrong words at the wrong times.

Sir Rory fixed things.

Now, he was checking his watch, and Daniel saw from the slight furrow in his brow that it was time to move. "They should be arriving," he said, a quick nod to Sir Bob conveying the need to continue the next step of their pre-arranged routine.

Daniel trailed behind them, feeling almost nonplussed about how his day was going – from errand boy to a seat at the big table in less than an hour. And, it occurred to him, if it had all been set up for the morning already, then it must have been planned. All without him suspecting a thing.

The three of them made their way to the front of the Foreign Office. The evening sunlight bounced off the Gothic Revival-style building and left Sir Rory resplendent in its glow. He stepped to the curb as sirens sounded from out of sight, his back straight and his chin up, ready to greet Lewis Everett and his retinue.

It was only a moment before two blacked-out, no doubt armoured Chevy Suburbans pulled into the inner courtyard and up to the entrance to the Foreign Office. Their Met Police motorcycle outriders whistled past, blue lights flashing and sirens blasting. As Lewis Everett stepped out of the second car in a magnificent Saville Row suit, he was greeted with a bear hug and a slap on the back.

"Welcome, Lewis; always a pleasure to see you, my friend," Sir Rory said. "How is Bridget? Your children?"

"Fantastic," Lewis replied with an easy smile as if the crushing hug had not taken his breath away. His nasal Milwaukee accent sounded strange in this bastion of Britishness, but he appeared completely comfortable here. It was far from his first visit. "Costing me a lot of money in boarding schools and purses, as always. But it's not personal financials we're here to discuss."

"No, indeed," Sir Rory said, accepting the segue. "If you'll follow me, I have a suite awaiting us with a little welcome on ice."

"Lead on," Lewis agreed, and Daniel found himself once again trailing after two of the most important men in the country – plus, this time, one of the most important men from another.

And he still had no idea what this meeting was about – or how difficult and politically dangerous the task ahead of him might be.

Chapter 2.

Uncle Beson's Shadow

The old-fashioned end-of-lesson handbell rang out with its joyful sound, signalling the end of the day for the kids, and it allowed Yash and his younger brother Hassan to pack their books. They were, in fact, leaving the same classroom, despite the fact that Hassan was two years Yash's junior at eleven. The school simply didn't have the space for each class to have their own room.

"Have you got everything?" Yash asked, looking his brother over. Hassan was his charge while they were at school, as per their mother's decree.

Hassan made a show of glancing at his backpack, checking his pockets, and nodding eagerly. "I'm ready."

"Let's go, then." Yash led the way across the school lot to the bus stop, stopping just shy of holding his brother's hand – that would be too much.

"Can we play a game when we get back?" Hassan asked. "I don't have much homework."

Yash shook his head. "Sorry," he said. "It's Thursday, remember? I've got Athletics Club."

Hassan's head drooped. "Oh, yeah," he said. It had only been eight weeks since their mother had finally relented and allowed Yash to join, after much persuasion. Yash felt like they'd hit a good rhythm, even though Hassan still wasn't used to it.

Besides, tonight was a strange night, anyway – with their parents away in Mogadishu at a teaching conference until the weekend, they were staying with Uncle Beson.

"Go right inside when you get there," Yash instructed Hassan. He paused for a moment, thinking. "Especially if Uncle is chewing khat. Just go right on in and don't annoy him."

Khat was legal in Somalia, and nearly everyone Yash knew chewed it. But Yash felt the khat had given his uncle demons since the death of their aunt a few years earlier. Uncle Beson hadn't been the same since. He'd disappeared into his grief, become rough with his words and his hands. He drank often. He wasn't very nice to his sister's boys anymore.

Whenever they visited, Yash's parents would hold their heads close together and whisper on the way home, exchanging concerned glances that they hoped their boys wouldn't catch. Yash had seen them from the back seat and he knew that something wasn't right with Uncle Beson. They had expected him to get better – they'd even said it out loud at first – but the years had only seemed to make him angrier and less patient.

But Yash knew how important and exciting this trip was for their parents, so he didn't fuss when they were told about it. It was only two nights, after all. Then they would come home from the Airport Conference Centre and everything would be back to normal.

Hassan was still a little too young to always remember to be quiet and small around Uncle Beson. That was what Yash was worried about. Getting home late left him no opportunity to prevent his little brother from annoying their Uncle and pushing him into something bad – whatever that might be – but this meeting of the Club was too important to miss.

The bus was pulling up at the stop, and Yash gave Hassan a gentle push. "This is the one," he said. He waited until he saw his little brother seated happily a few rows back, then waved at him through the window and turned back towards Noradin Primary School with a flicker of unease that he forced himself to dismiss. He needed to focus on other things, now. He headed for the rear of the complex, where the school's dusty running track had been carved out of the orange sandy dirt.

Yash lined up alongside the other members of the Athletics Club, testing his shoes against the track and scanning the few scattered watchers for anyone unfamiliar. The nearby city of Hargeisa, where he hoped to join the British International College once he turned fourteen, was at high altitude, so it neither experienced very hot nor very cold weather. This meant the region produced superb athletes who competed globally in diamond league and Olympic events. It wasn't unusual to find a scout watching the runners, looking for talent.

Whether there was a scout or not, Yash liked to do his best. He concentrated on the track, on the goal that lay ahead of him. Eight hundred metres away sat the finish line, and he would be the first to cross it.

The air felt cool on his face as he surged forward with the others, ignoring their presence and focusing on his own race. Everything else fell away: Hassan, Uncle Beson, the homesickness of waiting for his parents to come back, the homework waiting for him, his grades. There was only the air on his face and the ground under his feet.

He crossed the line and his head whipped to the side, seeking out the timer. His heart pattered rapidly in his chest as he waited to hear the time.

Then he grinned: a personal best.

He might not have jumped up and shouted and whooped like some of the others did when they won or beat their best times, but he felt the joy in his chest all the same, expanding and filling him up until he was fit to burst. *Pride*. That was what it was. And it would be all the sweeter when he could share it with his parents in a few days. He knew they would be so pleased with him that they might offer him a special treat or cook his favourite meal.

The real reward, though, was simply achieving. Being better than he had been the day before. That was what his father had taught him to always strive for.

Yash's smile stayed on his face for the whole bus journey to his uncle's home, even though he hated going there. He was too excited about his results to tamp it down.

Yash found his brother hosing out the pipework and septic tank in the yard. Uncle Beson was watching from the porch with a glass of home-brewed sugar rum and clearly chewing khat. Yash's shoulders slumped a little at the sight of it, but he still rushed over to help Hassan finish up the pipework, worried that Hassan might injure himself or do it wrong.

"Did you get your homework done?" Yash asked as he took over with the hose.

"It's finished," Hassan replied, his eyes lighting up when he saw Yash. No doubt, Uncle Beson had decided that without homework to do, Hassan was idle and needed putting to work. Yash was glad he had missed the yelling, but sorry that he hadn't been here to take up the chores and let Hassan rest in the first place. "How was the race?"

"I won! A new personal best," Yash said, grinning from ear to ear. He kept his voice low, knowing how much Uncle Beson hated loud children, but he hopped on the spot a couple of times – the one outward expression of his excitement and happiness that he allowed himself.

"That's amazing! I knew you could do it," Hassan said, beaming with pride for his brother. It was maybe just a little too loud, and Yash tensed up in anticipation.

There was a cough and a grunt from the porch before Uncle Beson got up and lumbered inside. Yash's shoulders relaxed slightly, but only slightly. That was a sign that their Uncle was about to make food, having judged that the outside chores were done. Hassan and Yash exchanged a tense look and followed him inside.

Uncle Beson's house was a three-room property—unkempt and clearly needing a woman's touch. The house was small and cramped, a far cry from the comfort of their own home. But Yash and Hassan made the best of it, finding solace in each other's company. They slept in the living room together.

Deep down, Yash hated his uncle. He dreaded what supper they were going to have. But, for Hassan's sake, he tried not to let it show.

Dinner was a tense affair. Uncle Beson, in his usual state, was grumpy and irritable. The boys ate the tasteless food quickly, avoiding eye contact and trying to keep out of their uncle's way. Hassan lowered his voice to a whisper to ask if there was anything they could add to the food to make it taste better, but Yash shook his head, an urgent message in his eyes to stop asking.

"What are you two whispering about?" Uncle Beson barked, his breath reeking of rum and khat.

"Nothing, Uncle," Yash replied quickly, hoping to diffuse the situation. "Just school."

"Better be nothing," he grumbled, turning his attention back to his drink.

Later that night, as they lay on their makeshift beds in the living room, Yash and Hassan spoke quietly into the darkness, careful never to make enough noise to attract their uncle's attention from his bedroom. They would have preferred to study a little later, but Uncle Beson thought that it was a waste of electricity to illuminate their books. Instead, Yash had tucked his favourite – a tattered old tome about famous explorers that his mother had given him – under his arm for comfort. He loved to read about the expeditions, analysing those that succeeded and those that failed, admiring the qualities of the best leaders.

"One day, we'll leave this place," Yash whispered. "We'll go to the British International College, and then who knows? Maybe even travel the world."

"I'd like that," Hassan said, his voice filled with hope. "I want to see all the places we read about in our books."

"We will, Hassan. We just have to keep working hard and never give up," Yash promised, determined to make a better life for them both. "We'll get out of Somalia and go somewhere better." He knew it wouldn't be easy, but with Hassan by his side, he felt ready to face whatever came their way. Together, they would carve out a better life, one step at a time. One day, they would go to the airport, just like their parents – though not for any conference. They'd get on a plane and fly away, together.

As Yash's eyelids fluttered closed and sleep dragged him under, his mind's eye conjured a sleek grey plane taking off into the air, and his face at the window, behind Hassan's.

If only he could make that plane come sooner, before anything bad came to interrupt their lives, before one more night with Uncle Beson, before fighting could come to Somalia again.

Chapter 3.

The Gates of the West

Alberto Lopez pressed the Sky Parlor button and rode in his Otis lift to the top floor of Alees, the most exclusive building in Gibraltar – and the place that Alberto called home.

He was off for his morning swim. Tall and athletic, Alberto's body was toned by religiously swimming three kilometres every morning. His mind performed better after a dip, although he'd already completed the Financial Times' cryptic crossword before leaving his apartment.

Leaving the lift, he walked through the gardens, meticulously planted with one-hundred-year-old olive trees at great expense. Using his phone, he turned on the jet pumps for his endless pool and quickly looked out over the magnificent Rif Mountains of North Africa. It was another beautiful sunrise. Up high above him, a plane split the beautiful colours of the sky with a white trail, reminding him that other people in the world were also awake and moving on with their days.

With a quick stretch, he dove into his generous two-tier, edge-heated terraced swimming pool overlooking the Straits of Gibraltar. The powerful water jets guaranteed that Alberto always had a challenging workout.

His target time was fifty minutes. Over the last five years, he had managed to reduce his time by nearly an hour through meticulous diet control and dedication to refining his freestyle technique.

Although he would never consider himself at an elite standard, nor ever have any desire to compete, he knew he was in the top two per cent globally.

Alberto was meticulous and deliberate, a trait drilled into him by his mother.

He pursued his goals with a tunnel vision few could match. Whether it was swimming, identifying undervalued assets in financial markets, or consulting on projects for governments and multinational corporations of extremely delicate natures, Alberto approached everything with the same intensity and precision.

As he left the pool, he dressed in his robe and sat down to drink his morning juice, thoughtfully prepared and left out by his loyal assistant Xaliima during his swim. Gazing out over the Bāb al-Maghrib, the Gates of the West, he took a moment to appreciate the serene view before starting his business day.

"Good morning, Alberto," Xaliima greeted him with a warm smile as she brought in his breakfast.

"Good morning, Xaliima. Any updates from the team?" Alberto asked, sipping his juice. He was skilled at hiding his true thoughts even from those closest to him, but today he was expecting bad news. He wondered if it had come in, yet.

"Yes, there are a few things that need your attention. I have the reports ready for you," she replied, handing him a tablet.

Alberto glanced at the tablet, scrolling through the latest updates from his company, Cryptropolis Corporation. Founded by Alberto, Cryptropolis had grown into a powerhouse in the digital currency world, attracting some of the brightest minds in technology and finance.

Alberto's journey to creating Cryptropolis was driven by a vision of financial freedom and security. With a background in computer science and economics, he saw the potential of blockchain technology early on. He surrounded himself with a team of exceptional talent, including cryptographers, software engineers, and financial experts.

Their latest project was the biggest yet. He'd had a lot of success with building an experimental blockchain system for a few countries before, but nothing on this scale – the kind of scale that would put his and his company's name into the records of history forever.

"Let's go over the progress on the new security protocols," Alberto said, motioning for Xaliima to follow him to his study. Clearly, the news he was expecting hadn't yet broken, but that didn't mean he couldn't start getting ahead of it.

As they entered the sleek, high-tech room, the walls lit up with holographic displays of data and charts. Alberto sat at his custom-built desk, which integrated various biometric security measures. He reviewed them all at a glance, feeling satisfied with what he saw, and turned to Xaliima for the rest of what she clearly wanted to say.

"Today's agenda includes a review of our latest encryption algorithms and a strategy meeting for our upcoming partnership with the UK and US governments," Xaliima said, pulling up the relevant documents for him.

Alberto nodded, his sharp mind already analysing the information. "We need to ensure that our systems are impenetrable. The stakes are higher than ever with the Veritian project." And it would be good to have the data at hand ahead of the meeting since they would inevitably ask about it.

“Yes, sir,” Xaliima murmured in agreement, apparently with nothing more to add.

"What's the status of our recruitment efforts for Veritian?" Alberto asked, his fingers tapping rhythmically on the desk.

"We've onboarded several top-tier engineers and cryptographers. They're currently undergoing security clearances," Xaliima replied, her eyes scanning the data.

"Excellent. We need the best minds working on this. The integrity of Veritian is paramount," Alberto said, his voice steady and confident. “What about my killer four?”

“They’ve all agreed to meet,” Xaliima said with a slight smile. She knew Alberto preferred briefings to remain calm and unemotional, but she must have known how good he would feel about his plans coming together. The four were essential to the project’s success. Without them, he could likely pull it off; with them, it was guaranteed.

With the morning briefing done, Alberto shifted his focus to the day’s tasks. He had a packed schedule, including meetings with international partners, strategy sessions with his executive team, and a keynote speech at a virtual blockchain conference.

"Remember, we have the Crypto Summit X conference coming up this week. Our presence there is crucial," Xaliima reminded him.

“As if I could forget,” Alberto replied, with a gently admonishing smile.

Crypto Summit X was the largest gathering of cryptocurrency enthusiasts and experts, held annually in Cologne. Alberto was a revered figure at the event, his company having a special, invite-only stand in Hall Twelve. The congress attracted over forty thousand delegates, including former US presidents, famous athletes, and IMF leaders. Not to mention the fact that that was where he would meet and recruit his killer four. He wasn't likely to let it slip his mind.

But first, there was an even more important meeting to tackle – briefing his team for the latest project entrusted to him by the British government, which, in fact, had been triggered by a meeting at Crypto Summit X some years before.

"Alright," he nodded to Xaliima, going over the documents in front of him one last time. "Patch everyone in."

With a few taps of buttons on Xaliima's end, screens positioned across Alberto's desk lit up with the faces of the various team members working with him on the Veritian CDBC project.

"Good morning, everyone," he began, and without much preamble, launched into his planned speech. "As you know, what we say here, and what we work on for the duration of the project, is not to be taken outside of this circle."

There were nods on various screens. "Yes, sir," a few of the trusted engineers and mathematicians murmured.

"I was invited to recommend and recruit each one of you by British diplomats and employees from the Bank of England," he said, fixing the camera lens with a stern gaze that would make each of the video call participants feel he was talking directly to them. "Some of you accompanied us on our first trip to Westover Airfield in Maine a few years ago; others of you are just joining us now. As the project progresses, it becomes more complex and requires new specialists to assist us. The current phase we are working on is the integration of the new security protocols we've developed."

Everyone was nodding. Alberto took that as a sign that there were no questions so far, and plunged onwards.

"We must stay ahead of the curve. Our clients trust us to protect their assets, and we cannot afford any lapses," he emphasised. "This is not just a matter of completing a project to the satisfaction of our clients – but one that would have international repercussions on an unprecedented scale if we fail. This is not just about protecting the system from the current threats – but about anticipating the development of future threats and putting safety measures in place before they can emerge."

"*Future* threats?" one of the newer recruits piped up, frowning slightly. Alberto did not mind the interruption – he encouraged free conversation and collaboration within his teams, empowering his teams to innovate and ask questions as much as possible. "How can we do that?"

Alberto smiled slightly. "And with that, I segue to our expert in future threats," he said, giving the cue to one of his more senior executive team members. "Could you explain, for everyone's benefit?"

He sat back, muting his microphone as the conversation flowed on.

Xaliima stepped to his side, leaning down to whisper into his ear, even though the others couldn't hear her. "Don't forget, you have a call with the Prime Minister's office at noon," she reminded him.

"Thank you, Xaliima. Please prepare the briefing notes," Alberto replied, appreciating her efficiency. As always, he would be doing at least two things at once – if not more – to keep up with his daily responsibilities.

That was just how he liked it.

With his other free hand – the one that wasn't holding the pre-prepared briefing Xaliima had already handed him – he flipped open a secure laptop, hand-built himself with biometric checks that would only prevent access by any other person. Not only that, but it would also wipe all of the data from the machine and make it completely unusable if any other hand touched the pad or keys. Everything that would be discussed at this meeting was already known to him: he was the architect, the mastermind, behind everything his company did.

Time to have a little fun on the side.

Chapter 4.

Spider's Egg

Daniel could only listen, rapt, as Sir Rory and Lewis passed the walk up to the Locarno Suite in discussion of a topic on which both men were experts: fine wine.

"What do you think of this year's Chateaux Latours en primeurs?" Lewis asked, seeming to pay no attention at all to his surroundings – despite the weight of history all around them. Daniel glanced behind at the feeling of prickling on his neck to realize that five others from Lewis' entourage, none of whom he recognised, were following them.

"Wonderful," Sir Rory said, with a hand gesture that seemed to encompass all that needed to be said on the subject. "Have you tried the latest Screaming Eagle?"

"I managed to get a few bottles before the price hit eight thousand dollars," Lewis said with a sly smile. Daniel could never hold his own in this kind of conversation – spending eight thousand dollars on a bottle of wine was so far out of his grasp as to be laughable. While it was true that he was one of the few Sir Rory trusted to fetch one of the four thousand premium wine bottles from the government's cellar from time to time, he was hardly invited to *sample* them.

"On the matter of price, I really should thank you," Sir Rory was saying. "The Sugar Shack Chardonnay you showed me at our last meeting in Washington was not just an excellent wine, but an excellent investment. I hear it's selling at five hundred dollars a bottle, now."

"Thank Olivia, not me," Lewis replied modestly. Daniel dimly recalled that Olivia was the name of his eldest daughter, though he hadn't been invited on the trip and didn't know anything else about her. Was he really the best choice for this meeting? "Her husband turned out to be a good investment, too – his wines are becoming quite renowned."

Sir Rory chuckled. "How fulfilling, to find that one's progeny has developed excellent taste!"

"I'm sure you have prepared something wonderful for us, today," Lewis suggested, his eyebrows lifting hopefully. Daniel could make out both men's faces even though they walked ahead of him, as both turned frequently towards the other.

"Of course," Sir Rory said, though not yet giving the game away on what. He gestured almost demurely to the doors of the Locarno Suite that had appeared ahead of them. "Right this way."

On entering the Grand Locarno suite, Lewis and his entourage were confronted with a mural picture by the artist Sigismund Goetze, 'The Britannia Republica'.

"This is not only a magnificent work of art," Sir Rory said. "But also a significant piece within global history. The figures in the mural represent various colonies and territories. You can see them offering their wealth and culture to Britannia, who stands tall and resplendent in the centre. The painting, with its rich colours and intricate details, serves as a reminder of the legacy and responsibilities carried by those who walk these halls. I hope that we shall never forget it."

Daniel wondered if Sir Rory's point was to remind Lewis that *his* country had once been one of those colonies; if it was, Lewis seemed to take it in stride. Perhaps he'd visited Sir Rory enough times already to be immune to all the showboating.

Continuing, they found their way to a grouping of elegant chairs around a vast table – just enough empty for everyone who had taken the stairs up from the cars, even though the table could seat twenty. Someone had rushed ahead, Daniel knew, to set up precisely the right quantity of chairs and glasses. Several of the remaining places were already taken by Sir Rory's team, though they did not yet move into introductions.

"I hope you will all take some port," Sir Rory announced with a flourish and a sly grin in Lewis' direction. "This is Kopke 1963, a delicious white port with quite the political history."

"Port?" a young woman, one of Lewis' followers, exclaimed. She was checking her watch, no doubt taken aback by the early hour. Though the others hadn't spoken up, they appeared just as dubious.

Sir Rory chuckled, gesturing expansively as he held court at the front of the room. Beside him, Bernie was studiously pouring glass by glass, serving the port with tonic water and garnishing each serving with a slice of orange and mint.

"White Port is a type of fortified wine made in Portugal's Douro Valley," Sir Rory explained, with the air of a man lecturing a specialised wine course. "It is made from white grapes, typically Malvasia, Viosinho, and Gouveio, and is fortified with brandy to stop fermentation and add sweetness. You may not know that white port comes in two styles: dry and sweet. The dry white port is light and crisp, with citrus and floral notes, whereas the sweet white port is richer and more complex, with honey, caramel, and dried fruit flavours. Perhaps you can guess which this is."

Bernie passed out a few glasses, beginning with Lewis as a mark of respect, and the sips began almost immediately. A few exclamations of appreciation rang out. Daniel was the last to accept his own, a gift he took with surprise but with no desire to talk them out of letting him have it. On sipping it, Daniel noted how rich and jammy the drink was, with a smooth texture. It struck him that this was the first time he'd been invited to actually try one of the drinks he'd brought for Sir Rory. It struck him, next, that he'd better not try too much of it, in case that and the newfound responsibility went straight to his head.

"This is sweet white port," Lewis answered, gaining a grin from his counterpart.

"Of course, I should have known I couldn't fool you," Sir Rory laughed. "White port has been associated with the British gentry since the seventeenth century. It was then seen as a sophisticated and refined wine and was often served on formal occasions. Sadly, it is overlooked nowadays, but I always enjoy a glass at this time of the evening."

Daniel watched the others closely, noting how some of them – particularly the young woman – couldn't hold back from pulling a slight face with the extra alcohol punch. Drinking alcohol at work clearly wasn't something they were used to – and then to be drinking port was an acquired taste that each of them would remember. He could hardly claim to be any different. He felt like the new kid at school, watching his peers closely so that he could follow their lead.

Lewis, of course, appeared unaffected. "This is absolutely delicious!" he exclaimed effusively. "What a tipple – absolutely magnificent!"

"I'll send you a bottle," Sir Rory said, his chest puffed out with pride.

"Now," Lewis said delicately. "The matter at hand…?"

Sir Rory nodded, appearing grateful for the cue rather than affronted by the interruption. The pair had worked together enough times over the course of their careers to have an easy flow.

"Allow me to introduce my team," Sir Rory said, going around the table with an open-palmed hand gesturing to each of the attendees in turn. "We have Peter Nichols - Executive Director, Risk, who leads our Risk Directorate at the Bank Of England; Barney Dodd - Executive Director for Markets; and Nikita Cowling – previously a rising star in Digital Networks at the National Crime Agency and now seconded to the Bank of England. And then Daniel Warren – Operations Field Manager: Foreign Office."

Daniel knew some of their names and faces already, but he quickly endeavoured to memorize them all. Peter Nichols appeared to have enjoyed one too many large lunches, whereas Barney Dodd was a short and wiry man who looked a little weedy. Nikita, meanwhile, with her beautiful complexion and disarming nature, was one of the UK's leading junior economists. Daniel had heard of her before, and now he saw that she was not just intelligent but also deeply empathetic, a feeling he took from her eyes. They held a mixture of determination and warmth.

That left Daniel, and he couldn't help but wonder what they all thought of him.

There were still several others in the room that Sir Rory had not introduced; he paused while greetings were exchanged with the US team, then continued.

"This is Anthony, and beside him, John," he said. "I'm deliberately not giving their surnames or specific roles, as they are part of the UK security services. I'll hand over to Peter Nichols, now, to lead the session."

Sir Rory sank into a chair as Peter stood, nodding and adjusting the button on his suit jacket.

"Thank you, Sir Rory. Please, let me begin by reminding you all that this meeting is classified as top secret." He paused to glance at every face in the room as if needing assurance that they understood. Daniel knew this would have been pre-agreed with Lewis, and that any required paperwork would already have been signed, but it was important to double down on any reminders. "We have an almost insurmountable task ahead of us, and I'm afraid it is of the utmost importance that we complete it. We have news of a threat to one of our joint ventures that cannot be ignored."

Peter again looked around the room. The hush of gravity had settled over the assembled faces. Daniel almost felt he dared not breathe or move, in case he disturbed the atmosphere.

He had the sense that this was going to be a long meeting, and that if he was going to make the biometric test he needed to be present for at seven in the morning, he could be looking at an all-nighter.

"It's come to our attention that Project Maia is at risk of being compromised." Peter straightened up, clasping his hands in front of himself. "Our Mexican contact has explained that the notorious Spider, a globally well-known cyber hacker, may have somehow, in spite of all of our precautions, woven his way into the fabric of the code and blockchain structural system. In essence, our source tells us that Spider has created a back door to the digital currency. And despite our very best computer coding and security geeks and leading blockchain experts, this could allow him to destabilise it to its core. Nikita?"

Daniel's ears pricked up. Project Maia was the internal name they were using for the flagship launch of: the cross-border, joint initiative, central digital bank currency, or CDBC known as Veritian – but that was all he knew about it. He needed to find out more.

Nikita rose to take over the explanation, her voice clear and confident. "Our analysis has led to several lines of enquiry," she said, her eyes scanning the room. "And we genuinely don't know how or why a random Mexican knew about Project Maia. There is a limited insider list who knew about the details and specifics of the project – all on a need-to-know basis – and none of them were responsible for any leak or infiltration point, according to our exhaustive investigation. This information was beyond concerning. Our agent in Tulum didn't have any more information to share, including Spider's identity."

"Who is this 'Spider'?" Lewis interrupted.

Nikita took it in stride. "Spider is an anonymous, almost mythical figure in the digital ecosystem. Whoever they are, they're famed and regarded as a villain in equal measure. It's considered highly probable that Spider was behind the Equifax Data Breach in 2017, which netted him over a hundred million dollars in ransom money, the hacking of the Marriott international database to steal over five hundred million customer profiles and financial records, the Sony Pictures hack in 2014, the Department of Defense data breach in 2017, and the Federal Reserve Bank of Minneapolis in 2020.

"In every hacking case, all that could be discovered was that a tell-tale Spider's egg had been left behind. This digital egg was left as a line of code in the script – hence the name the hacker uses. Over the years, Spider has risen to a high position on the FBI, MI5, and Interpol most wanted lists."

Daniel was impressed by Nikita's ability to explain the issues compellingly. He warmed to her, appreciating her expertise and the clarity with which she communicated the threat, despite the fact that she was one of the younger faces in the room.

"Spider eggs?" Lewis asked, with a raised eyebrow. He glanced around as if to confirm he couldn't be the only one left behind. "I'm sorry, this is above my head. What does that mean?"

"The egg is really a metaphor for how the code works," Nikita told him. "If they're tampered with at all, these tiny pieces of code will splinter into hundreds or even thousands of tiny code strings. Those strings will spread chaos and infiltrate global digital wallets for our new currency and their own cloud-based data systems, quickly infiltrating other networks. Just like a cluster of spider eggs hatching and sending the babies scattering throughout a room. In short, this could be the largest-scale hack in the history of the human race, with the most sensitive possible data stolen from anyone using our digital currency – and all monetary value within the system vulnerable to deletion. It would decimate any trust that the public place in government-backed currencies, in both our nations."

As her words settled like so much falling ash onto the heads of those in the room, Daniel saw a flash of an image in his head, remembered from history class: wheelbarrows in the Weimar Republic, filled with a rapidly devaluing currency.

It was clear that the stakes could not be higher – and with the economy already teetering on the brink, Project Maia was supposed to be the solution.

Daniel leaned forward in his chair. Whatever Sir Rory planned to call on him to do to stop economic disaster… he would do it.

He had no other choice.

Chapter 5.

The Coding Prize

Yash logged in for his online tutoring session, settling into his chair with his eyes fixed on the screen. His father had managed to find him an online tutor from Cambridge in the UK, a luxury they could scarcely afford but believed in wholeheartedly. This tutor had opened Yash's eyes to a world of mathematical possibilities and the vast potential applications in computing and beyond.

Maths was Yash's strong suit, whereas languages were Hassan's. He would often spend up to two hours each evening buried in books and problems, his mind racing to solve the puzzles laid out before him.

With Dr Williams' help, Yash hoped he could go to either Stanford or MIT in the USA. His aim was to study computer science, as he knew from his research these were the best institutions in the world for this field. He also knew that the US universities gave amazing scholarships to the brightest kids from anywhere in the world—a distant dream.

Getting access to Dr Williams was the first step. Living near the airport meant they had access to a local satellite linkup, allowing for high-speed, low-latency internet. This connection was a lifeline, not only for their studies but also for playing online games, something he and Hassan did as often as possible and with gusto.

"Good afternoon, Yash," Dr Williams said with a smile, his patient face filling the screen.

Yash sat up straighter, beaming. He loved these challenging sessions and how they made him push himself harder and dream bigger. "Good afternoon, Dr Williams," he parroted.

"Before we get started, I wanted to talk to you about the coding competition you entered," Dr Williams said, pushing his glasses up his nose.

Yash's heart leapt. He'd applied to the competition thanks to Dr Williams' encouragement – his tutor had been the one to find it, see it was open to participants from all over the world, and recognise that it would fit Yash's skills. Of course, it had been Yash's father who encouraged him to try coding in the first place. One of his favourite sayings was that a man should "build tools, not walls" – and coding could build not only tools but bridges between nations, between peoples, and between lives.

"Are the results out?" Yash asked, his words stuttering over themselves in his eagerness and nervousness to know.

Dr Williams smiled gently. "They are." Yash had needed an academic sponsor to enter, and so Dr Williams was the one they contacted when the competition was over. "It's great news, Yash. Are you ready?"

Yash's heart was thundering in his chest now. "Yes," he said, wanting Dr Williams just to spit it out.

"You won," Dr Williams said with a wide beam. "You won, Yash."

Yash couldn't help beaming back. He'd known, in his heart, that he would be disappointed with anything less than coming first. He was good at coding, good at maths – these were his skills. Teachers were always telling him he was the best in his class, but to find out he was better than students from around the world as well…

“It’s a prestigious competition, and winning it will significantly boost your chances of getting a scholarship," Dr Williams said with pride. “There are a number of top universities who I know first-hand have been watching the results with interest. This is the first step on the road to your future, Yash.”

Yash could only laugh with happiness, thinking of everything this would unlock for him. The future. Stanford, maybe.

There was a cash prize, too. Yash would hand over his earnings to his mother. The forty-dollar monthly cost for their internet service was roughly equivalent to a week's wages, a considerable expense in their household budget, and it was thanks to that sacrifice that he was able to enter at all. He always gave anything he won to her – even from the few esports tournaments he’d entered and performed well in, thanks to the time he spent gaming and practising with Hassan after they’d finished their daily studies.

Yash finished the rest of his tutoring session diligently, putting aside the excitement for later when he was able to run out of the school gates and find his brother. They could celebrate on the journey home before quieting down in time to avoid angering Uncle Beson. Whenever he was tempted to blow off a study session or take it less seriously, his father’s voice would ring in his head: “Education is the key to your future".

Yash had taken him at his word. He wanted a bright future. He wanted what his parents always lovingly and encouragingly told him he was capable of.

He had no idea, when he went to sleep that night with big plans filling his head, that it would be the last night his dreams held the same shape – before fate forced them to change forever.

Chapter 6.

Underlord

Artem had always been a thinker. A strategist.

As a boy growing up in the industrial back streets of Odesa, he had seen patterns where others saw chaos. The port city that was the backdrop of his early life pulsed with both hardship and resilience – and his childhood was marked by a deep love for computers, an obsession with problem-solving, and an ever-growing commitment to the Ukrainian identity and struggle for independence.

The players who came up against him in Dota 2 didn't stand a chance.

Even in exile, he never stopped playing. He climbed the ranks, became a known name in online tournaments, and eventually caught the right people's attention. His quick thinking and ruthless efficiency made him a perfect candidate for professional teams. In the digital colosseums of online battle, he first encountered the teammates that would change his life, characters with names like Tonka, AranaNegra, Phantom, and Luna.

A smile curved his lips as he saw the current game's trajectory through to its conclusion. Things were in motion, now. His teammates knew how to make the play.

They had won.

Tonka: *Yes, guys! We're almost there!*

Luna: *Stop talking and make the play, before you miss it*

AranaNegra: *Nice work, Underlord! We've got them in our web – now we just need to crush them!*

Luna: *Gross metaphor – and shut up!*

Artem smiled as his teammates' messages flashed across his screen, focusing on making the next play and doing what he was supposed to do. They'd rehearsed their strategies and plays so many times. Now, in the early stages of a tournament that would take them to the world stage, it was paying off.

A car backfired outside at the same time as a fireball exploded on his screen and Artem flinched, jolting, his hand slipping off the right buttons for a split second.

For a split second, he was there again.

He blinked and tried to focus, biting his lip, tapping the buttons he needed to, managing to avoid missing a beat.

This time.

Faces swam in front of his mind unbidden, faces from a treasured family photograph that had hung in their front room. Artem was the eldest of three. His younger sister, Lilia, was the artistic one, always drawing, always dreaming. His brother, Mikhail, was a fighter, stubborn and defiant, constantly challenging the world around him. Their mother, a schoolteacher, believed in discipline and education, pushing all three children toward excellence.

Their father, Yuri, a stoic man who had worked in metallurgy, instilled in Artem a love for precision and structure, but also a quiet resilience. When he thought about his family he missed them all, so deeply and dearly it was an unrelenting ache inside his chest, but he yearned to see his father again the most. Just one more time.

His family was never wealthy, but they had each other, which was enough. Losing that meant losing everything.

He still remembered the look on his father's face when they learned that his uncle had been killed fighting near Donetsk. His school had started teaching classes underground when missile alarms became a daily occurrence. He had friends who had left and others who had vanished.

Still, even in the face of all that danger, leaving had been the hardest thing Artem had ever done in his twenty-two years of life.

Artem was not just a gamer. He was a strategist. He saw how data moved, how systems operated, and understood the vulnerabilities inherent in every digital structure. While his friends obsessed over tactics in boring, less strategic video games, Artem saw a bigger game, the one being played on the world stage, where power wasn't just about politics but about who controlled the flow of information.

He had seen the writing on the wall. He had known that it was time to go. But that hadn't made it any easier.

Luna: *Underlord? Are you there?*

Artem refocused on the game, realising he'd missed a beat, after all, in his distracted return to the past. He shook his head to clear it, resuming a familiar stance, hands poised to make all the right moves. He'd been coding in Python since he was ten and gaming in esports since he was fourteen.

He played everything: Counter-Strike, Starcraft, League of Legends. But it was Dota 2 that captured his soul.

The strategy, teamwork, and sheer brilliance required to outthink opponents on the global stage were everything his analytical mind craved. Esports had no geographies, no languages, no faces. Each day he could be playing against someone from Argentina to Seoul. What united them was skill, passion and strategy.

Back home, Artem had enrolled at Kharkiv National University of Radioelectronics, one of Ukraine's top engineering, IT, and cybersecurity institutions. He honed his skills in network security, digital forensics, and advanced programming there, quickly rising as one of the most promising students in his field. His professors recognised his talent, and by his second year, he was already working on freelance cybersecurity contracts, applying what he learned in real-world scenarios. He understood how to defend and penetrate systems, knowledge that would later make him invaluable and dangerous.

He learned fast, working with underground hacker groups that had formed not for crime but for defence, digital partisans fighting against an enemy that sought to erase their identity.

He crossed into Poland with a single bag, his laptop, and a determination to carve out a new future. He took freelance security jobs, worked in backend development, and honed his skills in penetration testing. He didn't just want to build walls; he wanted to understand how to break them.

All the while, Dota 2 had been his touchstone: his home that was always waiting for him, no matter how much he moved around.
Artem's skill was undeniable. He wasn't just good, he was world-class. His ability to read opponents, predict movements, and execute strategies with machine-like precision weren't just gaming skills. They were the same skills that had made him a brilliant hacker, a cybersecurity expert, and a survivor.

And when the invitation came to join one of the world's best Dota 2 teams, to move to a city where he could play professionally and perhaps do more, Artem didn't hesitate.
He refused to be a victim of history. He would carve out his destiny, one move at a time.

Tonka: *Yes!!!!!!*
Phantom: *Hells yeahhhhhh*
Luna: *Nice work, team!*
Team Liquid Tundra – VICTORY

Artem smiled as the view on the screen moved, showing his team as the winners of the match – as he had always known they would be.

Artem didn't know where he would spend the rest of his life, or if he would ever know peace, or if there was some way that he could use his skills to give his people a voice and a place in the modern world. But he knew one thing for sure: his story was only just beginning.

Underlord: *Next stage, world champions!*

Chapter 7.

Biometrics

Daniel had barely slept, thinking about everything he had heard the night before. As he dressed and made his way from his apartment in Battersea Village, his mind buzzed with anticipation and anxiety. This mission felt different from anything he had tackled before.

He rode a Lime Bike to Westminster, the cool morning air doing little to calm his racing thoughts. The sun was just rising, casting long shadows over the historic buildings. As he approached 85 Albert Embankment, he couldn't help but feel a mix of excitement and nervousness. This was one of the most secretive places in the world, marked only by an unobtrusive brass plaque that read "SIS".

Normally, Daniel's visits to SIS involved dropping off handwritten memos from Sir Rory. Today, however, was different. As he walked up the stairs, he noticed the heavy security presence. The building had a time-locked door access entry system and numerous security procedures to prevent unauthorised access. Bag searches, bag scanners, and metal detectors were just the beginning.

After passing through the initial security, Daniel was given a special lanyard with a receiver attached, similar to an Apple AirTag. The implication was clear—they wanted to know where visitors were at all times. The inner chamber door operated on a two-door system: one door closed before the other opened. As he passed through, he was met by an official-looking man who said, "We've been expecting you, Mr. Warren. Please follow me."

Daniel headed for the lift, his nerves heightening with each passing floor. The building's airy appearance did little to alleviate the sombre atmosphere. CCTV cameras were everywhere, and people hustled along the corridors with their heads down.

He stepped up to the reception desk for Biometrics, where a woman with a pointy nose looked at him superciliously. "Name?" she asked, before he had a chance to say why he was there.

"Daniel Warren," he told her. He glanced around, then did a double-take. He was sure the man sitting on a plastic chair near reception had been in last night's briefing.

Daniel lifted a hand in greeting and acknowledgement, breaking into a smile. The man stared back at him blankly, not acknowledging him nor showing any flickering of recognition, until he looked down at the floor. It was almost pointed, as if Daniel wasn't allowed to know him, here. Daniel swallowed down the mistake and turned back to the receptionist.

"Department and date of birth?"

He gave her all of the information she asked for, watching her type it all into a computer screen until she finally nodded sharply.

"Move down the hall to the third door on the left," she said, her voice a quick patter that left him scrambling to remember it all. "You will find yourself in a private side room. Close the door, strip down, and put your clothes and other items into the locker. You will find a gown inside. You're to put it on and then walk through the other door into the examination room."

Daniel nodded mutely, trying not to be overwhelmed – or to feel too vulnerable at the idea of stripping down inside this building. Were there cameras somewhere in the room he couldn't see? He felt like someone was watching him with every movement he made.

He did as he was told, no matter how he felt about it.

Stepping through the next door in his gown, Daniel was greeted by another stern-looking woman. "I'm Dr Russo," she explained, gesturing towards a large table that poked out of a huge machine – an MRI scanner. "Please, lie down here. Our first step is to take a full-body scan."

Daniel lay down, feeling even more vulnerable as she strapped him down. He knew that you weren't supposed to move around in these things, but this was all quite intense. Even if he wanted to urgently get free of these bonds – which he probably couldn't – it wasn't as though he could go roaming around governmental buildings in just a thin, backless robe with nothing underneath. "Thank you," he murmured as she finished and stepped away because he didn't really know what else to say.

"The machine is very loud," she said. "We'll give you some headphones so that you can listen to something distracting. What would you like to listen to?"

Daniel thought for a brief moment. "Elton John?" he suggested.

Dr Russo only nodded and moved away, reappearing a moment later to put the headphones in his ears. "Remember," she said. "Try not to move. If you do, we'll have to start all over again."

As the familiar music played, she walked behind a screen and began the scan.

The machine hummed and clanked for about fifteen minutes. It meshed horribly with the music, turning it into a cacophony of off-beat rhythms that he wished he hadn't asked for. Daniel tried to relax, but his mind kept wandering to the mission ahead. What was Sir Rory going to tell him in the briefing today? He had a feeling there was a lot more to this Project Maia that he had yet to learn, and all of it was going to be essential knowledge now that he was part of it.

He was also uneasy about the project as a whole. Lewis Everett had started frowning halfway through last night's meeting, and there had been muttering and frowning even from people on their own side. Daniel had even noticed Sir Rory faltering slightly, unusual for someone who was usually so stridently confident. Something was happening under the surface of what he had heard last night, and he hadn't been privy to it, and that made him uncomfortable. It was akin to knowing someone was talking about you but not being able to translate the language they spoke.

After the scan, Dr Russo took his fingerprints, both the old-fashioned way and digitally. He was then moved to another table for a facial recognition scan, followed by an iris scan. Between each scan, Dr Russo logged data meticulously on her laptop.

Daniel couldn't help but be impressed by the thoroughness of the security measures. He understood their necessity. The public was not allowed into MI6 headquarters without prior authorization. Tours were strictly for those with legitimate reasons, such as journalists or researchers, and even then, they were rare. Daniel was experiencing the full force of the scanners, checkpoints, and contingency measures the approximately three thousand MI6 employees were used to, and it was not lost on him that this level of preparation indicated just how serious the project was.

"Alright," Dr Russo said, at last, looking up from the screen. "Please get dressed back in the room you came from. Once you're ready, head straight down the hall to Briefing Room Two. You can follow the signs on the wall."

Daniel nodded, more than happy to get out of the gown and back into his own clothes.

The room he found down the hall was modern, with sleek furniture and state-of-the-art technology. A large screen displayed a welcome message: *Project Maia – Briefing Room 2.*

Sir Rory entered, looking more serious than Daniel had ever seen him. "Good morning, Daniel," he said. "I trust you're ready for this?"

Daniel nodded. "Yes, Sir. I'm ready." *Whatever 'this' is.*

"Good. Have a seat. We're waiting for a few more people to join us."

As Daniel sat down, he couldn't help but feel a rush of adrenaline. This was it—the moment he had been preparing for. He glanced around the room, knowing he was soon to be surrounded by some of the most brilliant minds in the intelligence community.

Behind him, someone slipped into the room – a woman that Daniel recognised when he turned to look as Nikita from the meeting last night. What was her surname again…? She looked composed and put-together despite the early morning and late night, much better than Daniel was sure he came across. She was beautiful, in a haunting kind of way. He watched her tuck a loose strand of her straight, dark hair behind her ear, keeping everything perfectly in its place.

More people arrived in spits and spurts until the room was half-full. In response to some unspoken signal, Sir Rory finally began the briefing. "As you all know, we're dealing with a highly sophisticated threat," he said, launching right into a presentation that triggered a slideshow on the screens. "Spider is a brilliant hacker with a notorious reputation. He's suspected of plotting to destabilise the world's financial system through cyber-attacks."

The screen changed to display images of Spider's previous activities – the same attacks Nikita had described the night before.

"We believe that it is Spider's ultimate plan," Sir Rory continued, "to collapse the financial institutions that prop up the US and UK governments. He will use the Veritian platform to do so, making it unstable and using the chaos it will cause to his advantage."

Someone behind Daniel stuck up a hand. "Uh, sir," he said. "I'm a little out of the loop. Can you please explain the project and where Veritian sits within it?"

Sir Rory put his hands behind his back and cleared his throat, taking on a pose that made him look like an economics professor about to deliver a lecture. “As you will all know, the world's most common and most significant fiat currencies are the US dollar, the Euro, and the Japanese yen.

“But in recent years, the general population's trust has been failing, especially since the start of the Ukraine War and with the rise of China as a superpower. Couple that with almost record inflation in the US and UK, the failure of the tariff policies bringing down the value of the dollar to a record low, and China’s recent deal with Brazil. It’s fuelling whispers that the Chinese Yuan will replace the dollar on the world stage. A new currency would rekindle our countries' fortunes and keep our global economic superpower status. Without it, the general feeling is that the dollar will no longer be the global primary reserve currency.

“Over the last parliament and US congress term, the recently elected US President and our Prime Minister, with their two central banks, have been working top secret on building the necessary infrastructure, security, and protocols for a digital currency. This is called a CBDC – a Central Bank Digital Currency. As many of you will know, this is a new currency not backed by a physical commodity such as gold.

“The CBDC is called Veritian as a conjuncture between the words *Veritas* and viridian, calling back to the ‘green’ colour of the money we are used to. It is ready to launch to our respective countries and populations once they each receive their own democratic approvals. In public, significant propaganda has been published in the US and UK elections to educate and persuade our respective populations to switch to Veritian. The public now has a good understanding of how it will revolutionise our economies and be safe and secure. In fact, this was an electoral promise for our newly appointed Labour Prime Minister – and it is now in serious jeopardy."

Pieces were clicking into place in Daniel's head. He knew, of course, about the election promises – he thought anyone in the UK surely did, but he could be charitable: perhaps the individual who had asked the question had spent a few years undercover in a different country. But he hadn't quite thought about how badly not just the people, but the government, would be affected if this venture failed. If a financial catastrophe took place, the government would certainly take the brunt of the blame.

The last decade or more had already been bad enough. He didn't have to look far for an example: he thought of his own sister, struggling to afford her own home as the cost of providing food and clothing for her children weighed her down. He remembered her crying over the cost of formula milk and recalled wincing when he had to pick up a packet of emergency nappies for her on the way to a visit. Things hadn't improved since her children were babies, and even he, as a single man with a good wage, had felt the pinch.

"How has this risk developed?" a serious-looking woman in thick-rimmed glasses asked, pushing them further up her nose. She looked like some sort of analyst, Daniel thought.

"Our Veritian currency has been developed over the past three years with the cooperation of Cryptropolis Corporation, who are at the absolute top of this field. A specialist team was assembled based at a secret facility in Glasgow – that's

Glasgow, Montana, not Glasgow, Scotland. It's a city a hundred and ten miles from its nearest neighbour, with just five roads in and out, monitored daily by our joint security forces. In other words – secure.

"The highly specialist team from both our respective central banks is led by the brilliant mind and company of Alberto Lopez, the founder of Cryptropolis himself. He became globally famous, of course, for designing and building out BlockChainTropolis in 2014 at a young age. This system rivalled Bitcoin and was also known – key for our purposes – for its extremely high levels of security. To this date, it has never been hacked, even by Spider.

"On top of the already tight security protocols, absolutely no one has been permitted to work on the project unless they were fully authorised and there in person in Glasgow. Any and all electronic communications about the project have been encrypted, all employees were subject to stringent background checks, and there are guards and security cameras around every single corner and in every nook and cranny of the building."

Sir Rory paused for effect.

"Sir?" the analyst asked, frowning. "I still don't see how…"

"The long and short of it is, we don't know," Sir Rory said gruffly. "And that brings us to your assignments – because what we need to do now is get to the bottom of all of this and prevent Spider from unleashing his eggs."

"Sir," Nikita spoke up, drawing Daniel's attention immediately. "If I may – why don't we just pull the plug on the project and start again on the code, if the risk is so high?"

Sir Rory paused for a moment, looking down. "First," he said, his voice uncharacteristically quiet. He paused often, as if he was reluctant to answer the question truthfully but knew he had to. "The investment from both of our countries into this project so far is already in the hundreds of millions of pounds. If we were to stop now, the taxpayers would likely riot. We'd certainly lose the next election, and a change in leadership could well mean total upheaval of the project anyway, leaving us in a dire situation that could speed up the chaos in the economy."

"What about the digital vault?" someone else spoke up. "Isn't it common practice for the Bank of England to keep a digital vault version of any code, isolated from the working model, so that it can be reconstructed completely in the event of a hack or failure?"

Sir Rory looked slightly annoyed by the interruption, but he answered. "And how much trust would the public lose in the system in the meantime? We can't risk that happening. It would be a run on the banks, but so much worse. How does one withdraw all of one's money from a digital system that isn't even working? There would be riots, looting, anarchy."

Daniel couldn't stop himself. Sir Rory had been prevented from finishing his two points, and Daniel wanted to know how they ended. "And second?" he asked.

"And second," Sir Rory took the prompt, looking unhappy about it. "I should be fully honest with you. The US contingent does not believe such a threat exists. Lewis Everett made that clear to me before leaving us this morning. In fact, most of our government does not believe it exists. I met with the Prime Minister and Alberto Lopez, the head of Cryptropolis, a few moments ago. Lopez has assured us that there is no possible security breach, and the PM is inclined to believe him.

"I am, however, absolutely secure in the trust I place in our source. This threat is real. I know it is. Unfortunately, I am the only one, and so I am putting both my neck and my career on the line for this. That is how deeply I believe in this threat. Anyone who does not wish to join this team, for fear of risking their own careers, should leave now."

There was a long, tense silence. Daniel had no idea about the credibility of Sir Rory's source – he didn't even know who or what it was – but he trusted in Sir Rory. The man had never steered him wrong. He had looked after Daniel, brought him up through the ranks, and Daniel owed him everything he had. He wasn't going to return the favour by abandoning him.

If Sir Rory went down, so did Daniel. But if Sir Rory was right, this was likely the most important project he would ever work on.

Apparently, the others in the room felt the same, because not one of them moved.

"Good." Sir Rory said, nodding gravely. "Now: your assignments."

Daniel sat straighter in his chair. This was where he was needed, and he would do whatever Sir Rory asked. He sat tense, waiting, as Sir Rory handed out assignments to various people around him.

“Daniel,” Sir Rory said after what felt like an age, “you’ll be working closely with our team at GCHQ. Your first task is to review the data we’ve collected and develop a strategy for tracking Spider.”

Daniel nodded, feeling the weight of the responsibility. “Understood, Sir. I’ll get started right away.” He didn’t ask for more explanation or details – he would get that from the rest of the team.

He felt less daunted and more excited about the opportunity to show what he could do. As Daniel left the briefing room, he couldn’t help but feel a mix of excitement and anxiety. This was a high-stakes mission, one that could have significant implications for the world. He knew the road ahead would be challenging, but he was determined to succeed.

All that remained was to meet the team – and to get stuck in.

Chapter 8.

The Bomb

Early in the morning, the phone rang at Uncle Beson's house. It was still dark and quiet. The ringing phone woke everyone in the house.

Yash and his brother Hassan sat up on the sofa bed they slept in together, exchanging a confused look, as Uncle Beson talked to someone on the phone. Concern quickly crept into his voice. Something was wrong. Yash's mind began to race and he pulled Hassan closer to his side protectively.

Hanging up, Uncle Beson looked at the boys, tears streaming down his face.

He turned on the light and sat down on the edge of his battered armchair, facing them. "There's been an explosion," he began, his voice trembling. "Your parents... there was a bombing at the Airport Hotel in Mogadishu. They're missing, presumed dead, probably lost under the rubble."

Yash sat there, stunned. He couldn't believe what he was hearing. His uncle's words made no sense. It wasn't conclusive, but clearly, something terrible had happened. Perhaps Uncle Beson was mistaken. Perhaps he was playing a nasty trick on them. Perhaps there was a way to explain all of this. Yash hugged his brother, who was shivering and crying too. His mind was a rush of noise and nonsense, and he couldn't think well enough to even formulate a question.

Uncle Beson turned on RTN news on the TV. Reporters were at the scene. Yash and Hassan sat there in stunned silence.

Reporters on the channel were saying that the United States had conducted a number of airstrikes that evening. The first strike appeared to have targeted a suspected al-Qaeda convoy in the vicinity of Jilib, Lower Shabelle Region. The second strike appeared to have targeted a suspected al-Shabaab training camp near Janaale, Lower Shabelle Region. A third strike had targeted the Airport Hotel.

A spokesman for the US military was shown on the channel justifying these airstrikes as part of its counterterrorism campaign against al-Qaeda and its affiliates in Somalia. The American spokesman said that al-Shabaab was a threat to US national security. Yash's stomach was roiling, full of acid that made him sick. People had died. How could they respond so calmly? How could they pretend it was all okay?

The reporter noted that these airstrikes were the first time the US military had conducted airstrikes in Somalia since the 1993 Battle of Mogadishu. As if the distance of time made it okay for them to do such a thing again.

All of the information washed over Yash like a wall of sound. He understood the words and part of him dimly grasped the meaning, but he could barely hold onto it. He kept wondering if the screen would show an image of his parents walking away from the damage, perhaps covered in dust and even with blood on their foreheads like some of the other survivors, but alive.

He prayed for them to appear, his throat dry and cold sweat breaking out on his back and forehead with every new image, but the news seemed to go on endlessly, and they never did.

Yash sat in shock, realising that his world had just turned upside down. He clutched Hassan's hand in his own and entered a numbness that lasted for days, time seemingly losing all meaning and food all taste.

On the third day, they had a visit from a local official who sat Yash and Hassan down and confirmed the news they had feared but never quite believed.

Their parents were dead.

Chapter 9.

Hawthorne

The room smelled of freshly brewed coffee and tension. The polished mahogany table, lined with laptops and paper dossiers, reflected the dim overhead lighting. The walls of the secure briefing room were bare, save for a world map, a clock ticking methodically, and a flat screen that had been frozen on a document header that read *Project Maia - Cybersecurity Threat Intelligence Briefing.*

There was something incongruous about the old-fashioned building, with all its history, and the digital, futuristic nature of what they were about to discuss.

Daniel leaned back in his chair, arms folded across his chest, his sharp brown eyes scanning the room. Next to him, Nikita Cowling sat poised, her posture straight, eyes locked onto the screen as though memorising every pixel. She was serious, methodical, and sharp as a blade. If Daniel exuded relaxed confidence, she radiated precise calculation.

The other people in the room were analysts – people there to support their mission, but apparently, not part of it. Nikita was the only person Daniel recognised, and he'd only met her once.

He almost wished she'd sat somewhere else. She was distracting. He kept seeing the flick of her hair moving around her shoulders from the corner of his eye as she glanced around the room. She had a delicate scent of jasmine and rose about her, a perfume that was intoxicating without being empowering. He resisted the urge to lean closer. He was supposed to be focusing on the briefing, not the beautiful woman beside him.

“My name is Hawthorne,” the man standing at the front of the room, beside the screen, said. “I’m the lead investigator on this case. It’s nice to meet you both.”

Daniel privately thought it unlikely that the man’s name really was Hawthorne – he had the air of an MI6 strategist about him, even if he didn’t claim to be such – but he just nodded his head politely in greeting.

"Before we get into the details, you two haven’t worked together before. Daniel, this is Nikita Cowling, a cybersecurity and cryptography expert, recruited straight out of Harvard into national security before moving into other government departments,” Hawthorne said. “Nikita, meet Daniel Warren, one of the F and C’s up-and-coming stars, a Spanish speaker, and skilled in cracking problems. We’re putting you together because we need an unconventional approach."

Daniel turned slightly, studying his new partner. "You work by the book?"

"I write the book," Nikita replied coolly. One of Daniel’s eyebrows shot up. The more he saw of Nikita, the more intrigued she made him. Her beauty was uncomplicated and honest – her makeup was minimal, only there to enhance what she already had, and the bone structure of her face was noble and strong. Her character and her intelligence also seemed impressive, and judging by her background, she would be able to run circles around him in any contest of wits. It was difficult not to be intimidated.

Hawthorne continued, "As you know, you're both here because we've identified a potential breach in the Project Maia security infrastructure. The threat level is uncertain, but our concern is simple. If the system is compromised before its official rollout, we risk economic destabilisation and loss of trust in the new digital currency."

He tapped the screen. A few lines of network activity logs appeared. Daniel supposed they were working on the assumption that Sir Rory was right, as though there was no possible doubt. But even to him, the data looked like absolutely nothing – it could just have been a mistake or the innocuous activity of someone working on the project innocently continuing their daily tasks.

"This is what we've found so far," Hawthorne went on. "Whoever is behind this is good. Very good. Multiple VPNs, misdirects, layered encryption. It's like tracking a shadow through a maze. This is not the egg itself, but we believe it may well be a trace left behind when the egg was put in – a backdoor entrance that was closed on the way out."

Nikita exchanged a quick glance with Daniel. "What do we know about the potential breach?" she asked, her voice crisp, cutting through the room's thick air.

One of the analysts, a short man with thinning hair, adjusted his glasses. "The anomaly was detected five days ago. A series of untraceable pings to our blockchain network. Small, precise, like someone testing the doors before they kick them in. On inspecting the code, this was all we could find. We suspect whoever is doing this is a pro."

Hawthorne folded his hands together. "What we do know is that the attack patterns mirror techniques used in previous state-sponsored cyber incidents. Some intrusion attempts resemble methods used in the Shadow Protocol breach three years ago, though we can't yet confirm if it's the same actors. According to information given to us by an informant, however, this is the work of Spider."

Another analyst spoke up. "We've also intercepted fragments of encrypted communications from dark web forums discussing vulnerabilities in financial cryptosystems. Some chatter indicates that Veritian is a target, but whether that's just speculation or concrete intelligence, we can't be certain."

"Isn't Cryptropolis handling the main build?" Daniel spoke up, wanting to make some impact on the proceedings. "They're supposed to be the best in the world. Are they working on this?"

Hawthorne nodded. "We have heard from Mr Lopez, the founder and CEO of Cryptropolis, that they have their best people looking for inconsistencies. So far, this is the only thing that came up, and they argue that it doesn't actually show any evidence of an intrusion. They do assure us that they are, even as we speak, building new security defences against further incursions. It's worth noting that none of the supposed breaches committed by Spider in the past were against firms supported by Cryptropolis. They are doing what they can. In Sir Rory's opinion, however, it is not enough to simply expect the best hacker in the world to be beaten by the best security system in the world. He feels we should nip the threat in the bud before the security needs to be tested."

Nikita spoke up, though her expression was unreadable. "I imagine the people in this room are already the best in the country at this kind of tracing. Where do we come in?"

A senior stakeholder leaned forward. "We don't need textbook solutions. We need ingenuity. This isn't just about checking, rechecking, and securing a system, it's about outthinking whoever is trying to get in."

Nikita nodded slowly. She seemed to understand that as a directive, but Daniel was still lagging a little behind.

"And where do we start?" he asked, hoping for a definitive answer.

"We don't know exactly who's behind it. That's where you come in." Hawthorne glanced at a dossier in front of him. "You two have unique skill sets. Cowling, your history with cyber forensics and network security is unparalleled, and you have experience in leading missions in the field. You'll be the senior team member, guiding your own course through difficult and unpredictable circumstances."

If Nikita was pleased to be named senior, she didn't show it. Daniel shifted restlessly.

"What about me?" he asked, feeling as though he had a lot less to offer than she did – what had made Sir Rory suggest him for this mission instead of choosing someone who already worked directly in a cyber crime or digital networks space?

"Warren, your ability to navigate the underbelly of gaming communities and your untraceable experience means you can help unlock how these networks work without flagging up any concerns for anyone looking out for an expert. Your grasp of the Spanish language could also be invaluable. Between the two of you, you're going to find the answers we need."

Nikita crossed her arms. "Winning in video games and digital warfare isn't exactly the same thing." She'd clearly picked up on that one aspect of his history and ignored the rest like it was nothing.

Daniel smirked, not bothering to ask how they'd known about his gaming history – it was one of the things they were paid to know, after all. "You'd be surprised. A good hacker doesn't just break in. They make the system work for them. It's about strategy – and a lot of the time, it's about teamwork. With a big job like this, the hacker likely isn't working alone. Besides, my team is pretty special."

Hawthorne frowned at that. "Yes, we noticed as such," he said. "We were only able to identify you, Daniel, through the access we have to you and your devices – and according to the records, your gaming persona shows up as someone else entirely. All the other members of your team appear to be, well, ghosts."

Daniel grinned openly. So, they were good enough to fool the best minds the United Kingdom's government agencies had to offer. Excellent. He'd known Liquid Tundra ranked amongst the best, but this confirmation was beyond satisfying. It was a shame he'd never be able to tell the team how he knew. "That's our thing," he said. "We play under false identities so that if we ever get banned for the illegal tactics we use, we can just start again."

Nikita made a tiny scoffing noise – Daniel couldn't tell whether it was because she was astounded and impressed, couldn't believe he was using that level of skill just to play a game, or because she disapproved of the use of illegal tactics.

Hawthorne leaned in. "We need both of you thinking on your feet," he said with an approving nod as if they were already proving they could do it. "We're in uncharted territory. You must identify the hacker – be it Spider or somebody else – and bring them in."

Daniel tapped his fingers on the table. "If someone's probing the system, they're leaving traces. Have we been able to localise any of the pings? IP addresses? Even a general region?"

The analyst shook his head. "They're bouncing signals through multiple VPN layers, routing traffic through at least six countries before it reaches us. It's like tracing a ghost. The only thing we do know is that one access point seems to have been in Mexico City, and with our informant also pointing in that direction, it's the strongest lead we have."

Hawthorne leaned back. "That's why you two are here. We need you to dig deeper. Head to Mexico City in the morning. Follow our leads, meet with people on the ground who might have better access to the rumours we're chasing. Use your skills and resources in any way you can. Work fast, work quietly, and report back with anything you find. Dismissed."

Daniel and Nikita found themselves walking out together as the meeting wrapped up. The tension in the air between them had shifted, not quite camaraderie, but a recognition of each other's skill.

"So, you're an esports hacker?" Nikita said, a hint of amusement in her voice.

"And you're a cybersecurity prodigy?" Daniel shot back. "Guess we're both misfits."

"Misfits tend to be the best at getting things done." Nikita's eyes glinted. "Let's see if we can prove them right."

"What do you think he meant about using our skills and resources?" Daniel asked, pulling out his phone. His thumb hesitated over the icon for the group chat that Team Liquid Tundra used to privately communicate.

"I think he meant that we're allowed to do things that aren't exactly sanctioned officially," Nikita said with a wry smile. The smile lit up her eyes with a hint of mischief that made Daniel's pulse flutter momentarily.

"That's exactly what I was thinking," he said, opening the chat.

After all, he had access to not only some of the best gamers in the world, but the best hackers, too.

Tonka: *Need a favour. Got a digital ghost I need tracked. Can anyone help?*

They hadn't made it the length of the hallway before the reply came.

Luna: *You never ask for favours unless it's big. Send details. I'll see what I can dig up*

Daniel exhaled, rolling his shoulders. This was the first step. He and Nikita would start their hunt when they landed in Mexico City, but tonight, he was setting the pieces in motion.

“Let’s do this,” he said out loud, and Nikita nodded in approval, the very edges of her lips twisting up into a determined smile.

“I’ll meet you at your place for the airport taxi in the morning, Daniel Warren,” she said. “Don’t forget to pack a toothbrush.”

Chapter 10.

Liquid Tundra

The team had come together in the way most great things did: by accident, by necessity, and out of an unrelenting drive to win.

They were ghosts in the system, names without faces, voices without bodies. In the world of Dota 2, their handles mattered more than their identities. They hid behind fake realities, carefully constructed to fool competition judges, ensuring that they could easily compete again if they were caught bending the rules and banned. They lived in a world of pings, split-second decisions, and impossible strategies that turned five individuals into a unit that operated almost as cohesively as a single person.

And Daniel loved every moment.

AranaNegra: *Luna, ward placements. We need vision before they get the jump on us*

Luna: *I know. You worry about your lane, I'll worry about mine*

Daniel had to smile at his teammates' bickering. Luna could be spiky in the heat of the game, and AranaNegra was always in charge and in control. Both of them had perfect timing and sharp strategy, and Luna hated it every time AranaNegra tried to take the lead – and he tried to take the lead every time. This was only a warm-up game before they went into a major tournament round, but they all took it just as seriously no matter the stakes of the round.

This tournament wasn't just a game; it was a battlefield, a global phenomenon. It began as an experimental MMORPG – a massively multiplayer online role-playing game – with a new twist on an old classic. No one expected it to explode. But it did. It became the definitive multiplayer online battle arena, or MOBA, a format that fused real-time strategy with fast-paced action.

Why did it become so popular? Skill. No pay-to-win mechanics. No shortcuts. Just raw talent, knowledge, and mastery of over a hundred playable heroes, each with their own abilities and roles. It was chess at three hundred actions per minute, a battle of reflexes and intelligence where a single mistake could cost everything. It took time to learn and time to master, and both required dedication.

The game attracted the best. The boldest. The most ruthless strategists. And it rewarded those who could think five moves ahead, predict their opponent's decisions and adapt faster than anyone else.

And, of course, those who had the skills to covertly add code that would automate actions, allowing them to bypass the strict playing rules and add an extra dimension to their playing – requiring an even higher level of skill.

They didn't see it as cheating. Only as being more resourceful and talented than the rest. They were playing a whole other game on top of what the average player saw and understood.

Underlord: *No witty response, Arana?*
AranaNegra: *Focus! Tonka, you there?*

Daniel leaned forward over his keyboard. That was him – Tonka, a nod to his favourite childhood toy. Maybe AranaNegra had noticed, somehow, that Daniel's focus was elsewhere – worrying about the flight to Mexico City in the morning and what that meant for his normally carefully scheduled life.

Tonka: *Yeah, of course*
AranaNegra: *Strategy B, like we talked about.*

Even on their own private encrypted chat, they were careful not to openly discuss moves during games. If some of their own team members had the skills required to hack another team's chat and read their strategies – not that they needed to, to win – then they had to be on guard for others doing the same.

In Dota 2, every player assumed a specific role, typically categorised into positions one through five, determining which lane – or path – through the game map a player would take. These roles included the Carry, who dealt the most damage; the Midlaner, who dominated the mid lane running through the centre of the map; the Offlaner, who secured the hard lane, the shortest path in the game and therefore the most difficult to retreat from in a crisis; and the Support players, who assisted and protected their teammates. The game's complexity meant that coordination and communication were crucial.

Daniel was the wildcard of the team. He was the team's Support backbone, and his strategic calls could shift a dozen or more times in a game, flicking through planned plays until they found the combination that worked to take their opponents down.

Phantom was the team's joker, fun and creative, always finding new ways to taunt their opponents or distract them into making critical mistakes from the hard lane.

And then there was Underlord. The silent killer, their Carry. No wasted words, no unnecessary moves. He played like a shadow, disappearing into the jungle, reappearing just when he was needed most. He was the kind of player that made opponents nervous. The kind of teammate that made you feel safe.

They had fought their way up. From smaller online circuits, weekend tournaments, and casual ladders where they tested their chemistry. Then the stakes got higher. Major regional qualifiers. Knockout rounds. Then came the moment they had been grinding for: an invite to the International.

The International. The single biggest tournament in esports. A fifty-million-dollar prize pool. Global prestige. Every Dota 2 player's dream.

AranaNegra was the one to decide their tactics as the Midlaner, but it wasn't a dictatorship. He understood his teammates, their strengths and weaknesses. And Luna? She was the perfect Support foil to each of them, filling every gap the team needed, taking over any of their roles in a heartbeat if she had to.

She'd been a professional streamer, once, sharing her games live. When Tonka had invited her to join Liquid Tundra, AranaNegra had asked for one stipulation. She could no longer stream anything they did together. They had all developed their own ways of getting around the anti-cheating systems and could, in a pinch, force a win by doing something not strictly within the legal limits of the tournament. They didn't want that on camera. While she occasionally still went live for other games, Dota 2 was now off-limits – and any subscriber who asked her about it during stream quickly found themselves booted from the chat.

AranaNegra: *Phantom, if we pull off the split push this game, we need you to bait their offlaner. You can handle it?*

Phantom: *Baiting is my speciality lol*

Luna: *Yeah, yeah, you love the attention haha*

Phantom: *Don't be jealous because everyone's not looking at you*

AranaNegra: *Children... Tonka, thoughts?*

A pause. Daniel considered it.

Tonka: *It's a risk. If they counter-push hard, we'll need Underlord to play safe. We can't get drawn into a late-game fight if their core gets fed*

Underlord: *I can handle my lane*

And that was that.

They practised like they were already in the finals. Long hours, endless matches. They knew each other's habits, strengths, weaknesses. It was trust built in the fires of digital combat.

The tournament came down to the wire. Round after round, each game was closer than the last. Strategies that worked one round fell apart the next. They adapted. They survived.

They took down a Chinese powerhouse in the quarter-finals. The semifinals, a best-of-five bloodbath against the reigning champions from Europe. They won three against two. Barely.

Now, two games stood between them and the grand finals. The last steps before history.

The group chat was empty as they loaded into the lobby until one message flickered onto the screen.

AranaNegra: *We win this, we're in.*

Silence.

Daniel couldn't wait any longer. He'd wanted to tell them after the game, but it was eating at him.

Tonka: *I need to tell you guys something*

No one responded immediately.

Tonka: *I might not be here for the finals. Got work. I'm travelling last minute and I might not be able to get to my laptop.*

The silence stretched longer this time.

Luna: *... That a joke?*

Tonka: *No*

Phantom: *It better be a joke*

AranaNegra: *We will deal with that after this match. Right now, we focus*

As the game loaded, Daniel glanced down at a ping from a private message, sent directly by AranaNegra. No matter what he said to the group, he clearly had thoughts he wanted to share.

AranaNegra: *We've come too far for doubts. We need to win. And Tonka? You need to decide where your real priorities lay.*

Chapter 11.

No One's Son

"My stomach hurts," Hassan moaned again.

Yash gritted his teeth. "Uncle," he tried again. "Hassan's really sick. Please! We have to do something!"

Uncle Beson grumbled, lifting the TV remote and finally switching off his beloved shows. "You boys," he cursed, spitting. "Always want, want, want."

Yash had some choice words he could throw back at his Uncle about that statement.

Words about how Uncle Beson now got to live in a much larger home, since he was looking after Yash and Hassan, and he was even living off their parents' estate.

Words about how he didn't need to pay for their tuition, since it had been gifted to them by the English College in their parents' memory.

Words about how Uncle Beson never gave them anything they asked for: not the new athletic clothes Yash needed for his training because he had outgrown all of his old kit, not the money for school lunches they couldn't buy without his help, not time off from the household chores to study.

Angry words. Dirty words. Words he would never be able to take back.

Instead, he gritted his teeth against all of those words that threatened to spill out, and tried new ones: "Please, it's been days. This can't be right. He can't even get up anymore."

Uncle Beson muttered something about lazy children and wandered into another room, putting a phone to his ear. Yash listened until he was sure he was calling a doctor, then turned his attention back to Hassan.

"You'll be alright," he said, squeezing his little brother's hand. "The doctor is coming now."

"Maybe when I'm better, we can play on the computer," Hassan said, and Yash gave him a sharp look. He held a hand against Hassan's forehead and found it heated to the touch. Uncle Beson hadn't let them play games, or even use the computer, since only a couple of weeks after he'd moved in. He claimed it made them lazy, and that if they had time to play games, they had time to clean the house.

"Maybe," Yash said, not wanting to upset Hassan further right now – but he couldn't deny he was worried.

He talked to Hassan about nothing special – about school and friends and safe topics that wouldn't upset him – until the doctor arrived. Then he waited anxiously, seeing the doctor's frown deepen as he examined Hassan.

"I suspect he has a stomach ulcer," the doctor said. "You need to go to Mahdi Hospital immediately."

"Can you take us?" Yash asked.

The doctor shook his head, gathering his bag. "I have another call to make," he said. "Your Uncle will drive you."

But the moment the door closed behind the doctor, Uncle Beson was shaking his head. "I've taken khat," he said. "It's illegal to drive under the influence. I can't take you."

Yash packed a small bag and took Hassan on the bus, having to first wait two hours for its arrival. The whole while, his worry for Hassan and his anger at Uncle Beson grew. This was serious. Why couldn't Uncle Beson stir himself to help them, even just this once?

***

"I'm sorry to tell you this, but your brother is very sick," the doctor was saying, but Yash found himself shutting down again, the same way he had when Uncle Beson had told them their parents were dead. All he could do was stare numbly into the man's face. "We found multiple stomach ulcers, some of which have clearly perforated and ruptured. His bile is leaking into his wider system, including into his blood. He also has a chronic infection in the abdominal cavity. We're going to have to operate and keep him here for some time, and this is far from a simple case. Do you have a guardian who can sit with you and Hassan?"

Yash shook his head silently. The doctor patted him on the shoulder as if it was some kind of consolation, then walked away, leaving Yash standing outside of Hassan's room.

He could barely compute what the doctor had told him. Surgery. Ulcers.

All he could see in his mind's eye was the grave where they had buried his parents. A gravestone with room for more to be added later.

And in his mind's eye, though he wanted very much to stop, he saw Hassan's name carved there – and it took all of his strength to stay standing.

***

Yash had never wanted to be wrong about something more in his life.

He'd spent two days with Hassan in the hospital, never leaving, only slipping out of the room to find something to eat from the vending machines. He was there, sitting beside him, when the monitors finally began to ring out their alarms – and when the nurse turned them off, knowing there was nothing more they could do.

Hassan hadn't made it through the last surgery. They had known it was over. It only remained to let him quietly pass away, with his brother at his side.

Yash should have been able to protect him. That was his job. He was the big brother.

Now he was no one's son. No one's brother.

He was alone.

Returning to his home with no memory of the journey back, Yash walked in, saw his uncle sitting there watching a crass Mexican telenovela, and realised at that moment that he couldn't stay there any longer. He had to leave. He needed a new life. Everything he knew and trusted had changed within the space of three months.

He couldn't stay here until he, too, fell ill, and Uncle Beson just let him die. Like he wasn't a person at all, but an inconvenient piece of furniture he had inherited, that could be left out on the street once it broke.

Yash would never forgive that man, and if he stayed here, there were all kinds of dangers awaiting him. Not just the neglect of his Uncle, but the very real possibility that he would not be able to last for the rest of his days here without taking visceral revenge on the man who had let his brother die.

Yash walked past him and into the room where they kept the computers. He had heard stories at school of boys who had escaped to Europe. It was a dangerous journey, but at the end of it lay a new life.

That day, he began to research how to escape.

Chapter 12.

The Hunting Ground

The vast vaulted ceiling halls at Crypto Summit X were already filling up with delegates when Alberto arrived in the VIP entrance lane and showed his blackQ VIP pass. The atmosphere was buzzing, and even from the outside, it felt like this year's conference was going to be the biggest yet.

He could have walked from the stunning penthouse apartment he rented in the Cologne Kranhaus, the same one he rented each year, but he liked to arrive incognito. He'd had a car drop him off in the special VIP area, so he could walk right in without being recognised.

He would return to the apartment later, using it as a place to catch up with all his global friends in person. Importantly, it was also a great place for face-to-face conversations in the knowledge he or they weren't going to be overheard. With space for his butler Edward and assistant Xaliima, along with impressive three-sixty-degree views of the city from the seventeenth floor, it provided all he needed.

But that was for later.

Alberto was cloaked in his trademark public outward persona. He entered the congress wearing his usual black t-shirt, black-grey slim-fit Boss suit, and white Nike Air Force with his now customary and bespoke silver tick. He cut an elegant, tall, and athletic silhouette. He was quickly recognised by attending delegates, who began waving and talking about him to their neighbours - they all knew who he was. In his day-to-day life he shunned fame of any kind, but amongst his tribe – the crypto geeks – he welcomed their intellectual worship. He rarely gave interviews, however, and quickly stepped past the press lines without pause.

He waved off most of the attention as he headed towards his company's special stand in Hall Eight. It was built on two levels, with extra security to access the upper level. For good reason: there were forty thousand delegates expected to come from every corner of the world, and most of them wanted to be just like Alberto.

A satisfied smile lit his face as he took in the Cryptropolis booth, looming out of the crowd in front of him as one of the largest in the hall. It had been designed not just to impress but to intimidate. Sleek black walls with neon-lit cryptographic symbols framed the space. A massive screen looped a promotional video showing the "Future of Finance"—a carefully crafted montage of financial inclusion, technological breakthroughs, and optimistic quotes from global leaders.

The polished exterior hid an even more intimidating secret: this was not, as far as Alberto was concerned, a recruitment drive.

It was a hunting ground.

Alberto wasn't here to attend talks or mingle at networking events; he was here to identify talent, individuals who operated in the shadows of the crypto universe. Hackers, blockchain architects, penetration testers, AI developers—all gathered in Cologne under the veneer of professionalism.

Alberto had identified four potential recruits, and the first one was already sitting on the top floor of the booth inside a private office space, waiting for him. As he stepped up to the office, nodding to his security team, Alberto noted the shiny black exterior was working exactly as expected: no one could see through it, though the double-sided material allowed them to sit inside and watch the conference unfold around them.

"Viktor," he said cheerfully, opening the door and closing it behind himself immediately. The echoing noise of the halls, the cool air blowing through them, and the vaguely plastic smell of all the stands fell away as he sat down. In here, it was as though they could be anywhere in the world – a private room, not in the middle of a massive conference. "Or would you prefer I call you Phantom?"

Viktor Ivanov, a.k.a. Phantom in all of his online deeds, eyed him mistrustfully from his chair. "Viktor is fine," he said, a deep and throaty St. Petersburg accent marking his words. Viktor specialised in smart contract vulnerability exploits, and Alberto had contacted him through his own channels a while before, laying the groundwork for this meeting over the course of months.

That didn't seem to have bought him any trust, but he wouldn't expect anything less from a man who had stolen billions without getting caught.

"I'm impressed with the work you've done for me so far," Alberto said. They'd been working on a covert project for a short time, and though Phantom wasn't yet done with his task, it was clear that he was up to the job in all ways. "You're good at finding cracks, Viktor. How about you start building unbreakable walls instead? Come work for me, and I'll make sure your skills aren't wasted on petty exploits."

Viktor hesitated, a flash of anger crossing his face at the term 'petty'. "I don't need to work for someone who disrespects me," he said. His hands formed fists on top of his knees.

It didn't matter if he was reluctant, or even if he was considering violence. Alberto had already done his research.

"You've been sending money to an offshore account every month, to a sister studying medicine in London," Alberto said. "It must be hard, making so much money for your clients and only getting to keep a tiny percentage of it. Work for me, and she won't have to worry about tuition ever again."

Viktor was a man of few words.

He only nodded, his eyes glinting of steel in a stoic face.

That was the first one down, and Alberto had four more on his hitlist to go.

Alberto escorted Priya Nair to his office less than two hours later, after Alberto had the chance to watch her speak. Her presence on stage radiated both intelligence and confidence in an electric mix, but Alberto noticed something others didn't: she was frustrated. Her ideas, groundbreaking as they were, were being sidelined by short-sighted corporate executives.

Her discussion panel, titled "Post-Quantum Cryptography", was the first time he'd seen her in person. He'd heard about her skill and understanding of quantum-resistant blockchain algorithms, but given that she lived in Bangalore, India, they hadn't come into contact with one another until now. He'd spent years wondering about the best way to approach her; it was no coincidence the opportunity had arisen. He'd been the one to suggest her inclusion in the panel.

Nothing here was left to chance, and Alberto had gone to considerable effort to ensure that everyone was where he needed them to be.

After the panel, Alberto intercepted her in the networking lounge.

"Your algorithms are ten years ahead of the curve, Priya. Why are you letting these dinosaurs hold you back?" he asked, knowing that a direct approach was the best way to grab her attention.

Priya raised an eyebrow. "And you're offering…?"

"A chance to build the future without compromise. Join Cryptropolis, and I'll give you a lab, a team, and resources beyond your imagination."

She took one look at the rest of the guests in the lounge – none of whom were doing anything close to the innovation that Cryptropolis was – and held out a hand for him to take. "Let's talk," she said, and though the deal wasn't done right away, she was on the team by the time she left the Cryptropolis stand.

Alberto spent the rest of the day catching the occasional panel or workshop, overseeing the stand, and relaxing; he knew where to find his third target, and there was no rush to intercept him any earlier.

The exclusive conference afterparty was smoky and loud, with neon lights pulsing to the beat of deep house music. Alberto slipped through the crowd effortlessly, spotting Amir Rahman in a dark corner, sipping a cocktail.

"Nice work with the Dubai Exchange breach," Alberto said smoothly, without any other word of introduction.

Amir froze, his face pallid under the bright flashing lights.

"The Dubai hacker never got caught," he said cautiously.

"Exactly," Alberto replied. "You're brilliant at breaking systems. How about you start protecting one instead? A real one."

Amir smirked. "You want me to guard the walls I used to scale?"

"I want you to build better ones. And you'll be paid handsomely for it." Alberto glanced around at the dancing and drinking party-goers. "Let's discuss this somewhere we don't have to yell."

By the time they arrived back at the luxury penthouse suite, the others had already gathered. A discreet bartender was serving drinks, and Viktor and Priya were standing by the windows, talking in low voices as they looked down at the Rhine.

"Everyone's here," Alberto said, clapping his hands. The lights automatically changed, dimming at the sides of the room and brightening over a coffee table in the centre. A tap on the surface opened a hidden drawer, revealing a pile of black folders embossed with the Cryptropolis logo.

Inside each was a contract, details of their roles already personalised to the four targets Alberto had chosen, and, most importantly, a one-way flight to the US, where they would begin work on the Veritian project.

He handed them out one by one, meeting each of his new recruits in the eye. As they flicked through the contents, greedy eyes devouring the details, Alberto raised a glass of champagne into the air.

"To the future. To trust. And to secrets well kept," he pronounced, taking a sip.

The recruits exchanged glances, unsure whether to toast or run. But Alberto had already won them over. His magnetic charm, the promise of wealth, and the chance to be part of something monumental outweighed their suspicions.

Just one to go.

While the recruits mingled and Alberto played the perfect host, only one more person was missing: Artem Zheltonirvych, also known as Underlord. The two had been communicating via encrypted chats for months, and it was only now that Alberto had convinced the elusive gamer – and hacker – to meet him in person.

Artem was the real prize. The others were pawns – useful, brilliant pawns – but Artem was the piece that could tip the entire game board. Alberto retreated to his private balcony, the crisp Cologne night wrapping around him as his phone buzzed with a message on his secure ProtonMail.

Underlord: *Arrival confirmed for 8am. Hall 8.*

A smirk tugged at the corner of Alberto's mouth. The final piece was falling into place.

With Underlord as part of the team, this project would be unstoppable.

Chapter 13.

Mr and Mrs Drummond

Nikita sighed loudly, making Daniel glance over at her with a quirked eyebrow in the close confines of their seats. They'd been put on a commercial flight under assumed names, apparently the safest route for them to enter Mexico. Daniel wasn't sure whether the familiar circumstances were comforting or whether he would have preferred to be on a spy plane with all the other operatives, the ones who would supposedly be waiting to extract them or offer emergency help on the ground in Mexico.

Nikita caught his eye with a self-conscious smile. "I hate flying," she confessed. "It's not that I'm afraid or anything – I just get so bored and cramped up, without the option to get up and walk outside."

"You *could* get up and walk outside," Daniel joked. "It just might be a little chilly. And windy."

Nikita laughed, and he was glad to hear the musical sound of her voice when she was amused. "Do you think I could hold onto the wing for the whole eleven hours until we get to Mexico City?"

"Only one way to find out," Daniel suggested with a waggle of his eyebrows, determined to make her laugh again – and satisfied to succeed. Her laugh was charming, the kind of easy mirth that made others' lips quirk up even if they weren't in on the joke.

"Oh, god," Nikita said, her laughter dying away. "Seriously, I'm a terrible companion for long flights. Are you going to sleep?"

Daniel shook his head. "I don't think I'll be able to," he admitted. "I'm too wired."

"Me, too," Nikita said, sighing again – though lighter, this time.

"How did you end up working for the National Crime Agency?" Daniel asked. He had a fair idea of how she'd been seconded to the Bank of England – he could see Sir Rory's hands all over the positions of most of the members of their team – but beyond that, her background was a mystery to him.

"I graduated from Bristol with an economics degree, then took it to a PhD at Harvard," Nikita said. It was funny how so many years of hard work could be summed up in such a brief and glib manner. "How about you? How did you find your way to Sir Rory's right-hand side?"

Daniel smiled self-deprecatingly. "Left-hand side, maybe," he said. "The right hand is reserved for Bernie. I don't have any impressive credentials, I'm afraid – I never went to university."

He could see Nikita's mind working. "And you still worked your way up to where you are now?"

He ducked his head with a modest smile. "It was all a coincidence, really. I got a job instead of going to school, lost it, and sat drowning my sorrows with my Dad in the pub, moaning about it. Someone overheard and asked if I wanted an entry-level position that started the following Monday. Before I knew it, I was a jockey with the Foreign & Commonwealth service."

"Jockey?" Nikita repeated with a light frown.

"Post boy," Daniel explained. "That's what they call us. I was delivering international memos to all the offices, and I got talking to people while I was making my deliveries. I was good at my job, kept my mouth shut about the information I was shuttling around the city, and one of the people I got talking to was Sir Rory."

"And he recruited you, just like that?"

"Not at all," Daniel said with a wry smile. "He gave me a junior apprenticeship in the insights team. I did some research for him on a few different projects and worked my way up. Most of it was just being in the right place at the right time, but I slowly made it higher. Sir Rory helped a lot with making sure I could get through the ranks faster than I should have. He cleared red tape for me. I owe him a lot."

"That's impressive," Nikita said, her voice low and almost doubtful as if she was comparing herself to him.

"*I'm* impressive? You're a *doctor*," Daniel said with a grin. "I never had that kind of patience for school, so I'm always in awe of anyone who makes it to PhD."

"Not everyone's cut out for school," Nikita said, charming in her earnestness.

"School wasn't cut out for me," Daniel said, smirking wryly. "I have pretty severe dyslexia, and they didn't know what to do with me. The A-Levels convinced me I wasn't going to get anything out of doing any more exams."

Nikita chuckled, not mocking him but rather the unsupportive system. "I went to a state grammar school," she said. "There was no room for any weakness there, believe me."

"I believe it," Daniel said. There was a pause. "I always knew I wasn't stupid, though, you know? Just that the system wasn't for me. I was born in Spain, so I was bilingual before all the other kids at school."

"Oh, really?" Nikita asked. "You have no accent."

"No, we moved to South East London when I was four." Daniel smiled wistfully, remembering leafy suburban days. "I spent summers in Spain with my grandparents, but with an English father and Spanish mother, I ended up speaking English as my first language."

Nikita narrowed her eyes. "South East London," she repeated. "Your team?"

Daniel grinned. "Arsenal."

"Yes!" Nikita crowed, earning a look from the people in the row of seats opposite them. "North London forever!"

"Whatever the weather," Daniel completed the chant with a laugh. "I followed my Dad's footsteps in that one."

"I was worried I had a Millwall fan on my hands," Nikita joked, making Daniel shudder.

They passed the rest of the flight laughing and joking together, for the moment forgetting the serious task they had ahead of them. They were briefed and ready to go, and breaking the tension was the best way they could have prepared. The more they talked, the more Daniel came to realise he liked Nikita. She was easy to talk to, and her smile lit up the room in a way he'd thought was only a trite metaphor until now.

Their arrival in the late evening of Mexico City, however, brought that sense of urgency back to the fore.

As their taxi navigated the labyrinthine streets, Daniel observed the chaotic beauty of the city, street vendors illuminated by neon signs, murals of revolutionaries painted on cracked concrete walls, and crowds moving with the frenetic energy of a city that never slept. Everywhere he looked, there was something to grab his attention.

Nikita broke the silence in the back of the car, her sharp eyes catching Daniel's reflection in the window. "Focus, Daniel. We're not here to sightsee."

"Right," Daniel said, pulling himself from his thoughts. "We've got forty-eight hours, and I don't think Spider's going to make this easy for us."

"Did Sir Rory tell you the identity of the informant?" Nikita asked, her voice thoughtful.

"No," he admitted. "I wondered if someone would tell *you*, with your seniority."

That was a good reminder to himself. They were getting along well, and Nikita was beautiful, but she was technically his boss right now. Getting along was all it would have to be.

Nikita shook her head, the ends of her hair slicing around her face like knives. "They're keeping it under wraps. It's frustrating. If we knew, we could talk to them in person."

Daniel shrugged. "Maybe they're planning to introduce us later on."

The Grand Hotel Ciudad loomed ahead, its stained-glass domes glinting in the dim light. Their cover as Mr and Mrs Drummond had been carefully arranged by Langley and Vauxhall Cross, a thin veneer, but one they hoped would buy them time.

Their shared room was a modest suite on the fifth floor. The awkwardness began the moment they saw the beds—two singles pushed together to make one large double.

"Right," Daniel said, already moving towards the beds. "I'll fix this."

"Yeah, good idea," Nikita replied, unbuttoning her jacket and throwing it onto the armchair.

The scrape of bed legs against the floor cut through the silence as Daniel separated the beds and dragged them apart, leaving a chasm of neutral ground between them.

They both chuckled softly at the ridiculousness of it. The sound broke the tension, thankfully; Daniel wouldn't have wanted to spend the whole trip dancing around it.

"Room service?" Daniel suggested, grabbing the menu.

"Arroz al horno for me," Nikita replied. "And let's go over our briefing again."

As they ate, Nikita spread their notes across the small table—intelligence summaries, surveillance photos, fragments of encrypted messages.

The golden haze of the Mexican sunset faded, leaving the sprawling city beneath a blanket of flickering lights. The distant hum of traffic and occasional sirens filtered into the room through partially drawn curtains. Daniel leaned against the window frame, staring out at the city below. Nikita sat cross-legged on her bed, a stack of notes spread in front of her. Between them, a single lamp cast a warm circle of light, their shadows stretching across the walls of their shared hotel room.

As exhaustion crept in, Nikita leaned back, stretching her arms above her head. "Alright, let's sleep. Tomorrow's going to be intense. We need to track down these leads, try to turn them into something real."

Daniel turned off the lamp, the faint glow from the city lights painting their outlines on the walls. Nikita's voice broke the silence one last time. "Do you think we'll actually find him, Daniel? Spider?"

Daniel stared at the ceiling. "We have to."

Despite the exhaustion of the day, sleep came for him fitfully, that one thought circling around in his head like a vulture above a carcass: *we have to.*

Chapter 14.

The Smuggler's Price

A month after Hassan's death, Yash knew he had to start preparing to escape. It was clear from the chat rooms that the journey from Somalia to Europe was perilous and would include many challenges. He now knew that he needed good documentation and sound financial resources. He also needed a good sturdy bag and lots of luck.

He knew, above all, that he could not stay here, with the ghost of his younger brother in every room, around every corner.

Yash was committed to leaving the place that had been his home for all of his thirteen years. He had nothing to live for. He had to escape from his uncle and find a path to a new life. One that his mother had tried to create for him. One where his talent would be appreciated, where he had hope for a good future.

It was clear to him now that such a future could not be found here. Uncle Beson had not learned from Hassan's death but had become even more miserly, more violent. Perhaps, a dark part of Yash's mind suggested, he saw the opportunity to inherit all of his sister's estate by eliminating the only heir standing in his way.

Over the next few weeks, he began to prepare. He read online forums, sent secure and encrypted messages on Telegram to names that his school friends had shared, opened an online bank account, transferred his parents' inheritance so that Uncle Beson could not access it, set up a profile on Gmail and Facebook to document his journey, and stored away his birth certificate, taking a copy to his Google Drive. He picked up a mobile phone with a burner SIM.

He asked around the school playground to the older boys and was soon introduced via phone to Mohammed, who explained that the journey would cost upwards of five thousand dollars. He probably needed a further two and a half thousand dollars to pay bribes to the smugglers and traffickers en route. It was a steep price to pay, but a small price when he considered the potential of his future – and he had some of his winnings to go towards the cost.

It occurred to him, of course, that Mohammed could be the kind of man who would take all of his money and then take him nowhere – or worse, abandon him once he was far away from home. But what choice did he have? Stay here and never take the risk?

Enough people vouched for Mohammed taking their relatives away, and the relatives later sending home a little money, that Yash felt a tenuous trust in his services. And if there were stories about leavers who were never heard from again, surely that was just because they were enjoying a new life and no longer needed to talk to the people they had left behind.

The next Saturday morning, he visited the offices of the Red Crescent Society, a humanitarian group that would not report him to the authorities. They tried immediately to put Yash off the journey.

"It's too dangerous," a young woman behind the counter said. "Yash, you're very young. Why don't you wait until you've finished school?"

"*Years*," Yash told her, trying not to get angry. "You want me to wait in a situation I can't bear for *years*, just because I'm young?"

She pursed her lips. "You could die on the journey. Is it better to live through something difficult, or to die and never have the chance to see a better day?"

"It's better to die," Yash told her flatly. He felt his nostrils flaring but fought to keep himself under control. "How about you tell me some survival tips so that my chances are higher?"

When she saw he was determined, she gave in to his wishes and gave Yash advice on how to plan and survive the journey. She wanted to make sure that he had the right information. Much misinformation about the journey existed online, and many people could be tricked by traffickers or other criminals.

He met Mohammed on Monday, a man barely seen in the shadows of the early morning, hiding around the corner behind an old, uninhabited building near the school. Yash did not worry about his Uncle finding him missing – Beson would not be awake for hours.

He waited before he approached, checking for himself that there was no one else around. Overhead, a flock of birds were startled from a tree, flying over him. Beyond them, way back in the deep blue, he saw the tiny dot of a plane leaving a white trail behind it.

"The next bus to Nairobi leaves Saturday evening," Mohammed said, without much in the way of introduction. His words were rushed, his head whipping back and forth as he checked the streets for signs of movement. Yash couldn't help wondering right in the back of his mind whether Mohammed was one of the traffickers he had been told about, but he pushed it down. "You meet me here just before it goes."

Yash nodded. "We go from Nairobi?" he asked. He'd heard details of the routes, but he wanted to be sure he would not be abandoned and left to find his own way.

Mohammed's eyes glinted at him from the dark. "Nairobi to Juba, South Sudan. Then Khartoum, through the Libyan desert to Sebha, and on to Tripoli. You go through Algeria to Oujda, then to Ksar es Seghir in Morocco, and finally to Spain."

Spain. His new home, maybe. Yash fought down a shiver of excitement as he memorised the steps, just in case he would have to complete some of them on his own. "What do I need to bring?"

"Only one small bag," Mohammed warned him. "You can't carry more. You must bring me two hundred dollars. There will be about twenty on the bus."

Yash nodded. "Understood." He thought for a moment and opened his mouth to ask something more, but Mohammed was already gone.

Yash walked towards the school with excitement bubbling in his veins, fizzing in his head. It would be dangerous, but he felt better now that he had a plan, a purpose. Something his mother had always instilled in him. Whether he was aiming to win the next eight hundred metre race, beating the system with his algorithms, or aiming his education for

Stanford University, a plan was how he knew to operate.

He slipped into the school library and sat down at one of the computers, firing up his online game and logging in for what might be his last chance for a while. He sent messages to those he often played with, telling them that something had come up at home and he might not be back for some time. Their well-wishing warmed his heart, encouraging him further. People cared about him, even if they only knew him digitally.

He could do this.

He would do it alone because he had no one to stand by his side – but he could do it.

That Saturday, Yash turned his back on Hargeisa, on Uncle Beson, on his home, on his family history, on the ghosts of his brother and parents.

And said hello again to Mohammed.

Chapter 15.

The Devil's Bargain

Artem had always been a planner. He approached everything—gaming, coding, life—with a cold, calculated precision. But nothing about his journey over the last two days had felt planned. It felt impulsive, chaotic even.

After travelling to Cologne via Berlin, initially starting out from the seaside resort of Gdansk in Poland, the overnight train had arrived on time, at precisely seven thirty in the morning. Artem had disembarked and walked over the Hohenzollern Bridge, pulling his small case and carrying his backpack, holding between them everything he valued: his Razer Blade laptop, a selection of clothes to last a few days, and a stack of print screenshots of his chats with his summoner. Walking with other conference delegates, admiring the magnificence of the Rhine, his thoughts kept returning to the river in Kharkiv.

It had been too long since he had seen his hometown.

His time in Gdansk had been suffocating. He wanted a fresh start, away from the prison of language barriers and isolation. Perhaps his contact was about to offer him that opportunity.

The sun was out, and this early morning walk was the perfect antidote to stretch his legs after the long train journey. As he walked, he ran everything over in his mind again and again, rehearsing the plan.

He'd been playing Dota 2 online with Phantom for three or four years, now. He'd been invited to an already-established tournament team, replacing a player who could no longer commit to the hours of practice needed to be at the top. Phantom had been the one to invite him – Artem, in-game name Underlord – to join them, and now Phantom wanted to meet in person.

The messages they had exchanged had been cryptic, but intriguing. Standing at a road crossing and waiting for the traffic to clear, Artem flicked through their latest chat again with one hand.

Phantom: *You know, Underlord, your skills are wasted here. You could be doing something... something monumental.*
Underlord: *Like what?*
Phantom: *Something bigger than any game. Something that could change the world.*

Underlord: *What do you mean?*

Phantom: *I have a project. It's not a game, but it needs a player like you. Smart. Focused. Detached.*

Phantom: *You're coming to Crypto Summit X, right? Let's meet at the end of the second day.*

In fact, Artem had two meetings set up at the Crypto Summit X conference – one with Phantom, and one with the man who had sent him the train tickets and his attendance pass. Alberto Lopez, the genius behind Cryptropolis himself. Artem had no idea what this man could want with him or why he would invest in meeting him, but his heart thrummed with the excitement of finding out.

Arriving at the entrance, Artem showed his pass and walked inside Hall Eight. He saw where he was headed almost immediately: a sleek black monstrosity loomed over all of the other booths, the Cryptropolis logo emblazoned prominently on the front.

A security guard at the entrance to the booth escorted him to a small office unit built within the top floor of the booth itself. Artem sat up straight in his leather chair, his laptop in front of him as he gazed in wonderment from the soundproofed glass booth, leaning in different directions to get a glimpse of it all.

The chaos below him, with flashing screens, bright company banners, and hundreds if not thousands of delegates buzzing with industry chatter felt surreal. But here he was. Summoned by a higher purpose.

The glass booth felt sterile. Artem's palms were damp as he wiped them on his jeans. And then, the door swung open. Artem instantly recognised Alberto Lopez.

In stepped the man a hundred thousand tech boys would kill their mothers to meet: impeccably dressed in a tailored navy suit, his dark hair kept functionally short, his sharp brown eyes locked onto Artem with an intensity that felt magnetic. It was the second day of the convention, yet he looked fresh and energetic.

Alberto extended a hand, and Artem hesitated before shaking it. "Welcome to Crypto Summit X, and welcome to Cryptropolis," Alberto said. "I've been looking forward to meeting you, Artem."

Artem's breath hitched. "Thank you for the opportunity to visit," he said, remembering his manners. Even if this turned into nothing, he wanted to make a good impression.

Alberto sat down across from him, unbuttoning his suit jacket with effortless charm. "Let me start by being honest, Artem. I know everything about you. Your history in Kharkiv, your move to Gdańsk, your freelance coding projects, and your struggles to send money back to your family in Odesa. I know how much you've sacrificed."

Artem's eyes darted to his laptop, briefly considering whether he had walked into a trap. *Freelance coding projects* was a generous term. He'd broken some laws in the name of trying to fund his family's escape from the war.

"Relax. If I wanted to hurt you, I wouldn't have invited you to Cologne," Alberto said smoothly. He leaned forward, lowering his voice in spite of the soundproofed booth around them. "I've been watching you for a long time, Artem. In Dota 2, in your tournament performances. But more importantly, I've been watching your mind. The tools you built for your Liquid Tundra team — the HUD overlays, the stat analysis scripts, the predictive analytics — you're brilliant. And brilliance like yours doesn't belong in small tournaments or underpaid freelance gigs. It belongs here. With me."

Artem sat transfixed; here was one of the most famous men in tech, offering him a job – headhunting him! This was unreal.

Alberto handed Artem a tablet. On it, financial projections for Cryptropolis scrolled endlessly: charts, data streams, and flashing indicators of meteoric growth.

"This is the future, Artem. Governments are fighting over digital currencies. The US and UK have already approached me to build a secure infrastructure for their digital coin. But I can't do it alone. I need people like you. People who see patterns where others see noise. People who don't just play the game—they own the game."

Artem felt lightheaded. The weight of the offer pressed down on him like a physical force. He stared at the screen, trying to comprehend all of this at once. His analytical skills were hardly lacking, but the moment was completely overwhelming.

"And let's not pretend money isn't a factor," Alberto continued, his tone softening. "You've been struggling to send two hundred dollars a month back to Odesa. Join me, and you won't need to worry about your family again."

Artem swallowed. "I would like to be able to send them more," he said, his throat feeling raw with emotion.

Alberto pulled out a Razer Blade 16 laptop from under the table, brand new and custom-built. Even better than his own, a newer model. "This is yours, Artem. Your workstation. Your gateway to Cryptropolis. All you have to do is say yes."

In the back of his mind, Artem was thinking about Phantom. His Liquid Tundra teammate wanted to meet, and there was a chance that he, too, had an offer for him. But even if he did, there was no need to think about it. He would either take on both projects, if it was possible, or his teammate would have to be disappointed – though he would feel terrible to let down a friend, his family were more important.

“Yes,” he said, looking up at Alberto with absolute conviction. How could he turn down the offer of a lifetime?

“Then, here are your briefing documents,” Alberto said, handing over a discreet black folder. “You’ll need to start promptly tomorrow morning, but all of the details are inside. And, Artem?”

“Yes?”

“Welcome to the team.”

Alberto smiled, but Artem’s heart beat faster as he considered that his new boss had the smile of a wolf.

Chapter 16.

The Tulum Connection

Luna: *I have information for you*

Tonka: *Already? Luna, you're the best!*

Luna: *I don't think this channel is secure enough to discuss it. We should meet in person*

Tonka: *That might be a problem. I'm currently in a different country*

Luna: *I know. I've been tracking your IP address as well*

Luna: *You don't know this, but I live in Mexico*

Tonka: *OK. I'll just choose to ignore that you've been digitally stalking me... are you close to Mexico City?*

Luna: *Relax, I looked into everyone on the team. I had to. I noticed something about the data you sent. But I can't tell you here.*

Luna: *I'm in Tulum, but I know someone in Mexico City you should meet. Jezer. She's a contact of my girlfriend. She knows everyone and everything*

Tonka: *Can she be discreet?*

Luna: *That's her whole thing. She's connected. She has something on everyone. She can be trusted*

Luna: *She'll meet you in the Grand Hotel Cuidad atrium, tomorrow morning at ten*

Tonka: *We're here under false names. Tell her we're Mr and Mrs Drummond*

Luna: *I don't want to send my address over here. She'll give it to you. I'll let her know about*

Nikita tapped her pen against the printed message chain from Luna. "This Spider… it's like chasing smoke. Ten years of activity, hundreds of millions in crypto movements, and no one knows who or where he is. And now this Jezer comes out of nowhere with just the information we might need?"

Daniel chewed thoughtfully before replying. "If Luna trusts Jezer, we trust Jezer. For now."

"Don't you think you're putting too much trust into someone you barely know?" Nikita asked. "This 'Luna' – do you even know her real name?"

"It's… deeper than that," Daniel said. How to explain what it was like to be part of a team, to someone who didn't know anything about online gaming? "We've worked together for years. We've had to trust one another in pretty serious situations. It may only seem like a game to you, but we've entered tournaments with cash prizes – and had real success on the line. We've had each other's backs. And there have been countless hours of training, talking into the night, chatting even when we weren't playing."

"Still," Nikita said. "This is a matter of international security. There are *governments* resting on this. How well do you know her, really?"

"Well enough to know she can handle this," Daniel said. "Look how cautious she is. She understands the stakes. I trust her. Can you trust me?"

There was a long moment of pause; Daniel wondered if Nikita would say no. Finally, she ducked her head in what was almost a nod.

"Fine," she said. "We'll do it your way. But if there's any sign that we're being played, we back out."

"That's fair," Daniel agreed – but privately, he knew, there was no chance. He and Luna were the dual Supports for their team. They were the same, they thought the same way. She wouldn't betray him.

They walked down the street to their meeting place, both of them trying hard to be inconspicuous – and laughing when they caught sight of one another. Though it helped to diffuse their nerves a little, they both still felt the tension tightly wrapped around them. Covert meetings, code names – it was all a little like being in a spy movie, something Daniel had never anticipated when he agreed to join Sir Rory's research team a few years ago.

The Grand Hotel Ciudad was a relic of colonial grandeur. Its towering stained-glass ceilings created patterns of light on the marble floor while tourists milled about taking photographs. Daniel and Nikita took a corner booth overlooking the atrium, in a place where they would be less likely to appear in the background of any shots.

Nikita, wearing sunglasses, scanned the entrance casually. Daniel sipped his espresso, trying to look like a relaxed tourist and, he thought, likely failing.

Jezer approached them confidently. She was dressed in a flowing blouse and linen trousers, blending effortlessly into the hotel's cosmopolitan crowd.

"Good morning," Jezer said with a sly smile as if they had been friends for years.

Daniel gestured to the empty seat. "Jezer. How are you?"

It was a covert way of making sure that this really *was* Jezer, and her answering smile told him he had assumed correctly.

They ordered coffee and kept their voices low, all of them leaning forward over the table to hear one another better.

"I'm Daniel Warren," he said, holding out his hand for a shake, only to receive a swift kick in the ankle under the table from Nikita's side.

"This is my husband," she said through gritted teeth. "We're Mr and Mrs Drummond. *As you know*."

Jezer only smiled, and Daniel looked down, chagrined. He'd made a real rookie mistake. He needed to remember their cover – out here, even though they had a team waiting to extract them, things could go wrong quickly. He wasn't going to make the same error twice.

"You know a friend of mine," Jezer said. "You know her as Luna, I know her as Maria."

"I heard you're connected to her girlfriend," Daniel said carefully, trying not to use the wrong words this time.

"Eva reached out to me first," Jezer began, her voice calm but serious. "She messaged me on WhatsApp, saying we needed to talk about Veritian."

"You work with Eva on other matters?" Nikita interrupted, trying to get a handle on the nature of their relationship.

"Eva is one of my informants," Jezer agreed matter-of-factly. "But this is different to our usual conversations about high-up government meetings between her father and the power brokers who control the Mexican systems. My Langley handlers have instructed me to cautiously follow the lead she found."

Daniel studied Jezer carefully as she spoke, her voice low, deliberate, and razor-sharp with precision. Everything about her felt carefully constructed from the causal flow of her linen dress to the way she positioned herself slightly sideways, always aware of her surroundings but never letting her guard slip. Her eyes, an unyielding shade of steel grey, carried both exhaustion and an unnerving clarity, as if she'd seen too much but had learned to carry the weight of it without faltering.

He wasn't sure if she knew she was dropping them information they didn't have about Eva and Maria – even their names. Beside him, Daniel felt Nikita shift slightly in her seat. She was probably wondering what he was: exactly who Eva and her powerful father were.

"Do you know what the lead is?" Daniel asked. "Luna wouldn't tell us over chat – she was worried about our conversation being intercepted."

"Eva isn't naive," Jezer continued. "She knows how dangerous this, or, in fact, any, information is. But she trusts Maria with her life. And Maria picked up on something. Two IP addresses that shouldn't be here, both appearing here at the same time as your visit."

Nikita's brow furrowed. "Wait, so the key information came from Maria watching IP addresses?"

Jezer nodded. "It sounds thin, I know. But Eva doesn't exaggerate. And Maria isn't just some casual gamer, she's a strategist, an analyst in the gaming world. She doesn't miss things. I trust this lead. I can't say more just yet – I understand Maria needs to tell you some details that she's keeping close to her chest, even from me." Jezer shrugged carefully. "I wish she would give me the whole picture, but I understand. The rule here in Mexico City is to always assume every asset has already been compromised. That way, you're usually not disappointed."

She wasn't going to say more; they would have to wait for the rest of the story until they could meet Luna. But there was something else, something in the way her fingers fidgeted slightly with the edge of her napkin, the way she glanced toward the entrance every few minutes. She was scared. Not for herself, but for what she was about to hand over. Information wasn't just power in their world, it was a ticking bomb.

Daniel asked softly, "What do you or Langley know about Spider?"

Jezer took a deep breath. "Spider isn't just a hacker; he's a strategist. His operations are clean, surgical. He's held entire corporations hostage without leaving a trace. But here's the kicker—he's not just doing this for money. There's a cause behind it, a motive. And Mexico is central to it."

Daniel leaned forward. "What motive?"

"We aren't sure. It's just that the moves he makes – sometimes they're lateral, sometimes they go in an unexpected direction. He doesn't go for the biggest payoffs. There's something else driving his decisions."

"Why do you think it's happening here? Why Mexico?"

Jezer's expression grew grim. "Mexico is the perfect staging ground. It's a cybercrime hub, a crossroads of global financial flows. After the

Pegasus scandal, half the world's governments realised their systems had been breached by Mexican servers. Add in cheap labour from brilliant coders fleeing Eastern Europe and the Subcontinent, and you have a perfect storm."

Nikita nodded. "And with its proximity to the US, Spider has a front-row seat to the biggest financial network on the planet."

Jezer was still glancing at the door. Nervous. Daniel thought about what she'd said – that no one here could be trusted. Living like that had to be difficult.

Daniel leaned forward slightly, lowering his voice. "Jezer, I need you to understand something. I'm not here to catch you in a lie or to question your loyalty. I'm here because time is running out, and whatever you know might be the thread that pulls this entire mess apart. But for me to trust what you're telling us… I need to know that you trust me."

For the briefest moment, Jezer's mask slipped. A flicker of vulnerability crossed her face, followed swiftly by resignation. She nodded once, a subtle, almost imperceptible movement.

It was enough.

Daniel knew then, she wasn't just protecting herself. She had other people to protect, other stakes in the game. She wouldn't trust them right off the bat; they were no one to her. Strangers. Maybe enemies parading as allies. But she was giving him just a modicum of the benefit of the doubt, and it was all he could ask for.

"There's something else," Jezer continued. "Some of Spider's operations are running through shell companies registered here. We think they're being managed through encrypted systems located in romantic beach towns, like Tulum."

Nikita's eyes widened. "Could we trace him through those companies?"

Jezer handed Nikita a slip of paper. "This is Maria's address in Tulum," she said. It dawned on Daniel that this was a test – that if they really were friends with Maria, they would be able to meet with her and get the information. If they weren't, Jezer had risked nothing. "Eva's there with her now. You need to go. Speak to Maria directly. If anyone knows how to unlock this and determine what this Spider is planning, it's likely to be her. I don't understand the technical side – it's beyond me – but they tell me you're an expert."

Daniel looked at Nikita, wondering if he deserved the designation. She looked back at him blankly enough, so he nodded, accepting it. He was the expert here – he had to be. All those years of coding in his bedroom, doing it as a hobby, were now the foundation for something much more serious.

"What about you, Jezer?" Daniel asked.

Jezer smirked faintly. "I'll keep my ear to the ground here. And I'll see what I can dig up from Eva's contacts. Just don't lose sight of the bigger picture. Spider isn't just in Tulum or Mexico. He's everywhere."

The weight of her words settled heavy onto all of their shoulders.

"I may not see you again," Jezer said, getting up and glancing over her shoulder. "You can contact me through Eva if you need me."

Just like that, she was gone, lost in the crowd as if she had never been there at all.

Before leaving the café, Nikita paused. "Daniel… whatever happens in Tulum, we need to trust each other. No second-guessing."

Daniel met her gaze. "Agreed." He took a breath, examining the horizon as if it could tell them what they needed to know. "Let's get our bags and hire a car. We've got a long drive ahead."

Chapter 17.

Sahara Crossing

Yash's journey from Hargeisa to Nairobi took nearly thirty-four hours. The traffickers stopped twice for the passengers to refresh and pray, and to refuel the bus. The refuelling was carried out by a jerry can from the rear of a Toyota Hi-Lux.

In the interim, passengers also prayed on the bus, which caused chaos in the aisles five times a day. It was very hot, and acrid smells soon filled the cramped space.

It seemed strange to Yash to journey south first. But he also understood that travelling to Morocco via the western route was more manageable and easier to pull off.

In Nairobi, exhausted, the bus passengers slept overnight at the back of a gas station out of the city, in a district called Runguri. They awaited their departure with the next designated bus on the A1 road.

A lone Medicines Sans Frontiers aid worker was there at five the next morning, handing out food and water from the boot of her car. She disappeared when another car turned up, letting out a bigger man who introduced himself as Yaro.

Yash and the others each paid Yaro another two hundred and fifty American dollars; the money was needed to guarantee their journey to Juba. But he also asked for an extra fifty dollars as the bus apparently needed extra fuel. Yash understood this was an extra bribe.

Over the next twenty minutes, more people arrived and boarded the bus. They looked like central Africans. They were different in size and shape to Yash. He hadn't met people like that, and he wavered between excitement and fear at meeting these newcomers.

Most people on the bus were not chatty, but a guy who looked to be in his late teens – a few years older than Yash – sat down next to him and fixed him with a grin right away.

"Hi," he said. "I'm Rusanganwa."

Yash just looked at him, too scared to say a word. Were they supposed to learn one another's identities? Or was it better to stay silent and keep to himself?

When Yash didn't immediately return his introduction, Rusanganwa simply shrugged and leaned to the side so he could watch their progress through the front windows of the bus, and Yash did not need to say a word.

By the second day of sitting together, however, Yash found that he could be brave.

"I'm Yash," he said, finally.

The grin that split Rusanganwa's face wide open was joyful. "How are you, Yash?" he asked. "Where are you from?"

"Somalia," Yash told him. Rusanganwa's accent was strange to his ears, but English was a common language they could both understand, a bridge between them.

"I'm from Rwanda," the older boy declared. He pointed to the front of the bus. "Juba, this way."

Yash nodded confirmation of their next stop. "Are you alone?" he asked, his curiosity getting the better of his fears again.

Rusanganwa nodded. "My family – all gone," he said, looking down at his hands. His English was broken, but easy enough to understand. "You know the troubles?"

Yash shook his head, his eyes poring over Rusanganwa as if he could see any sign of it. They had their losses in common. Did it mark them in some way? Make them different?

"Hutu and Tutsi killing each other," he said, shaking his head. "My tribe, Twa, caught in the middle."

Yash didn't know what most of those words meant, but he nodded anyway. "My parents were killed too," he said. "And my brother."

"I'm sorry."

Yash nodded. "Me too," he said. Something about their shared loss made him want to say more; he hadn't spoken to anyone at all about what had happened, and though each word caused him pain, he felt the need for them to be said. "My brother got sick and my Uncle wouldn't take him to hospital. Then it was too late. And my parents, they died before that – when the Americans sent a bomb."

Rusanganwa made a noise under his breath, a tsking noise against his teeth. "*Americans*," he said. "They could have done something. President Clinton, he refused to help us. That's why Europe. I can't go to America. They never helped us."

Yash found himself nodding along. "I would never go there," he said fiercely. Americans had, after all, stolen his parents – and if his parents were still around, Hassan would never have fallen sick –

and if he'd fallen sick, he never would have needed to wait for treatment. They would all be alive, all of them, and Hassan would be living his normal life still. Happy.

The bus jolted over a particularly rough bump in the road, jostling Rusanganwa and Yash together. They exchanged a glance and a shake of heads. The roads were bad, it was sweltering inside the bus, and there was a lot of noise all the time. It was hard to hold a conversation, and almost impossible to sleep.

"It will be worse to cross the Sahara," Rusanganwa warned. "Very hot. I heard of people who don't make it. Too weak."

Yash nodded miserably. He'd read about the gruelling twenty-two-hour trip, almost a race; if they stopped for anything, bandits would attack. At the very least, their possessions would be stolen – but the outcome could be worse, especially for the women on board. Yash didn't want to think too hard about that.

The experienced bus driver would stop and pay people beside the road along the route. Human trafficking was clearly a lucrative business. He seemed to be on good terms with most of the sentries that blocked the path.

On passing through the town of Juba, even more people got on the bus, and Yash was glad Rusanganwa had chosen to sit next to him – so that he was not stuck with an odious seatmate. Desperate migrants huddled in makeshift camps as they passed, their eyes hollow with fear and hope. The caravan started under the cover of night, moving cautiously along Bahr el Ghazal Road. The road stretched like a black ribbon into the wilderness, flanked by checkpoints manned by jittery young men carrying ageing AK-47s.

In the day, Yash read his book over and over again – the tattered volume of explorers his mother had given him. Sometimes, he felt like he was an adventurer himself, exploring new territory bravely and heading off into the unknown.

But reality crashed down on him: the smells of the unwashed men and women around him, the constant fear at each checkpoint that they would not make it, the hunger and thirst, the exhaustion of sleepless nights in uncomfortable places. This was not a heroic, courageous journey that would make his name. No one would ever know he had taken this route. That was necessary for his safety, and for the safety of those who came after him.

This was not an expedition, but a nightmare, and the only thing keeping him going was the hint of safety and freedom at the very end.

From Juba, they headed towards Khartoum. With road signs counting down the mileage, both journeys were long and uneventful save for a few stops to refuel and to see the odd camel in the distance. And the Blue Nile, winding its way alongside their route through mainly arid land. Behind them, for miles, a plume of dust gave away their journey. Each mile burned away weakness, each checkpoint tested resolve, and every encounter with border guards or militia was a brush with death.

Yash observed everything—the smugglers' mannerisms, the patterns of bribery at each stop, the way each checkpoint commander's chest puffed up when handed a wad of crumpled notes.

After days of tense travel, they reached Khartoum. The city was chaos wrapped in the illusion of order. Smugglers herded them into an abandoned warehouse where the air reeked of sweat and stale urine. There was no comfort here—only waiting and fear.

And the Sahara was still to come.

Chapter 18.

Underlord's Detour

Artem was holed up in a converted cartel building, his Razer laptop perched precariously on an ornate mahogany desk. Lines of code cascaded down his screen as he worked furiously to decrypt the stolen files.

The Caracas safehouse was unremarkable, its plain exterior hiding the significance of the mission inside.

The hours passed in tense silence. Outside, armed guards patrolled the grounds, and somewhere in the distance, the faint hum of city traffic could be heard.

This whole trip had been strange, stranger, and stranger still. On landing in Mexico City, Artem had been met by a woman named Sofia – beautiful, wrapped in a red dress that looked like it cost more than everything Artem had owned in his life put together, and just as mysterious as Spider himself. She wasn't Mexican, that much was clear, but he had no idea who she was or where she came from – or where she'd gone, since he was now on his own.

Standing in a side street that was apparently a blank spot – he saw no cameras overhead, nothing pointed in their direction to record them – she had handed him a slim black case.

"What's this?" Artem asked, inspecting it with a practised eye. It looked like a hard drive, one of the most secure on the market.

"It's secure," she said, confirming his suspicions. "Quantum-encrypted, air-gapped, and designed to self-destruct if tampered with."

"Alright," Artem said. Spider had given him no instructions other than to get to Mexico City and look out for the woman in the red dress. "What do I do with it?"

"There's a warehouse about twenty miles outside of Tulum," Sofia told him, her eyes darting behind him, tracking the progress of tourists walking by the end of the alley. None of them turned in; Artem had the feeling this meeting would go very differently if they did. "You're going to meet a man named Emilio Sanchez. He has some files you will decrypt."

Artem's spine straightened, a tingling sense of danger rippling through him. "A man named Sanchez in a remote warehouse needs me to decrypt some files," he said. "I suppose these are stolen files."

Not for the first time, doubt struck him. What was he doing here? The money was welcome, yes, but Phantom had not been what he expected. A Russian accent, for one thing. He had almost turned and walked away in disgust when he heard it. The only thing that kept him listening was the fact that Phantom could help him save his family. The uncomfortable thought that he might be betraying the rest of his countrymen in order to do it was too heartbreaking to contemplate. What choice did he have? Family was everything.

For another thing, it was increasingly obvious to him that whatever Phantom wanted, it was probably utterly at odds with the goals of his other employer – Alberto Lopez and Cryptropolis.

Was he being a coward and a fool, undermining the work of a man who had given him an excellent job? Or would anyone do the same in his place, given the need for money to send back home?

Sofia inclined her head slightly, not quite a nod. "Sanchez is a dangerous man. A drug baron leading a cartel. He must not know why you are really here."

"Why am I really here?"

And Sofia had smiled and told him.

"Can you do it?" she asked, eventually, as Artem stood there wondering again what the hell he'd gotten himself into.

Artem nodded. It was too late to change his mind now. He knew too much. He would be a liability if he grew morals. "It'll get there."

Sofia's sharp gaze lingered on him. "Make sure it does. We've come too far for mistakes."

"You don't need to worry," Artem replied, pocketing the drive.

He turned and left, and caught a train to Tulum, then a taxi into the middle of nowhere.

That was how he came to be sitting in a warehouse, decrypting lines of stolen code, waiting for a chance to get the drive out of his pocket and do what he was really here for.

But something wasn't adding up. The warehouse wasn't just a random cartel warehouse. It wasn't full of drugs or weapons, at least as far as Artem could see.

It was full of servers.

Servers that were branded with the logo of Cryptropolis.

Artem's pulse quickened as he realised his work on the decryption was nearing completion.

Was this connected to Alberto? Was this connected to Cryptropolis? *Was he actually hacking his own boss?*

Suddenly, his secure chat window pinged.

Spider: *Finish the job, Artem. Time is running out*

Not for the first time, spine-tingling dread crept into Artem's mind. Was he being manipulated? Was Spider using him for something darker, something that would attack Alberto's operations? Was he here to break the project he'd been hired to work on? How could he look any other member of the team in the eye if that was the case – and what would happen if they found out he'd used vacation days immediately after joining the team to go off and hack them?

He closed the terminal, his eyes narrowing.

He had decrypted the file. It was now or never. If he didn't do what he'd been paid to do, he would miss the chance.

He glanced behind him. There was an armed guard outside the room, but his back was to Artem. Taking a chance, holding his breath in case the chair creaked and drew attention his way, Artem launched himself forward and inserted a USB cable from the drive to the computer tower on the desk. He watched as the files inside unzipped, processed, propagated.

He held his breath.

It was an egg.

One of Spider's infamous eggs.

He'd heard of them – but never had the chance to see one in action.

The egg was passed seamlessly, its significance hidden beneath layers of subterfuge. He watched as it erased all traces of itself, embedding itself into the project coding saved to the server, then almost disappearing.

The egg wasn't just malicious code, it was a masterpiece. Once embedded into the DGTX system, it fragmented into thousands of micro-subroutines. Each subroutine mimicked routine blockchain processes, rendering it undetectable.

Its activation mechanism was equally ingenious. The egg would lie dormant until triggered by a specific sequence of transactions—a sequence known only to Spider. Even Artem, having watched it at work, had no hope of triggering, deactivating, or even recreating the egg – the work was too complex, too advanced. Once activated, it could rewrite ledger histories, reroute transactions, or collapse the system entirely, all while leaving no trace of its origin.

By the time it reached the DGTX engineering team, the egg would appear as nothing more than a basic hardware update from the Mexican servers that handled the project's security. The engineers would integrate it without question, unknowingly completing the final step of Spider's plan.

The light from his monitor illuminated Artem's face, pale and uncertain. Had he just ruined his new boss? When he'd signed on at Crypto Summit X, Artem had had every intention of staying loyal to Cryptropolis. But even with the generous package Alberto Lopez had offered, what Spider offered was unimaginably greater.

Artem took a breath and tried to gather himself, looking at his screen and starting to close down programs that were no longer needed. As the window filled with the running details of his VPN –

a virtual private network, one that was untraceable to his real location – he hesitated.

Cold horror rushed through his blood.

The VPN was turned *off*, meaning that he was broadcasting his real location to anyone who cared to look.

Artem hit the switch to turn it back on as fast as he could, his fingers shaking. He thought back over everything he had done in this session – so much illegal activity that it was almost funny, except for how it absolutely wasn't. How had he managed to forget to turn on the VPN?

No: he hadn't forgotten. Retracing his steps, he remembered it clearly. That was why the window was open – because he'd carefully put all of his privacy systems into place first, before even beginning anything else.

So, how had it turned off?

There was only one way it could have been done. A hack on his machine, someone able to control it from the outside remotely. They could have switched it off without him noticing it – no alert would have shown up on his screen.

Artem looked around furtively, wondering if he was being watched and tracked even now, but a quiet beep from his machine dragged his attention back.

He glanced at the single new message that had just pinged onto his secure channel.

Spider: *Good work, Underlord. Now forget everything you saw.*

But Artem couldn't forget. And the trail he left by using his own laptop to decrypt Emilio Sanchez's files had already begun to unravel.

Chapter 19.

Manhunt Begins

Daniel flexed his hands on the steering wheel, trying to loosen up his cramped muscles, glancing in the rearview mirror yet again to check for any familiar vehicles. Beside him in the passenger seat, Nikita shuffled through a stack of photos.

She had always been methodical, her ability to piece together data one of the reasons Daniel admired her. But right now, all he could think about was the growing knot in his stomach. Who was Spider? Who were Eva and Maria, really? Was it just a coincidence that Maria – Luna – had stepped in to help just when it seemed that a trace of Spider could be found so close to her own home?

It felt like they were chasing ghosts.

But if that was true, then at least they were committed to the chase. They'd left Mexico City not long after they met with Jezer, hailing a taxi from their hotel. Daniel had watched the city fade into the distance as they drove towards the airport. Next stop: Tulum. The sun was rising, casting long shadows over the sprawling capital. Somewhere, Spider was watching. Waiting.

The warm glow of the late afternoon sun filtered through the windshield as their taxi went down the highway to Puebla International Airport, leaving Mexico City far behind. The sprawling chaos of the capital had given way to occasional glimpses of the squalor that surrounded this mega city.

Nikita had sat beside Daniel, sunglasses perched on her nose, her hair pulled back into a neat ponytail. Daniel sat flipping through a creased notebook filled with scribbled notes and hastily drawn diagrams, trying to make sense of everything, trying to guess what Maria had found.

It was about halfway through the drive that they'd realised they were being tailed.

The same car stuck behind them all the way to the airport, even when they asked their driver to take a shortcut or an unusual route. A black sedan, unmarked in any way, a little dusty and beaten up. Not one of theirs; they already knew that the operatives shadowing them had gone a different route, an attempt to throw off anyone who might suspect something. The glare of sunlight on the windscreen made it impossible for them to make out the features of the driver, but it had been unsettling enough for them to grab one another's hands and sprint as fast as possible through the crowds at the airport.

They'd even gone intentionally to the wrong gate, before turning and taking another path through the airport to the right place, trying to throw off anyone who was waiting to see where they would go.

Ultimately, they had no idea whether they'd been successful.

The flight from Puebla to Cancún International Airport had been uneventful but tense. Nikita and Daniel had stayed quiet for most of the short flight, their minds racing with fragmented plans and unresolved questions. Daniel's hand tingled where he had grasped Nikita's, a strangely intimate gesture given their circumstances and the short time they had known one another. Upon landing, they rented a modest white Ford sedan—something common enough not to draw attention – and started their drive south to Tulum.

The journey stretched over two hours, with the coastal road winding lazily through small towns, dense vegetation, and the occasional roadside food stand illuminated by flickering neon lights. The late afternoon sun painted everything in warm gold, the sky blushing pink and orange as the day began to fade. They relied on an old-fashioned paper map, leaving no digital trace of their journey, no GPS record.

So far, there was no sign that anyone was behind them – but Daniel had no way of really knowing if they'd managed to get out here without being noticed.

"This place feels… dreamlike," Daniel said, his eyes scanning the passing scenery. "Like paradise."

"It's like it can't decide if it's paradise or purgatory," Nikita said, her voice soft but thoughtful.

Daniel glanced at her. "It's both. Wealth and beauty stitched together with shadows and secrets. The perfect place for someone like Spider to hide in plain sight."

Nikita nodded in agreement, her hands steady on the wheel. "It's the kind of place where people come to disappear. Sunsets and secrets, that's Tulum in a nutshell."

They passed through Playa del Carmen, where luxury resorts sat side by side with crumbling colonial architecture. Occasionally, a sleek black SUV or an armoured vehicle would cruise past them—silent reminders of the cartel influence that loomed over the Riviera Maya. Though Daniel watched them closely, noting number plates and models, none of them appeared twice. It seemed they had lost that tail.

The road stretched ahead, empty except for their headlights cutting through the encroaching twilight. The silence in the car was thick, punctuated only by the faint sound of static from the radio.

Daniel broke it first. "Nikita… back in London, before all of this—you had a good life. A safe one. Why throw yourself into something this dangerous?"

Nikita smirked faintly, her eyes never leaving the documents in front of her. "You think the National Crime Agency is safe, Daniel? Half of my time was spent chasing ghosts, people who could destroy entire economies from behind a keyboard."

Daniel turned slightly in his seat to face her, though he kept his gaze on the road. "But you're not just doing this for the thrill, are you?"

She sighed, shuffling some photographs together into a pile. "My mother died when I was twelve. Cancer. My father, well, he disappeared into his work after that. I was practically raised by firewalls and encryption manuals. But there was one thing he always told me: 'If you have the skill to stop something terrible, you have the responsibility to try.'"

Daniel nodded slowly. "And this, Spider, the risk to Veritian, it feels like one of those terrible things, doesn't it?"

"Worse," Nikita said softly. "This isn't just about money or control. If Spider succeeds, entire systems will collapse. People will lose everything, and they won't even know who to blame. There will be riots, mass imprisonments, deaths – and all that just from the civil disobedience. Who knows what the quieter, longer-term consequences could be for those with nothing left."

Daniel made a faint noise of agreement, his hands tightening on the steering wheel. The repercussions of economic collapse didn't bear thinking about.

"What about you?" she asked. "Are you really just Sir Rory's dog, so desperate to please him you'll dive headfirst into whatever he asks?"

Daniel shifted and glanced at her. "Is that how you see me?"

"Is it how you are?"

Daniel hesitated for a long moment. How could he explain what he felt? "You know that I didn't take the usual route to this job," he said. "Sir Rory was the one who dragged me up from where I came from. He trusted in me from the start. He saw something in me that even I didn't know was there. I owe him everything I have."

"Owe?" Nikita asked. Her emphasis on the word made it clear that she was sceptical about just how much such a trust was worth, and whether it really amounted to risking his life. "You've used that word before."

"Sir Rory believed in me," Daniel said, seeing the need to explain it a different way. "Right now, no one believes in him. But I do. I'm returning that trust. If he's right, this is incredibly important – not just for Sir Rory, but for the world. The economic repercussions of this Spider hack could ruin a lot of people – especially working-class people, people that I grew up with. It's not just about what I owe

Sir Rory, but it starts there. And I really do believe that if he's convinced the egg is real, then it's real."

Nikita nodded, understanding dawning. "You trust him enough to believe the mission is needed, and if the mission is needed, you believe it's your duty to take part."

"That about sums it up," Daniel smiled. "Better than I could have."

For a while, they drove in silence again. But something between them had shifted—an invisible wall had cracked, and through it, a fragile trust was beginning to grow.

They pulled into a dusty gas station on the outskirts of Tulum as night fully embraced the sky. The flickering fluorescent lights overhead cast harsh shadows on the cracked pavement. A stray dog wandered between parked cars, and a man leaned lazily against the station wall, smoking a cigarette.

Daniel stepped out of the car, walking over to an OXXO convenience store beside the gas station. Inside, under the cold glow of the fridges and the faint buzz of a dying ceiling light, he purchased a cheap burner phone and a big packet of Lays crisps.

Back in the car, Daniel powered on the phone. Its screen glowed briefly before displaying the default home screen.

"You think she'll answer?" Nikita asked, her voice low.

"She will," Daniel replied, typing out a short message.

Eva, it's Daniel - Tonka. We need to meet. Tomorrow. Tulum. Let me know a safe place

They waited in silence, the faint chirping of insects outside filling the car.

A few minutes later, the phone buzzed. Eva's reply was short and to the point: *Casa Fryzer. Noon. Be careful who's watching you*

Daniel showed the message to Nikita, who nodded. Casa Fryzer was the address Jezer had given them – Eva and Maria's home. "Looks like we have our meeting."

Tulum at night was a paradox. The beachfront resorts glowed with golden lights, laughter spilling from open bars and rooftop lounges. But the further they drove from the tourist areas, the quieter and darker it became.

They pulled into a boutique hotel on the outskirts of town, a low-slung building surrounded by dense jungle foliage. Its sign, hand-painted in fading white letters, read "El Paraíso Perdido"—The Lost Paradise.

Inside, a sleepy receptionist handed them a single key to room seven. The room was basic but clean—two single beds, a ceiling fan, and a small window covered with wooden shutters.

"Safe enough," Nikita said, tossing her backpack onto one of the beds.

Daniel locked the door behind them and set the burner phone on the nightstand. "Alright. We need to go in prepared, tomorrow. And we'd better check in, let them know what's going on back home."

They sat cross-legged on the floor, papers, handwritten notes, and a tablet glowing faintly between them. Nikita's laptop hummed as she scanned encrypted network logs. Daniel had sketched out a rough plan on the back of a hotel flyer.

His secure laptop was wired into the intelligence briefing room back at the MI6 headquarters. They used encrypted satellite phones to guarantee connection and prevent hacking. He could see that the walls of the MI6 room had been adorned with maps of Mexico, which further hinted at the urgency of the manhunt.

Sir Rory was there, leaning towards the screen; Daniel knew there would be others in the room, outside of the view of the camera.

"Alright," he said, once they had finished explaining everything that had happened so far. "We'll do our best to support you on the ground. We have agents moving to join you in Tulum. They'll stay out of the way, but if you need extraction or emergency help, someone will be there."

"We can't trust them entirely," Nikita said bluntly, perhaps sensing Daniel's doubt that they would need the help. "Eva is well-connected, clearly, and Maria might be a genius online, but they're still civilians. They could be playing us, or worse, they could already be compromised."

Daniel rubbed his temples. "Agreed. But Maria's intel—if it's real—it's our best lead on Spider. Whatever Maria's found, it could be the first solid target we've had."

"And Eva?" Nikita pressed.

Daniel hesitated. "I don't think Eva is the enemy. I would guess she's scared—of Spider, of Jezer, of whatever game she's caught in. Jezer mentioned her father being important and dangerous, and that makes her both of those things by association. But we can't afford to misjudge her."

"The best case scenario is that this woman of yours turns out to have information that gets you access to Spider's infrastructure, or even his identity," Sir Rory said. "But in the worst case, it's a trap, and you'll walk right into Spider's web."

Daniel shuddered lightly at the mental image.

Nikita yawned and stretched her arms over her head. The digital clock on the bedside table behind her read 2:14 am. Daniel had lost track of what time it was at home.

"We should sleep," she said. "Tomorrow's going to be long."

Daniel nodded, and Sir Rory did the same before disconnecting. Daniel closed the laptop, making sure everything was fully turned off.

He was tired, too, but as Nikita lay back on her bed, he found himself staring at the faint glow of the burner phone on the nightstand.

Spider was out there, somewhere. Watching. Waiting.

Outside their window, the jungle buzzed with life, crickets chirping, leaves rustling in the breeze. Somewhere deep in the tangled shadows of the remote Mexican countryside, servers hummed in the dark, carrying secrets Spider had hidden from the world.

Tomorrow, Daniel and Nikita would start pulling at the threads. And somewhere in that tangled mess, Spider would feel it.

Chapter 20.

Escape to the Mediterranean

Rusanganwa and Yash were paired off and given instructions to walk along Army Road, crossing the White Nile and meeting their next Mohammed in the Al Hilal Stadium car park.

They boarded this time into a Toyota Hi-Lux, crawling under a heavy blanket nestled next to six rusty jerry cans of diesel fuel. They were warned to stay as long as they could under the blanket, to protect them from the desert sand and hot wind.

The Sahara was not a passive backdrop; it was an adversary.

The sun was not merely hot—it was vengeful, bleaching skin and stealing moisture from their mouths until tongues cracked like dry clay.

The sand was not just ground—it was a force of nature, shifting and swallowing entire tracks overnight.

The nights were not peaceful—they were bitterly cold, with frost settling on exposed skin.

In the truck bed, Yash wedged himself into a corner, his body curled against the metal siding. Sleep was impossible. Every bump sent shocks through his spine, and every sharp turn threatened to throw him overboard.

The men and women around him were reduced to little more than shapes—silent, hollow-eyed figures clinging to life with cracked fingers and whispered prayers.

One day, in the middle of an endless sea of golden dunes, their truck slowed to a halt. One of the migrants, a thin man with haunted eyes who had barely spoken since Nairobi, began to mutter under his breath. His voice grew louder, panicked, and then turned into an unintelligible scream.

The smugglers cursed in Arabic. One of them dragged the man out of the truck and threw him to the ground.

"Walk north," the smuggler barked, pointing towards the horizon.

The man clutched the air, his cracked lips mouthing pleas. But there was no mercy in the desert, and there was no time for weakness.

"You can't make him go," Rusanganwa spoke up, his own throat cracked and dry, turning his voice hoarse like everyone else. "He'll die out there."

Yash stared at him. What was he doing? No one else had said a word. No one else had drawn attention to themselves.

"Then you can walk with him if you want to keep him alive," the smugger said. When Rusanganwa did not move, he raised a gun and pointed it squarely at Yash's travel mate.

Rusanganwa looked at Yash wordlessly, but his eyes pleaded louder than any Yash had ever met.

Yash said nothing. Did not move. Barely dared to breathe.

He did not want to die in the desert.

He looked away on purpose, not wanting the smugglers to think that he was associated with Rusanganwa, that he should walk too.

Overhead, a vulture circled lazily, broad wings catching the hot wind.

Rusanganwa got down from the truck slowly, not saying another word. Everyone was still and silent. The smuggler got back into the truck, keeping his gun pointed behind them until the last minute, as Rusanganwa stood tall and unflinching under the sun.

There was a pause in which Yash thought surely it was a joke, surely they would let him back on.

The truck started up again, leaving Rusanganwa and the dying man behind—a shrinking silhouette in the rising heat waves.

Yash kept his eyes forward, but something in his chest tightened. It wasn't fear—it was anger. Anger at the way life had been reduced to a disposable commodity out here. Anger at the people who had created a world where this was possible.

Anger that he'd been forced to make that choice, to stay quiet to save himself.

But anger wouldn't keep him alive. His mind, sharp and relentless, was his greatest weapon.

At the next stop, when the smugglers began whispering about "excess cargo" and rationing water, Yash knew that silent survival was not going to be enough. He had to make his move.

The leader of the smugglers was a man named Omar—broad-shouldered, with a permanent sneer and a scar running across his jawline. He was cruel but not unintelligent, and Yash knew better than to confront him head-on.

Instead, he approached Yousef, one of the younger smugglers who had a nervous energy about him.

"Yousef," Yash said softly, speaking in broken Arabic. "The boss doesn't trust you, does he?"

Yousef bristled, eyes darting around. "What are you talking about?"

Yash pointed at the water barrel strapped to the side of the truck. "You drink more than the others. He notices."

Yousef's mouth tightened.

"But I can help you," Yash continued, his voice steady despite the pounding of his heart. "I heard Omar talking about a stash—under the spare tyre."

It was a lie. A calculated gamble. He'd seen Omar bending over near the tyre, glancing up and looking around to check that no one was watching him; when he'd seen Yash, he'd scowled and straightened up as if he had been doing nothing at all. But Yash knew there had to be something hidden there. Some prize that would help him survive.

Yousef's eyes flickered with greed. That night, Yash was given an extra piece of bread and half a cup of water, stolen from the stash he had been right about and shared between himself and Yousef. It was a small victory, but survival in the desert was made up of small victories. He would not starve, would not collapse with dehydration – would not give them a reason to leave him behind.

As days bled into nights, exhaustion and dehydration began to pull Yash's mind into strange places.

He dreamed he was back in Mogadishu, running barefoot along dusty streets. His mother was calling him from their doorstep, her arms open. But when he reached her, she dissolved into ash.

He dreamed was in a grand lecture hall, equations sprawling across a massive blackboard. His professors applauded, and his father stood in the corner, nodding with pride. But when he turned back to the board, all the numbers had turned to dust.

He dreamed of catching a bird and holding onto its tail feathers as it flew him away to freedom, but when it landed in the desert, he realised it was a giant vulture eyeing him hungrily, and he was not free at all.

Yash awoke each time drenched in cold sweat, his body aching, his mind racing.

After weeks of relentless travel, the convoy reached Tripoli, a decaying city at the edge of the world. Migrants were herded into an overcrowded warehouse that reeked of mildew and fear. There, they were all told that only those who had paid for the extra part of the journey would make it to Spain.

Mohammed hadn't said anything about an extra fee. Had he cheated Yash? Or just failed to tell him? Either way, Yash was stuck. He had no more money on his person and no way to make any.

Tripoli was a purgatory—a place where dreams went to die and hope became a scarce currency. Yash understood well that if he stayed here too long, he would never make it to a place where he could fulfil his dreams – his parents' dreams – his brother's dreams.

Ideas flashed through his head and disappeared as quickly as they had come. Could he find access to a computer somehow? If he could, maybe he could hack his way to a windfall. Perhaps he could send money from someone's account, or make it look as though he'd already sent a transaction before. Did the people smugglers even use bank accounts? What use were his skills here if this was a pre-digital world, based on paper to avoid being traced?

He had to think of something else.

That evening, he overheard a smuggler arguing about a paid seat on a boat left empty after a migrant had died. As he listened with bated breath, he heard them call the migrant *the Twa boy*, and realisation prickled through his nerves.

The Twa boy was Rusanganwa. No one had seen him die – but leaving him in the desert was clearly as good as the real thing, and they did not question his survival.

Yash could not believe his luck, and he could not let this opportunity pass. It was at Rusanganwa's expense, but he understood as well as the others did that his friend was not coming back. He approached the smuggler—a wiry man with bloodshot eyes.

"The boy who died—he was my cousin," Yash said, his voice trembling just enough to sound authentic. "He told me he'd bought passage."

The smuggler squinted at him. "You're not Twa."

"Our mothers were sisters, but my father was Somali," Yash said, thinking on his feet. "Rusanganwa's father was Twa."

"Prove it."

Yash reached into his pocket and pulled out his mother's scarf, clutching it tightly as if it were proof of kinship. He hoped the man had no way of knowing that it was nothing. The only other thing he had that could possibly help was a photograph of his family, but his mother did not look Twa, either. "Rusanganwa gave me this."

The smuggler hesitated for a long moment before finally nodding. "Be at the dock tomorrow early morning, before light. You'll pay extra for the change of passenger."

Yash exhaled, his chest heaving with a mixture of relief and fear.

Unable to sleep that night, Yash stood by the edge of the dock, staring out at the faint shimmer of the Mediterranean Sea.

The lights of the city flickered behind him, and the salty wind carried the distant hum of cargo ships.

At that moment, Yash made a silent promise.

I will survive, for my parents.

I will rebuild, for Hassan.

And one day, I will make those responsible for my suffering feel the same hopelessness I felt, for Rusanganwa.

As the night air hung heavy with salt and tension. Yash thought about his next steps, his next lie, his next survival tactic. He was no longer a scared boy from Somalia. The desert had burned away his innocence, leaving only steel in its place.

Chapter 21.

Luna's Discovery

The sun rose low over the horizon, casting Casa Fryzer in hues of molten gold and pale pink. The sprawling villa stood like a silent sentinel over Tulum's coastline, its infinity pool reflecting the waning daylight. Nikita leaned against the rental car's window, watching palm fronds sway lazily in the breeze. Beside her, Daniel sat behind the steering wheel, his brow furrowed in focus as he looked at their destination.

They'd left their motel just as the night began to give way to the day. A minute earlier, Daniel had turned onto a private gravel road, the tyres crunching underfoot. Casa Fryzer came into view, a sprawling white fortress, modern yet elegant, perched above the sea.

"Here we go," Daniel murmured, watching the impressive front doors swing open. They both got out of the car, ready to make the next move.

At the villa's entrance, now unveiled by the doors, Eva and Maria stood waiting. Eva, poised, confident, her dark hair falling effortlessly over her shoulders, wore a flowing white linen dress that seemed tailor-made for the Caribbean setting. Beside her, Maria, smaller and more reserved, stood in a loose T-shirt and denim shorts, clutching her phone tightly.

The four of them exchanged brief nods, layered with tension and meaning.

"Welcome," Eva said with a carefully rehearsed smile. "I hope you didn't have trouble finding the place."

Daniel extended his hand first, shaking Eva's firmly. "Thank you for agreeing to meet us."

Nikita, however, stood slightly behind Daniel, her arms crossed, her gaze sharp and analytical.

"Daniel," Maria said, his name rich on her tongue. It held a smile, a recognition. "It's strange to call you that. Strange to call you *anything*, in person."

When he reached to shake her hand, it was warmer, more like the grip of a friend. "Maria," he said with a grin. "Likewise."

"Come on," Eva said, casting a glance over the road behind them. Daniel turned, but couldn't see anything that might cause concern.

Eva led them inside. The villa was breathtaking: high ceilings, expansive glass walls, and an uninterrupted view of the Caribbean Sea stretching to the horizon. The living room was filled with natural light, expensive modern art, and carefully placed orchids.

But Daniel wasn't admiring the view. He was watching Eva and Maria, cataloguing their body language, their hesitations, their unspoken glances.

They gathered around a polished wooden table overlooking the infinity pool. The faint sound of waves crashing below filled the silence.

Nikita broke the tension first. "You'll forgive us if we don't trust you immediately. Your story, Jezer, what little you would tell us about the lead, the cartel ties, it's… thin. And thin stories get people killed."

Eva's smile faltered slightly, but she recovered. "I understand. Trust is earned, not given. But we're here because we believe you want to stop Spider just as much as we do."

"You do?" Nikita asked.

"What he is trying to do could destroy people around the world," Maria said. "Especially poor people. The people who are least deserving."

"So, you're just Robin Hood types, is that it?" Nikita asked. The challenge in her voice was unmistakable.

"Many hackers are," Maria replied, undaunted.

Daniel interjected, his voice softer but firm, before they could get into a real argument. He could sense that Nikita was uncomfortable and suspicious, but he did trust Maria. Getting into a fight this early on could compromise their ability to access the information. "Let's start with this, then. Maria, you said you saw something – an IP address. Tell us everything you know."

Maria shifted uncomfortably in her seat, her wide eyes flickering between Nikita and Daniel. It was clear she was intimidated by Nikita's sharp demeanour.

"Take your time, Maria," Daniel said gently. "We're listening."

Maria took a deep breath and began.

"At first, I thought it was just routing traffic," Maria said, her voice steady but quiet. "But the more I dug, the more I realised it wasn't random. Underlord's activity was… deliberate. Focused. Like he was trying to stay hidden, except from his own teammates. Or maybe he forgot that we would know how to find him, I'm not sure."

"Wait," Daniel interrupted. "*Underlord?* Like, *our* Underlord?"

Maria nodded grimly. "That's the only way I knew the IP address. Because I'd seen it before. I've tracked all of our team's IPs, making sure you were all ready for the tournament rounds. Maybe he doesn't know that."

"Team? Underlord?" Nikita said, looking between them. "I'm lost."

"Sorry," Daniel said, shaking his head. "Maria and I met on a gaming team – you remember that from the briefing, right? We compete in the tournaments together."

Nikita nodded. She might not have been up to speed on the names of the players, but that didn't make her slow. "So, Underlord is the gamer tag for one of your teammates?"

Maria nodded confirmation. "He's been with us for years," she said, her voice tinged with fear and sadness. "He's good at what he does – like all of us, that's how we found each other – but I never thought he would be wrapped up in something like this. When I started watching him, though, I noticed something else. The IP signature you gave me, the lead from your government – it was also there."

She went on to describe the moment of the slip—when Underlord's digital trace had overlapped with Spider's IP signature for just a fraction of a second. Maria had dug deeper into the clue, searching for software signatures and analysing fragments of intercepted data packets. They allowed her to both confirm the machine that left the trace belonged to Underlord and to pin him down to a precise address.

The location had been totally unexpected – unlike Underlord's usual haunts in Europe, it had pointed to a place not far from Maria's own home. A warehouse in Aldea Zama. An area notorious amongst the locals for cartel activity.

"It was faint, almost nothing. But it was enough for me to guess that they're working together. Or, at least… Underlord is being used."

Daniel and Nikita exchanged a glance. Nikita leaned forward. "How can you be sure about the location?"

Maria hesitated before answering. Daniel wondered whether she was thinking about protecting her method, or wondering how much she needed to dumb it down for everyone to understand it. She didn't realise Nikita could follow her easily.

"Like I said, it was server activity and data packets. The data coming from Underlord's communications was being routed through the warehouse servers before being masked and sent elsewhere. It's a relay point, but a big one. They're running something heavy from there—something important. For some reason, he didn't use a VPN on his personal laptop, like he normally would. I'm not sure why his defences were down. That's why I'm not sure whether it was purposeful, or whether someone dismantled his system in order to deliberately leave a trace."

"That sounds like it could be a trap," Daniel pointed out.

"Yes," Maria said with a helpless shrug. "But for who? Underlord wouldn't be involved in something like this. I'm worried he's out of his depth."

Nikita's expression hardened. "And you're sure this… Underlord is involved? He couldn't have just been visiting by coincidence?"

Maria nodded. "Yes, I'm sure. You don't just 'visit' those warehouses. They're cartel land. Anyone going there unaware would be risking their life."

"If the IPs overlap, doesn't that indicate it's likely that Underlord *is* Spider?" Nikita insisted. "Using two devices?"

"But I don't think he's Spider. He's… something else. A tool, maybe. But not the mastermind. I don't know that Spider was really there, with his trace being so fleeting, but Underlord definitely was. Maybe he was connected to Spider's network temporarily, which would definitely mean they overlap in some way."

Daniel exhaled, leaning back in his chair. The weight of the information hung heavy in the room. Could one of his teammates have been taken along for a ride by a criminal mastermind? Or was that just wishful thinking from Maria, not wanting to imagine the worst of the player that had fought alongside them? Could he actually have spent years playing on a team with Spider himself?

Nikita turned her attention to Eva. "And Jezer? How does she fit into all this?"

Eva didn't flinch. "Jezer works for the Americans. She's smart, but she's also afraid. This isn't a normal operation for her, it's personal. She's caught between protecting herself and doing her job. This isn't really her area – she's here for the cartels – but any information we can give her about Spider, she'd be happy to take to her boss."

Daniel watched Eva carefully. There was something else there, something unspoken.

"And you? Are you caught in the middle, too?" Daniel asked softly.

Eva hesitated. "I want this to end, Daniel. Spider, whatever his real name is, he's building something terrible. I've seen shadows of it, but even I don't know the full picture. What I do know is that Maria is right. Aldea Zama isn't just a server farm, it's a fortress. And whatever Spider's doing there, it's getting closer to completion."

Nikita's gaze was suspicious. "You're going to report whatever we find to Jezer, aren't you?" she asked. "Even if it's something we'd rather keep covert."

Eva shrugged. "I'm sorry," she said. "I don't want to mislead you. But, yes. It's a delicate situation. Whatever we find, I'm afraid I'll have to pass it on."

Daniel looked at Nikita. He could see that she was pulling away already, that she wanted to avoid telling Eva anything at all if they couldn't guarantee secrecy. But they were going to need help, and it would be much easier and faster to rely on people they knew personally than to wait for Sir Rory to send in a support team. "We need to report back," he said. "Come up with a plan."

Eva led them to a room that would serve their purpose: the furthest from the pool, where Eva and Maria promised to stay so that they would not overhear anything they shouldn't. As far as trust went, it was a thin promise, but a gesture that served well to warm Nikita up towards cordiality.

Daniel and Nikita debated, called Sir Rory and debated more – but, finally, they had a plan.

The group reconvened on the villa's patio as Eva served a light lunch – food that most of them could only pick at.

"So?" Maria asked at last, looking up at Daniel only. "Or, can't you tell us?"

"We can tell you," Daniel said, glancing sideways at Nikita and seeing no objection. "We're just trying to get our heads around the plan, ourselves."

"What do they want you to do?" Maria asked. Her voice quivered as if she sensed already that her friend was in danger.

"Tonight, under cover of darkness, we'll investigate the Aldea Zama warehouse," Daniel said, making Maria's eyes widen in fear. "We're going in."

"Alone?" Eva asked.

"Don't worry," Nikita said. "We won't ask you to come with us."

Daniel cast a look at Nikita, hoping she would understand that he wanted her to relax. "Just the two of us," he said. "Less likely that we'll be caught, that way."

"We still need you to do something for us," Nikita said, and to her credit, her tone was softer. "Maria, we need you to monitor the security systems. Help us avoid detection and, most importantly, tell us if the alarm is raised."

"I'll do better than that," Maria said, lifting her chin resolutely. "I can help you get a trace. Start hacking from the outside while you go in person. Their security system should be simple enough to fall to a brute force dictionary attack, and then I can have eyes on you and the whereabouts of all their guards."

"And you, Eva, too," Daniel said, raising his gaze to their host's. "We need you to keep communications open with Langley, just in case." If she was going to be passing information, anyway, they might as well benefit from it in the form of some extra security.

There was a long silence at the full reveal of the plan. Everyone in the room was, no doubt, considering the danger. The possibility that Daniel and Nikita would get caught, and what might happen then.

But, what was the alternative? They had been chosen for this role because they were the most skilled at this work. Once inside the warehouse, if they found computer systems, they were the best placed to take a look at what was on them and understand what they were looking at. No secret agent from any country would be as good as they were in that regard.

It had to be them.

"Well," Maria said, smoothing her hands over her skirt where she sat. "I guess if you're going to be risking your lives tonight, we should eat."

***

As twilight fell around the villa, Nikita adjusted her holster under her jacket, her face grim. "If we go in, there's no room for error. We can't afford to tip Spider off."

Daniel nodded, his eyes fixed on the darkening horizon. "We'll move at midnight," he said. "We travel there, watch the outside of the warehouse while Maria and Eva prepare, and then move in total darkness."

As the sun finally disappeared below the horizon, the villa's lights cast long shadows across the patio.

Daniel turned to Maria, his voice soft but steady. "What you've given us, Maria, it's more than enough. But I need you to stay sharp. If something changes, if you see anything, call us immediately. Then stop hacking the system. Get out."

Maria nodded, her wide eyes reflecting the faint glow of the villa lights.

Somewhere in the jungle beyond, the faint hum of servers pulsed silently through the night.

Chapter 22.

Partial Extraction

The night was thick with humidity as Daniel and Nikita crouched behind a wall of dense vegetation, their eyes fixed on the illuminated compound ahead. Aldea Zama's warehouse fortress stood in stark contrast to the idyllic Tulum beaches, high walls topped with razor wire, infrared cameras swivelling methodically, and armed guards patrolling the perimeter.

Maria's voice crackled softly in their earpieces. "You're clear to move. I've rigged the external cameras to loop a static feed for ninety seconds. Go now."

Daniel exchanged a quick glance with Nikita. "Let's move."

They sprinted low across the open stretch of gravel, their boots crunching softly against the loose stones. Reaching the edge of the compound, Nikita produced a compact laser cutter, carving through the metal fencing with practised precision.

Inside, the warehouse sprawled before them, half data centre, half cartel stronghold. Rows of servers hummed softly beneath cold fluorescent lights, while crates marked with cryptic serial numbers lined the walls. The faint sound of Spanish voices echoed from somewhere deeper inside.

"Alright, Maria," Nikita whispered into her mic. "We're in. Start your trace."

From her laptop back at Casa Fryzer, Maria's fingers flew across the keyboard. "I'm routing through the server logs now. Look for a terminal, something connected directly to the mainframe."

Daniel spotted a workstation tucked in the corner. "There. Nikita, cover me."

He slid into the chair, nudging a mouse sitting beside the computer. The screen blinked to life, revealing a series of encrypted files and chat logs. Whoever had been using this monitor hadn't been gone long enough for the machine to log them out automatically; he could still feel the warmth of their body in the chair. That probably meant they didn't have long before the user came back.

Maria's voice returned. "Search for communication hubs. Look for recurring usernames, timestamps… anything that stands out."

Nikita stood watch, her gun drawn and eyes sharp as she monitored the far end of the room. Daniel's brows knitted as he scrolled through the logs, fingers hesitating briefly over the keyboard before he began hitting arrow keys, moving through the file. A familiar name caught his eye. Underlord.

"I've found something," he hissed. "Underlord appears in the logs."

"Keep digging, Daniel," Maria urged in his ear as Daniel slipped a USB stick into the terminal and started copying files. "If it has Underlord's name on it, it must be something."

But then, a flicker on the security monitor caught Nikita's attention. Movement. Guards were headed their way.

"Daniel, we need to move. Now."

Daniel pulled his USB stick from the workstation, yanking it free just as the first voices reached their ears. Nikita grabbed his arm, and they ducked behind a stack of crates just as two guards entered the room.

The guards spoke in rapid Spanish, one shining a flashlight across the workstation. After what felt like an eternity, they moved on, disappearing into the shadows.

Daniel exhaled slowly. "That was too close."

"Do you have what we need?" Nikita whispered.

"I don't know," Daniel told her. "I got whatever was on that machine, but there may be localised logs or files that aren't shared with the network. Ideally, we'll want to find another terminal – more than one, if we can. It would be too easy if we just found everything we needed on the first terminal we came across."

"I have something on the security camera feed," Maria said into his ear. "There's another server bank at the opposite side of the warehouse. But there's a group of guards between you and those servers."

"We could distract them, lead them away somehow," Daniel said.

"How?" Nikita whispered. She shook her head. "It's too dangerous."

"Shit," Maria said, her urgent and hushed over the line. "I think we're being watched."

"What?" Daniel demanded, spinning to look at Nikita with wide eyes.

"The cursor on my screen just moved without me touching it," Maria said. "Get out. *Get out now.* You need to get out!"

Daniel and Nikita didn't need to be told twice. They ran for the door, keeping their steps quiet and their bodies low, but no one came running after them as they left the warehouse.

They slipped back out the way they came, retracing their steps through the broken fence and into the cover of the jungle.

Daniel kept looking over his shoulder, expecting to hear shouts or even gunshots – but there was nothing. They made it to the car and drove, hearts pounding. It was only once they were behind the wheel and halfway back that he looked at Nikita. They exchanged a glance, fuelled by adrenaline and the exhilaration of getting away with it – and then both of them burst into laughter.

"We did it," Daniel said, a flush of warmth spreading through him. They'd done it *together*. That made it seem all the more meaningful.

"We did," Nikita replied, her eyes crinkling with a grin that made her seem all the more alive, all the more vibrant. He almost reached out for her hand but held himself back at the last moment. She was still his superior on this mission. He wasn't supposed to be looking at her like that, and maybe it was only the adrenaline, and surely she wouldn't feel the same way?

Once they were back at Casa Fryzer, Maria and Daniel pored over the data they had retrieved. They immediately struck a problem.

The language used for the data was not all English.

"This isn't real," Nikita said, frowning at the screen. "It's a list of crypto wallet addresses and offshore accounts, but the numbers are wrong."

"What do you mean?" Daniel asked. They were all crowded around his laptop, watching closely. Maria had turned her system off completely, shuddering as she recounted the way her cursor had moved as if someone else was already hacked into her system even as she hacked theirs.

"Look at this number, for example," Nikita said, tapping the screen. "That's a Swift code for a bank in the Cayman Islands. But it has five digits at the end where it should have four. It's not a real bank number."

Daniel stared at the lines of text on his screen, comprehension slowly beginning to dawn. "This isn't data," he said. "None of it. The crypto wallet addresses, the bank numbers – they're all a code."

"Code, like hacking, or code, like cryptography?" Eva asked.

"Cryptography," Nikita said, turning to look at her in that intense way that, Daniel knew first-hand, could send a shiver down your spine. "Why?"

Eva blushed slightly. "I'm… kind of a cryptography nerd," she said. "It's what I studied. I love cracking codes. Do you want me to try?"

Daniel gestured for her to go ahead, stepping aside – and then tried not to claw his own face off with the frustration of being able to do nothing but sit and watch.

He checked in with Sir Rory, reassuring him that they had the data but were in the process of analysing it, and then sat back, snacking on tapas dishes that Maria brought out one by one and trying not to think.

He watched Nikita for a while; she barely moved, focused on Eva, watching her every keystroke. She'd positioned herself so that she could see the screen, could watch and try to catch Eva out in betraying them if that was her plan.

Daniel wanted to reach out and tell her to relax, but he knew Nikita didn't trust either of their hosts.

Maybe that was a good thing. Maybe he was too quick to trust. Maybe they needed a failsafe of doubt.

"Got it," Eva announced, looking around victoriously. "It was a tricky cypher to work out, but I have it. Maria, can you build an algorithm to quickly decode it all? There's a lot of text."

They swapped places, Maria using her expertise next. Within just a few minutes, she had a program running, turning the random numbers into real words.

Only, this time, they were in Spanish.

"Oh, no," Maria said, reading the first few lines.

"What?" Daniel asked, jumping up beside her – and then he saw it, too. "Oh, no."

"*What?*" Nikita demanded, looking between them anxiously. She was the only one in the room who couldn't read Spanish.

"This basically says we have twenty-four hours to decode the rest of the data using the encryption key, or we'll be infested with spider eggs," Daniel said. "It's a failsafe to make sure the data doesn't fall into the wrong hands. And this is a completely different layer of data. This Spanish text, it's all about some kind of planned coup in Venezuela. How they're going to use deepfakes of political leaders to cause civil unrest and then put their own puppet leader in charge."

"What's the point of setting that all up if it's not the real data?" Eva frowned. "Surely, anyone who reads the first few lines knows they haven't decrypted everything?"

"The way we got into the system is a little different," Daniel explained. "This should have popped up as a warning to enter a password – that should turn out to be the answer to the riddle posed by the text. But we've opened this file as raw code, so we can read the commands. The time limit and the consequence are all part of the code itself. We only have a warning because we went in there to grab the data and decrypted it here, instead of trying to read it on the computer inside the warehouse."

"So, how do we get the password?" Nikita asked, moving on to the next, most practical aspect of the issue.

"I guess we look for clues," Daniel said. "Can we print this, make copies to look at?"

Eva nodded. "Let me connect it to our printer," she said, leaning in to do the job.

There were a lot of lines of data; they divided the pages up, taking twenty each to start. Nikita couldn't help read them, so she sat with Daniel's laptop, trying brute-force attacks to find the password.

Daniel, Eva, and Maria concentrated in silence. The only sounds audible in the room were the turning of pages and the whirring of the laptop's fan, attempting not to overheat under such a heavy workload.

Something Maria read made her sit up straight.

"What is it?" Daniel asked immediately.

"It might be nothing," she said. "But there's a line here I recognise. It's from a poem, written during the Spanish Civil War. A rallying cry. I've read it before."

"Try the poet's name as the password," Daniel urged.

Maria stepped up to the machine, typed rapidly –

And the text on the screen mutated, dissolving and reforming into new words entirely.

"What the hell is this?" Nikita exploded. "Some kind of African language, now?"

Daniel lowered his head into his hands and groaned. "We should have known it wasn't going to be as easy to read as it seemed. Why bother protecting your data closely when you have security measures like this for anyone who tries to read it?"

"We're going to need the help of the team back home," Nikita said. "Unless anyone recognises this?"

Everyone shook their heads. "I'll make a call," Daniel said.

Sir Rory answered almost immediately, patching them through to the familiar room at HQ via video feed – making Daniel wonder whether any member of the team was actually getting any rest at all. Daniel explained the situation; they couldn't send the data across to anyone for fear that the spider eggs would infect more devices, but having it attack Daniel's would be bad enough. He had data on there already, connections to other devices, traces that would tell the story of where he had been and what he knew. They needed to beat the deadline.

Thankfully, one of the analysts ran a search and quickly identified the language used as Somali, and a translator was sourced within the building. Within ten minutes, they were watching as the man read from the screen in front of him aloud, watching the video feed pointed at Daniel's laptop.

"These are all proverbs," he said, after reading the first few lines.

"Is there anything that seems out of place?" Daniel asked, thinking about the layers they'd gone through so far.

The translator scanned ahead – then his eyebrows shot up. "Yes," he said. "There's one which is missing a word. It should say *shimbir*."

Daniel typed it out, asking him to spell it to make sure he didn't get it wrong – and waited with bated breath as he hit the enter key.

Password accepted.

A line of code appeared on the screen.

// if justice > collapse { legacy = redemption }

Then, just as quickly as it had appeared, it was gone. Daniel frowned, trying to memorise what he had seen as the blank white page was filled in once again. This time, it was English, and there was a collective sigh of relief in the room as they realised they'd found the true data hidden within all of the layers.

Lines of chat logs filled their screens, discussions about DGTX vulnerabilities, cryptocurrency wallet addresses, and a name that kept repeating: Artem.

There was one exchange that was particularly illuminating:

Underlord: *I don't know if I can do this. You're asking me to betray Alberto. I was only just hired.*

Spider: *Don't you want the money you were promised? Don't you want your family to be safe? Only I can get all of them out and find them a new home, Artem. You know even Alberto can't do that. He wouldn't dare to hack missile systems or stop orders going to the soldiers on their route out. He* *wouldn't dare interfere with war. Without me, your family are on their own.*

Underlord: *Of course, I want to save them... I just... I don't want to betray him. I'm sorry. I'll get the job done. Please don't leave my family behind.*

Spider: *Today for you, tomorrow for me. Hold up your end of the bargain and they will be safe.*

"Artem?" Nikita said aloud, looking over Maria's shoulder. "Do we know if that relates to a real person?"

"Yes," Maria replied. "Underlord's real name is Artem. He's been in communication with Spider, directly or indirectly, for weeks. And according to these logs, Artem started working for Alberto Lopez right before he came to Mexico."

"We've been chasing shadows," Nikita said quietly. "Artem isn't Spider. He's being targeted. Used because he has access to Lopez and Cryptropolis. That's the firm handling all the cybersecurity for the new currency system. It's a perfect trap. He's the one they'll use to implant the egg."

Daniel's jaw clenched. "Then we find Artem."

"I'm going to warn Cryptropolis that one of their employees has been compromised," Sir Rory said. "Good work. I'll let you get back to it." He rang off, cutting off the previous buzz of the audio connection and leaving them suddenly alone.

A heavy silence settled over the room.

They all knew what finding Artem meant.

More danger. More risk. And potentially exposing a friend who had been used as a tool by a criminal – an act that might end with him seeing jail time, even if it was unintentional.

But what choice did they have other than to track him down and at least try to stop any more damage?

Chapter 23

¡Alto! ¡Policía!

Yash was woken by a sharp nudge to his shoulder.

"It's time," someone hissed in Arabic.

His eyes snapped open, adjusting to the darkness. For a moment, he thought he was still dreaming—the past weeks of torment and survival had turned reality into a fragile, shifting thing. But no, this was real. Today was the day.

He rose from the tangled bush he had been sleeping in, brushing sand from his clothes. His tatty bum bag was already strapped to his chest—inside were the only things he owned: a torn family photograph, his mother's scarf, a few crumpled notes that were all that remained of his bribe money, the book about explorers now even more battered than before, and a pocket-sized laminated card with basic Spanish phrases scribbled on it.

The others—men, women, even a couple with a child—moved cautiously down the hillside toward the beach. Yash fell into step with them, his eyes scanning the surroundings, his ears tuned to every sound.

The beach wasn't empty. A skeletal black RIB (Rigid Inflatable Boat) lay pulled up on the sand, its flimsy sides rippling slightly in the ocean breeze. Next to it stood Khalid, the pilot—a wiry man in his forties with hollow eyes and a voice like sandpaper.

"Listen!" Khalid barked in Arabic, raising his hand to silence the small group. "We have one chance at this. One chance. If anyone moves, if anyone panics, we all die."

The group nodded. The fear in their eyes said more than words ever could.

"There are five rules to the crossing," Khalid continued, holding up five fingers. With each rule, another finger dropped down, until he had made a fist. "One: sit where I tell you. Do not move. Two: if you need to relieve yourself, do it where you sit. Three: one small bag only. No loose items. Use the rope to strap it to you. Four: wear these life jackets. Keep them uninflated until I say. Five: phones off. If a light goes on, you'll be thrown overboard."

Yash tightened his grip on his bag, his pulse drumming in his ears.

"Do you understand?" Khalid's gaze swept over them.

Yash nodded rapidly along with the others.

Khalid's tone softened slightly as he pointed towards the horizon.

"Look at those lights. Spain. A new life. A better life. But you'll have to earn it tonight. Now… get in."

The RIB was smaller than Yash had expected. Inflatable sides, a tiny forty-five-horsepower outboard engine, and just enough room for eleven people to huddle together. It felt less like a vessel and more like a child's pool toy.

Yash climbed aboard, his foot slipping slightly as he stepped into the rubber hull. Khalid handed him one of the Jerry cans filled with petrol, muttering, "Hold this steady, boy."

The others boarded silently, a couple from Eritrea, a man from Nigeria, and a terrified teenage girl who clutched her knees to her chest the moment she sat down. Khalid gave one final look toward the distant hills before pulling the starter cord on the outboard engine. It spluttered and roared to life, the smell of petrol thick in the cold air.

"Bismillah," someone whispered.

The boat pushed away from the beach, the sound of the engine blending with the slap of saltwater against the rubber sides.

Darkness swallowed them.

Yash squinted toward the horizon. The lights of Spain looked impossibly distant—tiny pinpricks in an endless black canvas.

Yash repeated a phrase to himself, whispering it in the quiet of his own mind: *Mi nombre es Yash. Yo tengo trece años y me gustaría vivir en España.* He'd learned it from Hassan, who had always been better at languages. Now, Yash had to learn for the both of them. He'd kept the sentences on his cue card, but it was only now that he dared enough to hope he would be able to use it.

The sea was deceptively calm at first, the boat gliding forward in smooth arcs. But then came the swells—massive rolling waves that lifted the RIB high into the air before letting it crash down, water spraying into their faces.

Khalid yelled over the noise. "Sit still! SIT STILL!"

A sharp cry erupted from the teenage girl as she lost her grip and slid slightly across the rubber hull. Yash reached out, grabbing her arm and steadying her.

"Hold tight," he hissed.

Time lost all meaning. The salt stung their eyes, their clothes were soaked through, and every second felt stretched taut with tension. Yash's mind whirred, cataloguing every flicker of light on the horizon, every sound, every movement of Khalid's hands on the tiller.

At one point, the boat passed beneath the towering bulk of a cargo ship, its lights blazing high above them like a floating city in the sky. The hum of its engines vibrated in Yash's chest.

For a moment, he allowed himself to dream—of walking on solid ground, of speaking Spanish with confidence, of leaving the past behind. Yash marvelled at the bright lights of the Gibraltarian skyscrapers as they passed by.

But dreams were a luxury.

The boat drifted into calmer waters as they neared the Spanish coast. Khalid's eyes scanned the shoreline ahead, searching for the prearranged signal.

Suddenly, a torchlight flickered—a rapid sequence of flashes, almost like Morse code.

Khalid nodded. "Hold tight. We're going in."

The RIB surged forward, the engine whining as it pushed against the tide. The coastline grew clearer—low hills, faint house lights, and the dark outline of what looked like an inlet.

The moment the hull hit the sand, Khalid jumped out, his boots splashing into the shallow water. "Run!" he barked. "RUN!"

Everyone scrambled over the sides. Yash hit the wet sand running, his legs shaky, his lungs burning with cold air.

Behind him, Khalid disappeared into the shadows. The RIB was abandoned, bobbing uselessly in the shallows.

Yash sprinted up the beach, his feet slipping on loose pebbles. Others scattered in different directions, some running inland, others doubling back toward the rocks.

Suddenly, he heard shouting—Spanish voices, sharp and commanding. Blue and red lights sliced through the darkness.

"¡Alto! ¡Policía!"

Yash's breath came in short gasps. His desperate eyes scanned the terrain ahead—he spotted a narrow path leading up a hill. Without thinking, he veered left and bolted upwards.

His chest burned, his legs screamed in protest, but he kept going. Behind him, he could hear heavy boots pounding against gravel.

At the top of the hill, Yash realized his mistake. He wasn't running inland—he was running between two narrow streets, boxed in by patrol cars at either end.

A female officer stepped into his path.

"¡*Alto*! Hands up!"

Yash skidded to a halt, his breath ragged. He forced his face into a mask of calm and raised his hands.

"*Hola*," he said, his voice trembling. "*Mi nombre es Yash. Yo tengo trece años y me gustaría vivir en España.*"

The officer froze, her eyes widening. Migrants rarely spoke Spanish—especially not young boys with a face still untouched by adolescence.

Her voice softened. "*Deja que te ayude*… Let me help you."

He had a choice to make – but it was really no choice. He could do nothing other than submit, to follow her gesturing hands, to get into the back of the police car. To allow his hands to be cuffed in front of him, even though that trapped him more than before. He had no way to escape. It was trust her, or nothing.

Yash sat in the back of a police car for the first time in his life, his hands still trembling. It felt like being in very bad trouble, even if the offer had been one of help. The officer who had spoken to him sat in the front seat, her colleague driving in silence.

They pulled into the outskirts of what he would later learn was Estepona, a sleepy Spanish town bathed in the glow of streetlights.

At the Migrant Processing Centre, Yash got out of the car and was led to a small, fenced-off outdoor pen. The officer unlocked his cuffs and gestured for him to sit.

"Someone will come for you," she said softly. Then she stepped back as if that snatch of conversation was all she could risk for him.

Yash nodded, scanning the pen, already cataloguing exits, people, and opportunities. He was in Spain. He had made it. But this was only the beginning.

As Yash leaned against the wire fence, staring out over Estepona, the dawn started to rise, casting the town first into silhouette and then in a gentle, soft light that slowly illuminated details. Behind houses and villas lay opportunities, danger, and a world waiting to be conquered. His story was far from over.

"I will survive," he said, quietly, just to himself. "I will rebuild. And they will pay."

Chapter 24.

Soho House

As the rising morning sun turned the corner and cast its inevitable glow across the exotic Playa Ruinas beach, Eva packed up her beach bag, kissed her girlfriend Maria goodbye, and slowly walked across the white sand and up the rickety wooden stairs, that led towards the cliff top. She turned her back on one of Mexico's most idyllic coastlines, so used to seeing it that it no longer fascinated her.

She walked along the sandy path in her flip-flops, navigating her way past other beach visitors to the minor road that brought the traffic in and out of this stunning national park. All the while, she was aware of Maria behind her, still helping Daniel and Nikita.

Despite completely different upbringings, the girls had been friends for over eighteen years. They'd first met at the local Padel and Tennis Centre in the summer of 2005. They were thrown together into the long summer camp by their parents as a way to avoid parenting during the long summer holidays. They'd become friends almost instantly. Later, they had become more.

Eva walked past the entrance to El Castillo, an ancient Mayan castle, then passed through the beach area entrance barriers and walked up to her classic Porsche 911 Targa. A beautiful sand beige colour. This elegant classic car was a gift for her twenty-fifth birthday from her disgustingly wealthy daddy. That had been before she moved in with a woman and stopped seeing him so often.

She lifted the car's front boot and took out her beach bag. She switched into her lime green Adidas sambas to drive in. It was difficult to drive this classic 1967 Porsche in just a pair of Havaianas, with the pedals coming out from the floor and demanding a solid foot press. Unclipping and removing the black targa roof, she folded it and placed it on the rear seat. She climbed in and checked her phone. Her meeting was still on.

Roaring the car into life, she took off down the beach road for the twenty-minute drive to meet her handler at Don Caeftos. She was also looking forward to drinking a refreshing cup of Chayagra. It had been a tiring day and night with a lot of drama and tension, and the stairs and walk had parched her mouth and throat.

She liked it at Don Caeftos and knew she could grab a bite if she fancied it. She always wanted to meet up with her handler in public locations. Mexico was a place where secrets were tough to keep. It is almost impossible to protect without the threat of extreme violence. With wealth so wrapped in just a few families and the infamous drug cartels, the trade of information for money could transform everyone's lives, so it was hard to trust anyone.

Even for many, trusting family members was foolish. Every street in every town seemed to have a wannabe sicario eager to phone in and report anything out of the ordinary to someone who traded information. So, Eva had always preferred to be out and about. Be seen to live life. She was a well-known face in the town. In fact, she was a famous face in Mexico. A chatty girl who also knew how to keep secrets, but appeared to have many friends.

Parking in Calle Orion Sur behind an old blue, black, and slightly beaten-up VW Beetle, she opened the car door, deliberately leaving the Targa roof open. She locked the doors manually and walked around the corner to Don Caeftos in a flowing beach dress with her bikini underneath. The dress caught the evening sun, and it lit up her figure. Eva had an amazing athletic body. At five feet and eight inches, she was much taller than the average Mexican woman, who stood at five-two. In fact, at five-eight, she was taller than the average Mexican man. With her dark hair and tanned skin, she turned eyes wherever she went.

The setting sun still bathed the street and provided ongoing warmth. Her handler was already there, sitting under the large reed roof at one of their high tables with two stools. Jezer was always early. A friendly double kiss greeted her arrival, and Eva sat down.

In her blue and white beach dress, Jezer also blended in with the pre-beach vibe at Don Caeftos. Just two girlfriends meeting up. She was always dressed to blend into the situation and look anything other than the agent she was.

Eva ordered her refreshing and now eagerly awaited drink. Jezer had already ordered and was drinking a cenote margarita through a straw.

They initially chatted about a well-known telenovela called *Vencer La Culpa* and the appalling love life of the leading actress Monica Martin, who had been adorning the pages of *Hola* with yet another Mexican playboy millionaire. To the outside world, there was nothing unusual about their meeting at all.

After finishing their drinks and a quick bite in the form of two chorizo quesadillas, the ladies got down from their stools and walked back around to the Porsche.

They climbed in side by side and drove off towards the coastline, passing several hotels before turning on the beach road. The Caribbean sea was lapping up close to the beach road.

They parked beside a deserted eco-resort and walked onto the beach. Eva knew they could walk and talk here.

"My bosses were interested in your information about Spider," Jezer said. Her tone had shifted from the chatty, informal best friend they had pantomimed at the café into a cold and information-hungry spy. "I had a faster response from Langley than I've ever anticipated."

That, in itself, was surprising. Eva had passed a lot of information along to Jezer since they'd met at Soho House in Mexico City a few years earlier, where Eva had been working for her father's communications business. She'd graduated as a lawyer from one of Madrid's top universities, then come right back to help with the undersea internet cables operation.

The two of them had met casually by the outside rooftop pool bar at Soho House. An innocuous encounter, Eva had first thought. It was a friendly place. Located in the up-and-coming creative centre of the city, the Roma Norte district, often people would introduce themselves out of curiosity and to make new connections. Jezer first appeared to Eva as an uber-chic businesswoman.

Jezer had said she was involved in fashion. She said she worked in a division of LVMH, sourcing the very best leather for their Alma and Pochette Metis bags. Both were popular amongst the ladies of Defenos, the nickname most Mexicans gave their capital city.

Jezer had used traditional and centuries-old 'source development' techniques to slowly convince Eva to be an informant for the US. She won her confidence with drinks, an occasional dinner, and her unforgettable shopping trips to the fabulous malls in Miami and Atlanta before slowly asking her to give up information and betray her father's wealthy friends. By the time Eva realised that Jezer was looking for information, Eva had already given her crucial blackmail material through misplaced trust.

Eva's father was one of Mexico's wealthiest men, with a fortune estimated to be in the tens of billions gathered when the Mexican state's telephone company was privatised. And then, as mobile telephony had exploded onto the scene, he had a near monopoly, crushing anyone who tried to muscle in on this patch. His group of friends befitted his status as one of an elite group of individuals who controlled the state. His money and power could assign or dethrone a president. Many believed he had.

And despite all Eva could tell her about her father’s friends, *this* was the information that had most impressed them at Langley?

“They want more details as soon as you have them,” Jezer continued. “Any logs, footage, anything you uncover. The raw data. They have their own experts who can analyse it, of course. And no one must know."

"It will be difficult," Eva said. She was thinking about Maria. Daniel wasn't just an information source – he was Maria's friend. This was a betrayal of a new order: a line she had never crossed before. "I have no reason to access the data, no way to understand it. It might raise suspicions if I start to take more of an interest."

"Need I remind you of what is at stake?" Jezer asked quietly.

She rarely brought it up. She had more class than that.

But there it was: the reason that Eva told Jezer everything she discovered, usually without pause.

Eva had known she was gay from a young age, but she kept her relationships a secret. She knew her family, especially her father, would not accept her if they found out. University in Madrid had been the chance to explore, to finally be herself freely and even begin dating.

Jezer had caught Eva kissing her friend Maria on the lips in the toilets of the infamous nightclub La Santa - which was the information Jezer needed to start to blackmail her. Jezer told her that she knew about her relationship with Maria and that she could either tell her father or she do some basic work for her as a society informant. Networking – that was what Eva had believed.

It was only much later, when she was already in too deep, that she discovered Jezer was, in fact, working for the CIA. Eva was one of many informants Jezer had collected over the years – and who knew how many of them were working against one another.

"I'll see what I can do," Eva said. Her father still didn't know about Maria. He didn't visit her. She'd told him she needed to live her own life, away from him and the company, and fought with him so much that he eventually gave her the freedom to live on her own at a distance. They spoke on the phone, and Maria stayed quiet or left the house so she wouldn't give herself away. When her father planned a visit, Maria moved out to a hotel temporarily.

They'd kept it secret so well, and for so long, and Eva still lived on her Daddy's money.

She couldn't give that up.

If he'd known about his daughter's living arrangements – worse, if his *friends* had known – there would have been serious hell to pay. Maybe even her life.

"If you give me Spider, this is it," Jezer reminded her. "No more blackmail. No more informing on your father and his friends. You'll be free, truly free. I won't ever contact you again. If you give us information that leads to Spider, it's all over."

Eva would have to get her hands on whatever Daniel and Nikita had uncovered, and find a way to get it to Jezer – no matter the risks.

Chapter 25.

Shadows and Light

After their late night at the warehouse, the sun was rising, casting warm golds and deep oranges across the sky. Nikita stood barefoot on the balcony of their rented beach apartment, a glass of wine in her hand from the local OXXO.

Below, the waves rolled gently onto the white sand, their rhythm steady, calming. Behind her, Daniel was inside, focused on exfiltrating some of the remaining data files through covert channels on his laptop. Nikita took a deep breath, her eyes narrowing slightly as memories from her past surfaced. In this quiet moment, with the sun fading and Daniel nearby, she felt something she rarely allowed herself to feel. The ghosts of the past, hovering over her shoulder.

It was at the National Crime Agency, the NCA, amid flashing monitors and encrypted chat windows, that Nikita became one of the youngest field cyber security operatives in the agency's history.

But the digital battlefield wasn't as clean or precise as code. Nikita had seen victims of human trafficking whose movements had been tracked by spyware, bank accounts emptied overnight, and governments brought to their knees by ransomware attacks.

This wasn't just technical work. It was deeply, painfully human.

She cared because she had seen what happened when no one did.

She once found herself staring at the pixelated photograph of a young girl on a trafficker's encrypted server—alone, afraid, and utterly lost in the cold machinery of digital crime. Nikita had worked seventy-two hours without sleep to locate her. They'd found her, eventually. But Nikita never forgot that face. That moment became a wound that never fully healed.

Nikita turned and looked back inside the apartment, and Daniel smiled at her briefly before returning to his work. At that moment, she realised something startling: she felt safe with Daniel. In their world of encrypted messages and hidden motives, safety wasn't something she felt often. But here, with him, she did.

Their apartment in Tulum was secluded, surrounded by dense greenery and overlooking the turquoise Caribbean Sea. The tension of their mission hung between them, but there was also something else: a fragile, growing intimacy.

Daniel was smart. Almost intimidatingly so. She was used to men who flaunted their credentials without the ability to back them up: degrees from here or there, who they were classmates with at Eton. Daniel was completely different. He had no badges to wear on his chest, but his intelligence was quiet and practical – and he surprised her at every turn.

He was dangerous for her, she thought. Distracting. She almost thought he might be a match for her, and that wasn't a good thing to think on a mission where focus was imperative.

"How's the reading going?" Nikita asked.

Daniel offered her a self-deprecating smile. "The computer's doing all the work. I've got it scanning for anomalies or matches so we can see patterns in the chat logs. I don't know why I'm watching it so closely. It will finish when it finishes."

It was a rare moment of peace in the eye of the storm. But beneath the warmth of their conversation, there was something else, a slow, delicate thread of trust weaving between them. He could be vulnerable with her and tell the truth. She wanted to do the same.

She watched as Daniel poured two glasses of wine and joined her on the balcony, replacing her empty vessel.

The air was warm, filled with the faint scent of saltwater and flowers.

"There's another warehouse," he said. "Another set of traces leading to a second location. Some of the chat logs initiate from there. I think we need to check it out next."

Nikita nodded. "Tonight, then," she said.

"We'll sleep and then head out."

There was a pause, a moment in which they drank and said nothing, neither of them rushing to sleep and prepare for another night of danger.

"Do you ever wonder," Nikita said softly, swirling her wine, "if we're just… pretending to be heroes in a world that doesn't want saving?"

Daniel set his glass down, leaning on the balcony rail beside her. "I think everyone's pretending a little, Nikita. And I'm not sure I would ever call myself a hero. But I don't think that makes us any less real."

There was a long silence. Then Nikita spoke again. "You're different, Daniel. You care, even when it hurts you. That's rare."

He looked at her, his expression unreadable in the dim light. "So do you."

The moment hung heavy in the cool morning air. Everything was upside down. They'd been up all night and needed to sleep all day in preparation for tonight. Daniel leaned on the balcony next to her like it was late evening, like they were just having a casual glass of wine after dinner, a calm moment before retiring to bed. Nikita felt herself leaning closer, and before she could second-guess herself, their lips met.

The kiss was slow, hesitant at first, but then deeper, more certain.

"We shouldn't," Nikita said softly, though her tone had no confidence behind it.

"We shouldn't," Daniel agreed. "But will we, anyway?"

She answered him only with another kiss.

They moved inside, the curtains billowing softly in the breeze behind them.

In that fragile, fleeting moment, the walls they had both carefully built around themselves crumbled away. Daniel's gaze was questioning as he led her towards the bed, and Nikita answered him in full force.

As they lay side by side afterwards, Nikita traced faint circles on Daniel's shoulder and whispered, "Don't let me fall, Daniel."

And Daniel, half-asleep, murmured back, "I won't."

Nikita woke before sunset. She sat on the balcony, watching the horizon shift from bright blue through ever-darkening shade, letting Daniel sleep just a little bit longer. This time, she had no glass of wine. She sat and stared at the beginning pinpricks of far-off glimmering stars as they pierced the gathering darkness and remembered the cases where she had made a difference, the moments she was proud to call her life. She wondered if she would add this one to the list.

Daniel emerged from the villa, his hair tousled, holding two mugs of coffee. He handed one to her silently, and they stood together, side by side, watching the moon grow a steadier glow as the sun's light disappeared completely.

But Nikita felt it, the creeping shadow of inevitability. She had seen how these stories ended. She had buried friends and attended briefings filled with euphemisms like "acceptable losses" and "calculated risks."

And in that moment, she realised something.

She might actually love Daniel.

Not in a loud, fireworks-in-the-sky kind of way. But in a quiet, aching way, the kind of love that made every glance linger, every silence feel sacred.

But love was a dangerous thing in their world, and it was so early. They'd only known one another such a short time. Something in his soul called to hers, and she could feel the aching possibility of more – but this was work, and she had no idea what he was thinking after what they had done, and they couldn't afford any distractions.

She looked at Daniel and almost said something—almost confessed what she felt. But she stopped herself. There would be time, she thought. There would be time…

As they prepared to leave the apartment and head to the second warehouse – Maria's messages while they slept indicated that she had identified as belonging to the same cartel, with similar spikes of electrical activity perhaps denoting more servers – Nikita paused in front of the mirror.

She studied her reflection, the strong lines of her jaw, the faint scar above her eyebrow, the eyes that had seen too much.

She whispered softly to herself, "Stay focused. Stay sharp."

But somewhere deep in her gut, she felt it, a shadow, a premonition, a sense that their mission in Mexico would change everything.

Nikita stepped out onto the gravel driveway, joining Daniel as the rental car engine roared to life. They drove towards the second warehouse, the sun rising behind them, casting long shadows across the empty road.

Chapter 26.

Arana Negra

Yash's time in the migrant processing centre in Estepona felt both brief and endless. Days bled into each other as he navigated the routines—language classes, paperwork, and interviews with immigration officials who probed every corner of his story. Some spoke to him kindly; others treated him like an inconvenience.

But Yash was sharp. He knew when to speak and when to stay quiet. He learned the names of staff members, noticed who was kind and who wasn't, and made sure he left an impression on anyone with authority. It wasn't just his Spanish—it was his poise, his careful way of speaking, and his ability to make himself useful.

When Yolanda, the police officer who had arrested him, reappeared, Yash felt a flicker of hope. She greeted him with the same soft warmth as before.

"You've been assigned a family, Yash," she said. "Their names are Paco and Nuria. They're waiting for you in Bilbao."

Hope flared inside him at last. Not for a new family – surely he could never replace the family he had lost – but for the better life his parents had always dreamed of for him. Perhaps now, at last, it could finally begin.

The journey to Bilbao took him through Spain's sprawling countryside—rolling hills, golden fields, and ancient towns that blurred past the train windows. Yolanda sat beside him for most of the journey, occasionally breaking the silence with questions.

"Why Spain, Yash? Why not somewhere else?"

"Because Spain feels… possible," he replied after a moment of thought. Yolanda was silent in response to this, as if she was considering whether it was true or not, or perhaps trying to understand the possibilities that being born here had afforded her.

Later, she broke the silence again. "Where did you learn Spanish?"

"At school," Yash said. Her surprise was something he stored away inside his mind, a hint of information. Did she believe that he must not have had a good education, or that he hadn't gone to school at all, because he was an immigrant? Did she imagine him living in a mud hut before he came here?

When they arrived in Bilbao, the air was crisp, and the city bustled with energy. The mountains in the distance loomed large, their peaks shrouded in mist. Yolanda guided him off the train, her hand lightly resting on his shoulder.

Just before they walked down to find his new family, Yolanda stopped Yash with a squeeze of her hand. "Here," she said. "I have something for you."

Yash reached up and took it. It was a frame – a small and plain one, just the right size for the family photograph he'd carried with him from Somalia.

The gift touched him more than he could say. Yolanda had seen him holding the photograph and thought to protect it, to protect his memories.

A tinge of wariness flashed through him: would his new family want him to display a photograph of the old one, or would they want him to discard his old life completely?

On the platform, Paco and Nuria waited. Yash recognised them immediately despite not knowing what they looked like ahead of time – their nervous and expectant faces, the way they stood close together and examined the train, the way their faces lit up with tentative hope when they saw him walking towards them with Yolanda. Paco, a broad-shouldered man with thick glasses and kind eyes, smiled warmly. Nuria, slender and sharp-featured, held her hands together anxiously, perhaps to stop them from shaking.

"Yash," Yolanda said softly after shaking their hands, "this is your new family."

"Hello," Yash told them, in fluent Spanish which made them gasp in pleased surprise. "Thank you for welcoming me into your family."

The journey from the station passed in a blur. Yash was caught between trying to memorise the route through an unfamiliar city, picking up as much as he could about his new 'parents', answering their gentle and trivial questions about his trip from the centre, and a surprising tug of regret at Yolanda disappearing behind him. Too many friendly faces had disappeared behind him already.

Their home was a charming, sunlit apartment in the heart of Bilbao, just a short walk from the Nervión River. It was warm, filled with books, plants, and the faint smell of Nuria's cooking.

"Welcome home, Yash," Nuria said softly as they showed him his new room, a modest space with a desk, a window overlooking a quiet street, and a neatly made bed. When he placed his framed photograph on the windowsill, neither of them stopped him or tried to take it down.

For weeks, Yash remained cautious. He answered questions politely, ate his meals quickly, and spent hours sitting by his window, staring out at the world he had fought so hard to reach. But Paco and Nuria were patient.

Their home was a wonder to him. Familiar: four walls, doors, windows, tables and chairs, beds – all the things a home should have. And yet so different to life in Somalia: the decorations, the shapes of the furniture, the fabrics used for upholstery, the traditions and customs that moulded their daily lives.

Best of all was the floor: extremely polished wood that was Nuria's pride and joy. It was so special that they even had to wear felt slippers as soon as they came in from the outside. As they walked, the slippers would polish the floor further, keeping up its sheen – and, crucially, they wouldn't be at risk of falling over.

Yash saw an opportunity to test: when Nuria and Paco weren't looking, he took off the slippers and stood experimentally in his socks, seeing what would happen. The floor was so shiny underfoot that his socks slipped and slid across it.

With a grin, he saw what he needed to do.

He ran forward from the door, then stopped running, allowing momentum to carry him forward: he slid all the way across the room in his socks, gliding as if he was on ice. He laughed out loud, and the sound startled him.

It was the first time he had laughed since his brother died.

Guilt drew over him like blackout curtains, shielding him from the joy of the slide, from the innocence of childhood. Hassan could never laugh again. Hassan would never see the shine of the polished floor or slide across it just for fun. Yash's parents would never laugh or slide or see their sons smile again.

How could he pursue such foolish joy, when he carried the weight of their expectations – for two sons now, not just himself?

One evening, Nuria sat across from him at the dinner table.

"Yash," she said gently, "you're safe here. We want you to feel like you belong."

And slowly, Yash began to believe them.

Paco was the one who brought up the idea of changing his name.

"Yash," he said one afternoon while they were walking through Parque Etxebarria, "names have power. They can open doors or close them. In Spain, a local name might make things… easier for you."

Yash nodded thoughtfully. Over the following days, they discussed possibilities. Names were tried and discarded—Miguel, Javier, Carlos. Nothing felt right.

When Paco finally suggested a name that Yash thought he could live with, he accepted it without complaint. He knew he would always remain Yash, inside. Whatever they called him on the outside barely mattered.

The next step was school enrolment. Paco and Nuria explained that the Basque Country wasn't always the most welcoming to outsiders. But with a strong name, good manners, and sharp intelligence, Yash could carve out a space for himself.

He started at IES San Ignacia, a secondary school known for its emphasis on science and technology. The building sat at the edge of the city, close to the Aizkorri Mountain—a towering peak where students often went climbing on weekends.

Yash walked into his first class with his shoulders squared and his head high. He was nervous but determined.

The Spanish education system was rigorous, but Yash thrived. His porous mind absorbed everything like a sponge – mathematics, physics, programming. Teachers took notice.

In computer studies, Paco's influence became evident. After school, Paco would spend hours with Yash at the dining room table, helping him to study programming languages like Python, C++, and Java with ever-more complex books and guides.

Machine learning fascinated Yash. He devoured textbooks on artificial intelligence, neural networks, and cryptography. He studied pioneers in computer science—Alan Turing, Linus Torvalds, and Ada Lovelace—and wrote endless scripts to test his theories.

Paco, watching Yash's brilliance bloom, often said, "Your mind is a gift. Don't waste it."

In mathematics, he outperformed everyone. He won district competitions and was invited to represent his school at regional events. Teachers began calling him "*El Genio del Cálculo*"; the genius of calculation. And his foster father would take him to evening lectures at one of Spain's leading maths schools.

But school wasn't just about academics. Yash was athletic, fast, and determined. He joined the rugby team, excelling on the wing, and became a standout climber, scaling the cliffs of Aizkorri with precision and confidence. Whatever he did, he was determined to excel. He had not fought his way through the desert and left Rusanganwa behind just to be second best.

During the summer, he ran; long stretches along the Bilbao estuary, his breath steady, his mind clear.

At night, Yash would retreat to his room. The powerful Lenovo Legion Pro 7i laptop that Paco and Nuria had bought him sat open on his desk.

This was his world now, a glowing screen, lines of code, and the infinite possibilities of the internet.

Yash had always been curious about the dark corners of the web. He learned how to mask his digital footprint, how to create untraceable scripts, and how to exploit weaknesses in poorly secured systems.

And then came online gaming.

Yash quickly became a legend in Spain and globally. His tactical mind and near-supernatural ability to predict opponents' moves made him a formidable player. He played in underground tournaments, earning small but consistent winnings.

But to him, it was more than a game—it was a training ground. Every match honed his ability to strategize, to think three steps ahead, to anticipate and exploit weaknesses.

When he wasn't gaming, he was exploring. He slipped into corporate servers, government databases, and encrypted files. At first, it was curiosity. Then it became something more—a hunger for knowledge, a desire for control.

It was during one of these late-night explorations that Yash stumbled upon the concept of blockchain technology.

Decentralised. Immutable. Transparent.

To Yash, it wasn't just a technology—it was a philosophy. A way to build systems that couldn't be corrupted or controlled by greedy hands.

Paco noticed his interest and encouraged him. He wanted his adoptive son to be happy; he knew nothing of the dark web, of the power of the internet, of how dangerous it could be. He did not have the knowledge that Yash's parents might, of how to keep such an inquisitive and intelligent mind safe from the dark corners that beckoned. He only cared that Yash's lips almost moved to the edges of a smile when he completed a successful build.

Yash became obsessed. His gaming sessions grew shorter, and his hacking sessions grew longer. At Christmas, Paco presented him with the gift he had asked for, handing over a printed document with bemusement: proof that Yash was the proud owner of a silly little digital token, something Paco himself had never heard of but thought might be connected to the games Yash loved to play. A Bitcoin.

"This is it," he whispered to himself one night, staring at a blinking cursor on his screen as he experimented with building his own blockchain script, reverse-engineered from the examples already beginning to bloom online. "This is my future."

Yash sat on his balcony overlooking Bilbao. The lights of the city spread out before him, and the sound of distant laughter drifted up from the streets below. He was no longer Yash, the frightened boy from Somalia. He had become his online alter ego—brilliant, focused, and unafraid.

"The world will know my name," he promised himself, even if it wasn't his real name. "AranaNegra."

Chapter 27.

Finding Artem

The coordinates Maria had traced led Daniel and Nikita to a sprawling compound deep in the jungle, a fortress-like estate owned by one of the cartel's senior leaders. It was a place of excess and brutality, with high walls, watchtowers, and guards armed with military-grade weapons.

From a safe vantage point on a nearby ridge, Nikita surveyed the compound through binoculars. “This isn’t just some hacker’s hideout. Maybe it used to be a warehouse, but it’s had some serious upgrades. This place is fortified.”

Maria’s voice came over the radio. “I can disable the perimeter alarms, but only for a short window. You’ll need to be quick.”

Daniel nodded. “We’re not going in yet. We just need confirmation—visual confirmation that Artem is here.”

Under the cover of darkness, they crept closer to the compound. Maria temporarily disabled the external sensors, allowing Daniel and Nikita to inch their way towards the edge of the estate.

Through a narrow gap in the dense foliage, they spotted him.

Artem.

He was seated near a firepit, surrounded by two heavily armed bodyguards. His pale face was illuminated by the flickering flames, and his fingers drummed nervously against his knee.

"That's him," Nikita whispered. "He matches the ID photograph Maria showed us. That's Artem."

Daniel's pulse quickened. "He's right there. We should distract the guards and get Maria to dismantle the security system. We could get him out."

"Why?" Nikita asked.

The question was so unexpected, so cold, that Daniel turned his head and simply stared at her.

"I know you want to save him," Nikita said, her tone gentler. "But *why*? Because he's worth the risk? Because he will give us information? Or just because he's your friend?"

Daniel's jaw clenched. "Isn't it worth saving him just because he's a friend?"

"You barely know him." Nikita's eyes dropped to the ground momentarily before searching his out again. "He didn't tell you he was here, or about any of this. He doesn't know your real name, and if it wasn't for Maria tracing his activity, you wouldn't know his. And he's not in any danger if Spider is protecting him. We're alone, unarmed. We have no backup."

Daniel considered what she was saying. It made no sense to him. "You're saying we should abandon him?"

"No," Nikita said forcefully, reaching out to touch his hand. "I'm saying I want you to stay safe. We can send one of Sir Rory's teams in to extract him. They're only an encrypted call away, and they can be here within twenty minutes. This isn't a task for us. We're just the tech experts. That's why Sir Rory *sent* them – so they can do the things we can't."

She was right, of course, and her concern for him was touching. They weren't super spies with exploding pens and sniper rifles hidden up their trouser legs. They were just good at decryption and digital tracking. They'd been given small handguns for protection, but Daniel didn't even really know how to use his. They weren't this kind of hero.

Daniel nodded, conceding it at last, though it tugged an ache into his chest to leave Artem behind. "We have his location. We can pass it on to the rest of the team when we get back to the apartment. There's no chance we're getting inside to hack anything. Let's get out of here."

But as they turned to retreat, a distant voice barked out an order in Spanish.

"*¡Alto! ¡No se muevan!*"

Spotlights flared to life, cutting through the darkness and pinning them in place. Daniel and Nikita bolted instinctively without even discussing it, the sharp crack of gunfire splitting the night air.

They dove for cover, bullets tearing through the underbrush. Nikita turned and fired back, dropping one of the guards in a display of marksmanship that made Daniel's eyebrows shoot up. He was scanning the area behind them for another sign of someone coming after them when he heard it.

A soft gasp.

Daniel turned to see Nikita stumble, blood blossoming across her shirt as she held a hand towards the wound. Her expression was one of shock. Apparently, he hadn't been the only one not to realise the guard had hit his mark before she dropped him.

"No!" Daniel lunged forward, catching her as she collapsed.

Nikita's breaths came shallow, her hand clutching at the wound.

"Daniel… you have to… finish this."

"No, stay with me. We're getting out of here." Daniel grabbed the government-issue phone from his pocket and hit the quick dial, the number Sir Rory had given them for emergency situations. "We need an extraction. Now!"

But Nikita's grip on his arm weakened, her eyes beginning to lose focus. Daniel tried to shift her in his arms, but as he did so, his eyes caught on the rapidly expanding pool of blood on the ground below her. More blood than he could have thought possible.

"Don't let him win, Daniel…"

Her hand fell away, and her head slumped forward.

Daniel's world went silent. Around him, the jungle still echoed with gunfire and shouting voices, but he heard none of it.

He laid Nikita down gently on the forest floor, his hands trembling.

It had been so fast. Too fast. There had been no time to process it. No time to say goodbye, to say anything at all.

She looked almost like she could be asleep, except for the pool of blood and the ashen pallor that was already sinking into her face.

For a long moment, he knew only panic.

Would she just open her eyes? Wake up?

He didn't say it out loud, didn't beg. He knew.

In his heart, he knew.

Nikita was gone.

Something cold and sharp settled in his chest.

Nikita was gone.

Chapter 28.

The Final

Yash picked up his headset – though his teammates rarely used the voice channel, preferring to stick to more secure methods of communication – and slotted it over his head, settling back into his gaming chair.

It had been almost twenty years since he'd first arrived in Spain with nothing, and yet he still felt that appreciation every time he did something like this. That he could now afford a computer, a comfortable gaming chair, a headset all of his own – top of the line, always up to date – and even that he could afford the time to spend on such a frivolous pursuit as esports.

Not that he entirely believed it was frivolous, of course. Gaming built hand-eye coordination and reflexes, tested strategic thinking, and this particular game had helped him a lot with his coding and hacking skills. Most of that had been before they started entering proper tournaments as a team, of course – back when he'd been seeing what he could get away with, without getting caught.

They all had the same kind of background. Hackers and coders turned ace players who actually needed no hacking or backdoor coding to win – because they were just that good at strategy and teamwork.

Though setting up a custom code to automate actions once in a while didn't hurt.

The prize money also helped him not to consider the games frivolous, and this time, they were up to share in a big pot.

He logged in. A message flashed up on the screen in front of him.

WELCOME, ARANANEGRA

He clicked on the start button and entered the lobby, waiting for the rest of Team Liquid Tundra to join him. One by one, they appeared beside him: Luna, Phantom, and Underlord.

He waited. And waited. Finally, he typed out the first message to hit their encrypted chat.

AranaNegra: *Where's Tonka?*

Luna: *I haven't seen him.*

Seen him? That was a little quick and a little specific, wasn't it? Surely, she was expecting to *hear* from him over chat? Perhaps she meant that she hadn't seen his avatar pop up or an online status.

Phantom: *I don't have any messages from him. Anyone else?*

Underlord: *Nothing*

AranaNegra: *Nothing here, either. Do you think he overslept or something?*

Phantom: *Didn't he say he was going on a trip and might not be here?*

Underlord: *Yeah, but that was for the final, not for the last round. Right?*

AranaNegra: *Maybe he meant he wouldn't be around at all. Luna? Do you know?*

Luna: *No, I don't know anything. He didn't tell me he wouldn't be here, either. I'll send him a* *message now*

There was a long pause, all of them silently considering. Yash had no way of knowing what was in his teammates' minds, but he quickly came to a conclusion that he hoped the rest of them shared.

AranaNegra: *If he's not here, we'll just have to play without him. Luna, can you adjust the team plan to cover him?*

Luna: *We can't play without him. The tournament rules state we need a minimum of five players. If he doesn't show up, we can't compete.*

Underlord: *Does anyone know any potential subs?*

Phantom: *I might know some other players*

Luna: *Up to our standards, though? They can't have played in any other game in this tournament for a different team*

Underlord: *All they have to do is stand in a corner, we can make up for Tonka's slack ourselves*

Phantom: *Let me get online and ask, I don't even know what time zone they're in but we can try*

AranaNegra: *The game begins in less than ten minutes. If they aren't literally sitting at their computer ready to play, it's already too late*

Luna: *Do you have any better ideas? Or do you just want to forfeit?*

Yash swore under his breath. It would have to be a quick setup, but he could do it. He decided to ask permission – or forgiveness – later and grabbed a second laptop from under his desk. He started getting it ready as fast as he could.

Underlord: *Luna, has Tonka read your message?*

Luna: *No, he's not there*

There was a blip on the screen, and a second later, a new player stood beside the team.

Luna: *Woah*

Phantom: *Who's that?*

AranaNegra: *This is my... 'friend'. He's fully registered as a player with fake documents, don't worry. The officials will think he's real.*

Luna: *Wait, that's you? You're going to play two accounts at once?*

AranaNegra: *You just want him to stand in a corner, right? Pretty sure I can do that.*

Luna: *This is crazy. We're going to get caught and booted out of the tournament*

Underlord: *Well, the alternative is we forfeit anyway, so I say go for it*

Phantom: *Can you really play two at once, dude?*

AranaNegra: *We've got three minutes to go. I don't think there's a choice at this point. The worst that happens is they catch me and ban us from playing, and we just make new accounts on new IPs and carry on anyway*

Luna: *But I like being Luna*

AranaNegra: *You trust me, right? You know me. You know what I can do. They're not going to figure it out unless someone tells them, and none of us are going to do that.*

AranaNegra: *If it comes down to it and we have to explain, he's just a guy I work with who was registered but not very experienced, and he subbed in but stayed out of the way because he knew he wasn't up to our level*

AranaNegra: *Okay???*

Underlord: *Okay by me*

Phantom: *Okay*

Luna: ... *Okay, I guess. But if we get caught, I'm blaming you and denying all knowledge*

Yash settled back in his chair with a grin. One minute to go, and then the chaos would begin.

He was looking forward to the challenge.

Truth be told, he'd been building up his side character for a while – and he was pretty sure he could do more than stand in a corner and watch with the second account.

It was time to explore what he could really do.

Chapter 29.

Hollow Victory

When the end screen came up declaring victory for Liquid Tundra, Maria stood up in shock.

"What is it?" Eva asked. She was sitting in a room across the hall, lounging on a sofa with a fashion magazine in her hands, but she had clearly been paying more attention to Maria than the words on the page. She was tense – they both were. When Daniel and Nikita hadn't come back from their mission, the communications system shutting down unexpectedly amidst the sounds of gunfire, it had left them both in a state of fear and uncertainty.

"We won the game," Maria said. "But Daniel didn't show up."

Eva bit her lip. "Do you think he's…?"

Maria shook her head immediately. "I can't think it," she said. "I can't."

"Maybe he's been extracted by his government," Eva suggested delicately, and Maria nodded.

A ping from her computer drew her attention back to her second screen, to the chat log she kept open at all times.

AranaNegra: *Have you heard anything from Tonka yet?*

Maria checked her private chat. There wasn't any indication Daniel had been online.

Luna: *Nothing*

Her stomach churned. For good measure, she sent Daniel another message, one begging him to get in touch if he could – just like all the others she had sent last night, throughout the morning, and before the tournament round.

Underlord: *Do you think he needs help?*
Phantom: *He's just on vacation with work, right? Why would he need help?*

Maria's stomach churned. Underlord knew more than he was letting on – he had to. He was asking too much, and Phantom was right – other than Maria herself, none of their teammates should have been worried at all about his failure to attend. He'd warned them it could happen while he was away from home.

Maria was the only one who knew that the trip away from home had brought him here, to Mexico – and that Underlord was lurking somewhere in the shadows, too.

Maria typed out a message to Underlord – *I'm sure Daniel doesn't need anything else from you* – and then deleted it before she could send it. All she would do would be to alert him to the fact that she knew who he was and where he was, and that would put her and Eva in even more danger.

The only reason she'd been able to swallow down her bile and play alongside Underlord, knowing who he was and the fact that he could be involved in Daniel's *death*, was to keep up her cover and pretend she knew nothing.

She had to keep that pretence up now.

Luna: *Phantom's right. He did tell us this might happen. Tonka's probably just on a beach somewhere and lost track of time. He'll log in tonight and apologise, I bet*

AranaNegra: *I hope he makes it back for the final. I'm good, but I don't know if I'm tournament-winning good all on my own*

Phantom: *Dude, if you are all on your own, what are we? Huh?*

AranaNegra: *You know what I mean!!*

Underlord: *Your "friend" did pretty well, honestly. How did you do it? Scripts?*

AranaNegra: *Yeah, I was queuing scripts for my main account and then switching over to queue scripts for him, then back. It was pretty heavy. My fingers hurt from the typing haha*

Phantom: *Does that mean we're allowed to cheat now?*

Luna leaned forward to interject, annoyed. They'd all agreed on the rules, before the start of the tournament. They would win this one fair and square, prove that they were the best because they were the best – not because they were good enough coders to get past the anti-cheat checks.

Luna: *No!! We said no cheating. We all agreed!*

AranaNegra: *This was a one-off. Let's be honest, we would have won easily if Tonka was here. We'll have him back for the finale, I'm sure*

Underlord: *You're right. He wouldn't miss it.*

Underlord's last message blinked on the screen over and over again as Maria stared at it, trying to decide if it meant something.

Was Underlord saying that Daniel was alive? Did he have him captive, or had he witnessed him getting away free from the warehouse? Was he really positive that Daniel would show up for the last round of the tournament, or was he just pretending that he knew nothing for the sake of the others in the team?

Or for her?

Did he know who she was, who she really was? Was he baiting her, goading her, playing a game where they both pretended they had no idea what was going on?

She had to know.

She couldn't help herself any longer.

Someone had hacked her back when she was watching the warehouse security. They'd infiltrated Daniel's computer with the eggs on the USB stick, and if they'd poked around before the files were decrypted, they would have seen the chat logs between him and Maria. Not to mention the location of her IP address. She was as good as busted, anyway. She had nothing to lose.

She had to know.

She opened up a private chat log with Underlord.

Luna: *Did you do this? Did you hurt Daniel?*

There was a long pause.

Underlord: *Daniel? Is that Tonka's real name?*

Luna: *Don't mess around with me, Artem. I know who you are and where you are. Spider made you entrap him, didn't he?*

Underlord: *Entrap? What are you talking about? Tonka isn't on holiday?*

Maria took a breath. Either Underlord was talented at lying, or he was being serious. Which was it? Her nature was to trust people and take things at face value, but she wasn't sure she could do that here.

Luna: *He's in Mexico. Tulum.*
Underlord: *WTF? That's where I am*
Luna: *I KNOW*
Luna: *What are you doing???*
Underlord: *I just took a job. Phantom – I met him in person in London and he said he had a job for me, but it turned out to be working for Spider*
Underlord: *I'm decrypting some files for a cartel. I know it's stupid, but Spider said he'd help my family. I'm probably going to get shot in the back of the head before they let me leave, but I couldn't turn it down*
Luna: *PHANTOM is involved in this too?!*
Underlord: *I don't know how much he knows, if he was just connecting us or what, I haven't spoken to him since*
Luna: *So you don't know anything about Tonka?*
Underlord: *I have no idea what you're talking about! Why would Tonka be involved with Spider?*
Luna: *He's trying to CATCH HIM, Artem. And when he heard you were here, he wanted to go rescue you from the cartel. He didn't come back from that mission and now no one's heard from him. I think Spider might have killed him*
Underlord: *What?!?! There's no way... this has to be a joke...*
Luna: *is the cartel a joke? Is SPIDER a joke???????*

Underlord: *Oh my god*
Underlord: *I have to go*
Underlord: *I'll find out wht happened but I g2g rn*
Luna: *Artem?*
Luna: *Artem????*
She waited five minutes and tried again.
Luna: *Artem??????????*

There was no response. Underlord's icon flickered grey, indicating that he was offline.

Maria groaned, buried her head in her hands for a moment, and opened up her private chat with Daniel once again.

Luna: *Daniel, please tell me you're alive. I can't bear it. If you have the chance to reply at all, please just say anything – even one word – so I know you're out there, somewhere.*

The cursor in the chat box blinked steadily, the only movement on the screen. It beat like a heart, taunting her. No message popped up in response.

She sent over a copy of the log of her conversation with Underlord, just in case Daniel was out there and it could help him – but in her heart, she didn't know whether he was still out there at all.

Maria shut down her computer, walked over to sit beside Eva, and, without any warning, threw herself into her girlfriend's arms and sobbed.

Chapter 30.

Political Promises

Alberto settled in at his desk, allowing himself no trace of weakness as he clicked the button to turn on his camera and add himself to the virtual meeting room.

The screen flickered to life almost immediately, showing him a solemn and impressive scene.

The Prime Minister of the United Kingdom, Sir Michael Hargrove, sat at the head of the gleaming oak table in the Cabinet Office Briefing Room. The air was thick with tension, the kind that settled in when titans of power convened to decide the fate of nations. Alberto could feel it even from behind a screen and in a different country.

Across the Atlantic, a parallel meeting was taking place in the White House Situation Room. The President of the United States, Karen Hales, was similarly surrounded by her closest advisors, their faces etched with the same gravity. The window containing their delegation popped up on another of Alberto's screens, allowing him to give them both his full attention when needed.

This was no ordinary day, and certainly no ordinary meeting.

"So, where are we?" Hargrove asked without preamble, his clipped tone barely masking his frustration. Clearly, he had done away with the political niceties; Alberto read the urgency as nearing desperation. Hargrove adjusted his tie, glancing at Sir Rory Brown down the table from him. Next to Sir Rory sat Sir Bob White, the Head of MI6, and Peter Nichols, Executive Director for Risk at the Bank of England. Nikita Cowling, the Bank of England's cybersecurity expert, was conspicuously absent; Alberto remembered her face from earlier briefings, but she was not in this room.

Alberto missed nothing, not even the small details of changing staff members.

Sir Rory cleared his throat. "Prime Minister, as you know, Veritian has been in development for over six years. Its launch isn't just a financial milestone; it's a cornerstone of yours and President Hales' administrations and election promises."

"Why are you telling me something I already know?" Hargrove barked.

"I want to underscore just how important this project is," Sir Rory said. He was a little slow in the way he talked, a little too dedicated to laying out all of the details. Alberto had noticed it before; in certain situations, it allowed him to control the room with ease. But Hargrove was irritable and impatient, and clearly not interested in waiting for an old man to finish a long sentence.

"We've spent billions ensuring its success," Peter Nichols interjected, his voice firm; he had clearly sensed what Alberto did. "The infrastructure is rock-solid. We brought in Alberto Lopez, the world's leading blockchain architect. Cryptropolis's involvement has given us credibility and the technical edge. Every system has been triple-tested. GCHQ and NSA have certified it as impenetrable."

Alberto's spine tingled a little at the mention of his name. He sat up a little taller in his chair, though he hadn't intended to. He fought hard not to let his mouth twitch. This was no reality television show, where contestants were encouraged to smile and mug at the camera whenever their name was mentioned. This was a room full of the most important people in the world.

Hargrove leaned forward. “And Spider? What about this supposed infiltration? I’ve got half my people telling me to absolutely ignore what the other half say. Is there actually any proof that there’s any risk of an attack?”

Sir Bob hesitated, exchanging a glance with Rory. “We’ve had reports, Prime Minister. But… Spider’s involvement is, at best, speculative. There’s no concrete evidence that he’s breached the DGTX framework. Our intelligence suggests his operations are untraceable, which makes proving them very difficult.”

“Speculative?” Hargrove’s voice rose slightly. “Gentlemen, we’re about to launch a digital currency that will underpin the economies of two superpowers. Speculation isn’t good enough. Are you telling me that you’re asking me to stop the launch of the most important financial project of this century so you can go on a wild goose chase?”

His words threw silence in their wake, Sir Rory and Sir Bob exchanging panicked glances and then casting their eyes down to notebooks on the tables in front of them. If they had anything concrete, they weren’t confident enough to say it.

Alberto bided his time. He knew the security of his company, knew what they could promise. He wouldn’t speak up and seem desperate to please. He would wait for them to ask.

Across the Atlantic, President Hales leaned back in her chair, her steely gaze fixed on Treasury

Secretary Angela Collins. The President seemed to sense the need to take charge of the conversation. "Angela, what's the latest on Spider from our end? Do we have a direct threat to Veritian, or is this another phantom?"

Collins glanced at the Director of National Intelligence. "Madam President, Spider's reputation precedes him. Yes, he's a threat in cyberspace. Yes, he's capable of sophisticated attacks. But our cybersecurity teams, bolstered by Cryptropolis, have sealed every possible backdoor. If he's out there, he hasn't breached us, and we have no reason to believe he ever will."

The President frowned. "Karen," said Vice President Grant Mitchell, his deep Southern drawl cutting through the tension. "We've been selling this to the American people as a game-changer. We've promised transparency, security, and a better economic future. If we delay now, it'll look like we're not in control."

"Not just the American people," Angela Collins agreed. "The IMF, the World Bank, and Wall Street are watching us, not to mention stock exchanges around the entire world. A delay will send the markets into chaos."

The President was nodding, clearly agreeing with her team.

Back in London, Hargrove's advisors echoed similar sentiments. "Prime Minister," Peter said, "Veritian isn't just a financial tool. It's a geopolitical lever. If we falter now, we lose the first-mover advantage. China and Russia are already developing their own digital currencies. We cannot afford to look weak. This idea of a threat has been explored, and nothing has been uncovered. If there were some kind of egg to be found, wouldn't Sir Rory's crack team have uncovered it by now?"

"Our team on the ground have uncovered encrypted messages," Sir Rory began, his face slowly turning pink.

"What messages?" Hargrove interrupted, his voice a blade slicing through the air.

"Between Spider and a Ukrainian hacker currently operating out of Mexico," Sir Bob said, hastily taking over. "They imply a connection, a task the two are working on together."

"Is this Ukrainian linked to Cryptropolis in any way?" Hargrove asked. For the first time, his gaze swung to a new part of the screens he was looking at, and Alberto sensed his moment.

"Sir Bob, do you have the full name of the hacker?" he asked.

"Artem Zheltonirvych, also known as Underlord," he said, reading from the page in front of him.

Alberto smiled. "As I thought," he said. "I hired Artem recently to act as a go-between, a decoy, to throw Spider off the scent. He made contact at my behest and told Spider he would do take part in an attack. In reality, Artem is my hired man. There is no threat from that quarter, only a distraction to keep Spider busy."

Below the desk, out of view of the camera, Alberto turned a hand in Xaliima's direction and softly raised it up and down twice – a signal. She nodded in her peripheral vision and silently rushed away. She would have the full file on Artem – his movements before and since he was hired – in front of him within minutes. If Artem was doing something he shouldn't, Alberto would know.

No sense in sharing that information with the men and women on his screen, of course. Absolute confidence: that was all Alberto could show them.

"Do you have any proof that Spider is not manipulating you both?" Sir Rory spoke up. There was a harsh edge to his voice, something Alberto had not expected from their previous meetings. Was the man getting to the end of his tether? "We've sustained casualties on the ground. Whatever Spider is doing, he certainly seems to believe that he's about to be successful."

Alberto maintained his politically correct smile, turning it full force on Sir Rory. "How can I prove a negative?" he asked. He turned his head just slightly to address the full room, looking directly into his camera. "I can personally assure you that there is no vulnerability here. In all of the years Cryptropolis has been operating, we have never suffered a Spider attack to our systems. We are the best in the world – I promise you that. Spider is not capable of breaching what we have set up. All the expense, all the secrecy – this was all necessary to ensure that Veritian would be safe. There is no stone left unturned in our quest to create the most secure digital financial system the world has ever seen. You have my personal promise that there is no hack, no egg, no vulnerability, nor will there be by launch day."

Peter leaned forward. "Prime Minister, this isn't just a launch. It's a statement. The UK and the US leading together, forging a new era of financial stability. The world is watching. This isn't the time to show hesitation."

Across the Atlantic, President Hales voiced a similar concern. "This isn't just a financial decision," she said, addressing her team. "It's political. It's personal. We've campaigned on this. We've promised change, equity, and control. If we falter now, it'll define the rest of my presidency."

"Madam President, Prime Minister," Angela Collins said, "with respect, Veritian is ready. The NSA has run every test imaginable. Alberto Lopez himself has assured us there's no vulnerability. What more do we need?"

Sir Michael Hargrove turned back to the room. "Rory, Bob, Peter, what's the contingency if Spider strikes?"

Sir Bob spoke first. "Immediate lockdown of affected systems. We've created redundancies within the blockchain. Any breach would isolate compromised nodes before they could spread. We could then revert to a digital vault version if necessary to reset all breaches. Communications teams are ready to control the narrative. We'd frame it as a temporary disruption, an expected hiccup in a new technology and assure the public that no data or funds were compromised."

"And the financial markets?" Hargrove pressed.

Peter Nichols answered. "We've engaged key financial institutions. The Federal Reserve and the Bank of England have coordinated to stabilise currencies if there's volatility. We'll flood the markets with liquidity if necessary."

Hargrove nodded slowly, his gaze sweeping the room. It was clear that everything had been covered. "Then we launch. And I suggest we move ahead of schedule, to prevent Spider from getting any foothold, just in case he has plans afoot. Can you do that, Lopez?"

Alberto inclined his head. "My team is ready to launch at your convenience. We moved ahead of schedule in order to leave some room for extra testing just in case it was requested, but all of the necessary tests have been completed."

In Washington, President Hales reached the same conclusion as her counterpart. "We launch early. Tell the NSA and Treasury to be on high alert. And let's make sure Cryptropolis has all the resources it needs. No margin for error."

Back in London, the Prime Minister leaned back, a faint smile on his lips. "The world will remember this day, Madame President. We're about to redefine global finance."

Hales nodded, her jaw set. "Let's make sure they remember it for the right reasons."

As the meeting concluded, the leaders of two nations prepared to unveil a new financial era, one that promised transformation, stability, and hope. But in the shadows, Spider watched, waiting for his moment to strike.

Alberto turned off his monitor, accepting the bundle of files from Xaliima, ready to double down on ensuring his vision for the project was completed. Whatever it took, he would be ready for that launch.

"Send a message to our server-side team in Mexico," he told Xaliima. "We need to deal with Artem. He's become a liability."

PART TWO: VENOM

Chapter 31.

Breakdown

The cool night air clung to Daniel's skin as the British Airways plane lifted off from Cancún International Airport, its engines cutting through the silence like a blade. The seat next to him was empty. It shouldn't have been. Nikita should have been there.

Daniel stared out of the window, the reflection in the glass catching his eye. His face was pale, drawn tight with exhaustion and grief. The weight of failure pressed against his chest, suffocating him. He clenched his fists so tightly that his nails dug into his palms. The pain grounded him, but only barely.

The events of the last forty-eight hours replayed in his mind like a cruel, unrelenting loop. Back before his extraction. Before an anxious time hiding in the beach apartment waiting for the team to find him. The ambush at Aldea Zama. The frantic firefight. Nikita's blood on his hands, her body limp in his arms. Her last words, whispered so softly he had to strain to hear them.

"Don't let him win, Daniel..."

The memory sliced through him again, and he leaned forward, burying his face in his hands.

Back in London, the city felt alien. The rain blurred the lights of St. James's Park as Daniel walked to Vauxhall Cross. He had not slept since returning, spending hours wandering aimlessly through the streets rather than going home, a shadow of his former self.

He turned back from Vauxhall Cross, unable to face it, and carried on walking, anywhere but home.

Finally, his feet would take him no further.

He had to go back.

His flat felt cold, empty. The coffee mug Nikita had used before they left for Tulum still sat on the counter, untouched. He reached for it once, only to pull back as if it might burn him. Instead, he retreated to his bedroom, shutting out the world.

For days, he avoided contact with anyone, skulking in the shadows of his flat with the blinds drawn and the lights off. Sir Rory called repeatedly, leaving terse voicemails demanding a debrief that Daniel half-listened to and then hung up on. Jezer had sent encrypted messages asking for updates, but Daniel couldn't bring himself to reply. Eventually, he turned off notifications altogether and ignored his phone, spending half of his time sleeping and the other half feeling as though he would never sleep again.

Food was an afterthought. He ate nothing until he found himself so ravenous that he devoured foods he should have eaten in moderation: a tub of ice cream that brought him no joy, endless takeaways that he requested be left in the lobby late at night so he could sneak down to pick them up without needing human contact. He didn't bother showering, shaving, changing his clothes. There didn't seem to be a point.

He lay awake on his sofa, unable to sleep, and his laptop caught his eye. He remembered Nikita teasing him about his disorganized home screen as they booted up, ready to decrypt the latest download.

"Seriously, Daniel?" she had said, pulling his laptop to her. "Train maps right next to birds' nests? That's sacrilegious."

Her laugh had been warm, disarming. She had replaced the laptop, her fingers brushing his as she did. "You have to learn to organise your chaos," she had said, smiling at him in that way only she could.

The memory brought tears to his eyes. He sank to the floor, clutching the laptop. "I'm sorry," he whispered into the silence. "I should have saved you."

That night, Daniel sat at his desk, staring at his laptop. He opened his Dota 2 account for the first time in weeks, his fingers hesitating over the keyboard. Gaming had been his escape once, a way to lose himself in the strategy and camaraderie of the virtual world.

Could it be enough – could anything ever be enough – to distract him from the depth of this loss?

He still didn't even know if the device was safe to use after decrypting the files and avoiding the spider egg bomb, but did it really matter if all he was doing was gaming?

As he logged in, he saw familiar usernames: Underlord, Luna, Phantom, AranaNegra. A notification popped up.

Luna: *Haven't seen you in a while. Everything okay?*

For a moment, Daniel considered ignoring it. But something about her message felt different. He knew there was an undertone to it – that she really wanted to ask him what had happened after the raid, but couldn't do it here. The messages they sent here were encrypted, but only for outsiders; anyone who managed to hack into their supposedly secure server could read them. In fact, she probably had no way to be sure that it was even really Daniel she was talking to.

She had played it safe, and he would do the same. Maybe he could exist in a place where nothing really had happened, for a while. Just for a while.

Tonka: *Been busy. You?*

Her reply was immediate.

Luna: *Same. Just finished a tournament with some new tactics. You'd love it.*

Daniel frowned. New tactics. Was that supposed to be a hint about something that had happened back in Mexico? Or was she really talking about the game?

AranaNegra: *Daniel! Where have you been? You missed the last round of the tournament!*

Underlord: *We won, though. Don't worry. You're here now*

Daniel sucked in a breath. Underlord was here. He'd half expected the other player to have disappeared, perhaps aware that he and Luna had been tracking him down in person. But here he was, acting as though nothing had changed.

But what was Daniel supposed to do? Just as he couldn't talk to Luna openly here, he also couldn't confront Underlord. He'd read the chat logs Maria had sent him, and he knew now that Underlord hadn't known what he was getting into. But was that all real, genuine? Or was Underlord still trying to play them?

Better to play, and keep an eye on the chat or Underlord's actions, to see if anything came up.

Tonka: *Sorry. Yeah. I'm here now.*

They played as they always did: sharing strategies, encouraging each other in the chat, taking the other team down one by one. Halfway through the game, Daniel was finding his bearings after defeating a particularly tough opponent when the chat window pinged again.

AranaNegra: *Keep an eye on the game, people! I need help before you get back to your lanes. Today for you, tomorrow for me.*

Daniel's blood ran cold. The phrasing and the tone mirrored something he had read in the encrypted Spider logs retrieved from Aldea Zama.

It was just a saying – but it shot him back to reality.

He sat back abruptly, his mind racing. Nikita didn't want him to sit around in his flat, playing video games with strangers from across the world and pretending she had never existed. That wasn't what she had died for.

She wanted him to find Spider.

He had to do what she needed him to do. He had to find Spider, or he wasn't worthy of her memory.

AranaNegra: *Tonka! Are you still there?*

Daniel blinked, sitting forward again and grabbing at the controls. He spurred his avatar on the screen back into action, jumping back into the game rather than replying to the message. He glanced over the logs and saw he was supposed to be helping Luna with a two-player action, quickly getting back into formation so that he could do what was needed.

For the rest of the games they played that night, he felt a renewed focus like no other. He took down player after player until there was no one left.

Until they were standing victorious, all of their avatars in a loose circle on an empty field, the winners of the semi-final.

They'd done it.

Underlord: *Final tomorrow, guys!*

AranaNegra: *We're all going to be there, right? There's a lot of money on the line. Tonka, you'll be there?*

Daniel could take one more day. One more day to get his head on straight. One day to go over his notes and prepare himself for the debrief Sir Rory kept calling about. One day to win this tournament, to remind himself that he could do this, that he wasn't about to be defeated by some cowardly hacker who hid in the shadows and bought Mexican crime lords to do his dirty work.

He was Daniel Warren. He was his father's son. His mother's son. Sir Rory's protégé. Above that, he was his own man. Someone who had fought his way from the bottom to the top. A man who could hack with the best of them, break into cartel warehouses and get out undetected, shake hands with governmental officials from multiple countries around the world.

He was Tonka. He was a gamer about to win the top tournament prize in his field.

There was nothing he couldn't do.

Once he'd remembered that, he would do whatever Sir Rory needed him to do next to take down Spider – and he would do it in Nikita's name.

His hands curled into fists on his desk.

One day, one tournament victory, and then Spider was going down.

Chapter 32.

Collapse

The digital stage was set. The Dota 2 International Finals, a spectacle watched by millions on Twitch, loomed large on every screen, drawing the collective attention of the gaming world. For Daniel, still hiding behind his Tonka persona, the match was just another step in his carefully maintained cover. But tonight felt different.

This was serious. If he won, if he proved to himself that he was still alive and still strong even without Nikita, he knew he would be able to see this through to the end. He knew he could take Spider down.

He logged into the team's private channel, the familiar avatars lighting up as each member joined. *Luna. Phantom. Underlord. AranaNegra. Tonka.* Together, they had dominated the tournament, a juggernaut of strategy and precision. Yet, as the countdown to the match began, the usual banter and camaraderie were noticeably absent.

Luna: *Everyone ready? Let's go over the opening.*

Phantom: *Sure. Same as semis, yeah?*

AranaNegra didn't respond immediately, his status icon flickering briefly before stabilising.

Tonka: *Arana?*
AranaNegra: *Yeah, yeah. Same plan.*

Daniel felt a pang of unease. AranaNegra's tone lacked its usual confidence, and his clipped response seemed almost dismissive.

Luna: *Alright, let's focus. Top lane pressure early. Underlord, you push mid. Arana and I handle vision. Tonka, you're the anchor. No overextending.*

The plan was solid, one they'd used countless times. But something about the energy in the group felt off. Tonka could feel it through the quietness of the chat logs, the terse way they discussed strategy. Maybe it was the pressure of the final, the seriousness of it.

Or maybe he wasn't the only one with real-life issues getting in the way.

As the match began, the cracks were already showing. Underlord's positioning in the mid lane was too aggressive, allowing the enemy team to draw first blood.

Luna: *What the hell, Underlord? Pull back!*
Underlord: *Relax. It's one kill.*

But the ripple effect was immediate. The enemy team capitalised on Underlord's early death, taking control of the mid-lane and forcing Luna to abandon her usual rhythm to cover. This wasn't like Underlord at all. He was usually more cautious, more cunning. Was it the fact that he'd gone to Mexico that was making him reckless?

AranaNegra: *Stick to the plan.*

His words were sharp but hollow. Daniel could feel the tension bleeding through the chat channel.

Tonka: *We're getting flanked bottom. Luna, need you here.*
Luna: *I'm still covering mid. AranaNegra, rotate.*
AranaNegra: *On it.*

But AranaNegra's rotation came too late, allowing the enemy team to secure another kill and take the bottom tower.

The usually fluid synergy between them had vanished, replaced by hesitation and second-guessing.

Tonka: *We're too spread out. Luna, call it.*
Luna: *I'm trying, but no one's where they're supposed to be!*
Phantom: *Maybe the plan sucks*

The jab hung in the air, unacknowledged but not forgotten.

Daniel tried to salvage the game, focusing on farming and fortifying their defences. But the damage was done. The enemy team, emboldened by their disarray, began systematically dismantling their strategy.

Luna: *AranaNegra, why didn't you drop the ward? We have no vision!*
AranaNegra: *I'm not your damn babysitter!*

Daniel's eyes narrowed. The AranaNegra he knew, the calculated, unflappable leader, was unravelling.

Tonka: *This isn't working. We need to regroup.*
AranaNegra: *No time. Push mid.*

Against his better judgment, Daniel followed AranaNegra's call. It was a disaster. The enemy team ambushed them in the jungle, wiping out their entire lineup.

Underlord: *Great call, AranaNegra. Genius move.*
AranaNegra: *Shut up, Underlord. Maybe if you weren't feeding kills—*
Luna: *Enough! Both of you!*

The tension was palpable, even through the chat logs.

Daniel stayed silent, his focus shifting from the game to the dynamics of the group. The fractures between them were widening, and AranaNegra's erratic behaviour was at the centre of it.

With their base under siege and their strategy in ruins, they all knew it was over. Underlord's avatar flickered out of life on the screen again. He would reappear soon enough, but there weren't enough of them left fighting to defend their last base.

AranaNegra: *Es la gota que colma el vaso*

Daniel's heart skipped a beat. The words were innocuous enough on the surface, but he knew their weight. AranaNegra was slipping, his mask cracking under the pressure. And since when did he speak Spanish? Arana had always told them he was English, living in the UK in London's time zone, just like Daniel. With everything that had gone on with Underlord, Daniel found his stomach churning.

Tonka: *Do you speak Spanish?*
AranaNegra: *It's something I picked up from a friend. Focus.*

But Daniel couldn't let it go. The Spanish words, coinciding with the trip both he and Underlord had made into Spanish-speaking territory, left his mind racing.

The enemy team stormed their base, tearing through their defences with ruthless precision. The match ended in their first-ever loss, the word 'DEFEAT' emblazoned across the screen like a death knell.

The chat was silent for a long moment before Underlord spoke.

Underlord: *That was pathetic.*

Daniel blinked. That didn't sound like Underlord. He was usually more composed, more hopeful. He supposed, now he knew who Underlord really was, that it came from surviving a war. A loss in a game was nothing compared to real-life gunfire. Daniel knew that first-hand too, now.

But what was going on with him? Was it Mexico? Or something else?

Or was this who he had really been all along?

Luna: *We're done. I'm logging off.*
AranaNegra: *Fine. Go sulk.*

The infamous and formerly undefeated team dissolved, each player retreating into their own world of frustration and disbelief as the chat went silent.

Daniel leaned back in his chair, his mind buzzing. The loss was significant, but it was AranaNegra's slip into Spanish that consumed him. Mexico. The word was a hook, a thread connecting everything he had been chasing. It was like everything in the universe was conspiring to remind him of Nikita's dying wish.

He had to act.

They had lost the tournament, but it meant nothing. It didn't change who he was or what he valued.

Nikita had to be avenged, even if it cost him everything to do it.

He logged off, ignoring a new barrage of messages from the team chat. There was no time to dwell on the loss.

He had to go see Sir Rory.

Chapter 33.

Back in the Game

The rain battered London's cobblestone streets, a relentless rhythm that mirrored the turbulence in Daniel's mind. He had returned from Mexico only a matter of days prior, but the ghost of Nikita and the shadows of the mission in Tulum clung to him like a second skin. MI6's headquarters, Vauxhall Cross, loomed ahead, its brutalist facade reflected in the shimmering Thames. Tonight, it wasn't the river that drowned him; it was the weight of his next assignment.

Sir Rory didn't mince words when Daniel finally walked into the briefing room.

"You're late," he snapped. "By several days. I was about to send SCO19 to bring you in. And you look like hell."

Daniel sat heavily in the chair opposite him, his jaw tight. He couldn't hold back the words that wanted to burst out of him. "I lost her, Sir Rory. She died because I wasn't good enough."

Sir Rory's gaze softened, but only slightly. "Nikita was one of the best. Don't dishonour her by wallowing in self-pity. Now, tell me what you've learned."

For the next two hours, Daniel relayed the events in excruciating detail. The ambush, the cartel connections, the encrypted servers in Aldea Zama, Artem surrounded by armed guards, the conversation Luna had sent over, the tournament.

He left nothing out, his voice steady despite the storm raging inside him.

When he finished, Sir Rory leaned back, folding his hands. "You did what you could," he said. It sounded like high praise if only he'd actually said something that could make Daniel feel any better. He paused respectfully before continuing. "We've got something. The Americans intercepted chatter about a Venezuelan connection to the Mexican operatives. They're confident it's Spider. Something big is brewing in Caracas, and they've asked for our assistance."

Daniel's heart clenched. Venezuela. The heart of so much instability. A new lead. A chance to keep his promise to Nikita.

He'd worked there before, not long ago, on a diplomatic mission – an entirely different kind of task. But he had connections, and he spoke the language. What more could he need?

Daniel got to his feet, his resolve unshakable. "Send me to Caracas," he said. He was ready to go, then and there, to walk right out of the room and go to the airport.

Sir Rory raised an eyebrow. "You're not fully recovered, Daniel. You've been in hiding for days. This isn't just about chasing Spider. It's about stability in the region. If you're not ready—"

"I'm ready," Daniel interrupted. His voice was cold, steady. "Send me."

Sir Rory studied him for a long moment before nodding. "I thought you would say that, and I haven't yet briefed anyone else to take your place. The Americans have a contact waiting for you in Caracas. She's been tracking cartel movements linked to Spider's operations. Find her. Work with her. But tread carefully."

"What's the pretext?" Daniel asked.

"You'll pose as a freelance journalist," Sir Rory said, sliding a slim folder across the table. "Your cover story is that you're writing a piece on the resurgence of Venezuelan art and culture. We've arranged for you to meet Marisol Díaz, a gallery owner in Caracas. She's the one. You'll be guided by Rafael, the agent who watched over you during your last visit."

Daniel opened the folder. The first page featured Marisol's profile: sharp cheekbones, dark eyes, and an enigmatic smile. Her gallery, La Espiral, was a well-known hub for contemporary artists and, apparently, intelligence operatives.

On Daniel's previous visit, he had been more or less confined to governmental buildings and diplomatic quarters; that would work in his favour. He hadn't met anyone outside of the delegates assigned to deal with their visit. Now, he could still operate undercover without anyone recognising him.

"And Spider?" Daniel's voice was tight.

Sir Rory's expression darkened. "We've intercepted communications that suggest Spider's using Caracas as a staging ground. Likely a relay point for his network's operations. We need you to find out what's going on and what he is planning – and shut it down. We can give you this."

Sir Rory slid a small black case across the table. Inside was an unassuming flip phone, a secure satellite communication device disguised to look like an outdated relic. Alongside it was a sleek USB drive embedded in a pen, a tool for extracting encrypted data. And an extra passport.

"I think I need a new laptop," Daniel said. "Mine could have been compromised by Spider's team when we stole the data from the warehouse."

Sir Rory nodded. "Our analysts thought you might say that," he said, hefting a larger case from the floor. It hit the table with a clunk, a sure sign that it was a heavy-duty secure device. Daniel recognised the branding on the case as the same as his previous model.

"When do I leave?" Daniel asked, closing the folder.

"Tonight," Sir Rory replied. "There's a direct flight to Lisbon, then a connection to Bogotá. From there, you'll cross into Venezuela by bus. The cover must remain intact. We can't risk drawing attention."

So, he'd already scheduled the travel arrangements when Daniel had called to arrange the meeting. Sir Rory's confidence in his abilities of persuasion knew no bounds. Daniel wasn't even unsettled by the fact that he'd been right.

Daniel took the case and nodded a goodbye, already turning to leave.

"Wait," Sir Rory said, halting Daniel before the door. "This is a long shot, but it's our only lead. It might not pan out."

Daniel thought he understood his concern. Sir Rory was beginning to doubt himself, perhaps, but Daniel had seen enough now to believe that Spider was all over the Veritian project. "I understand. I can handle that."

"Even if it's not the thing that leads us to Spider," Sir Rory said and then paused, choosing his words carefully. "It's still progress. Ruling this out would still bring us closer."

Mexican cartels, Venezuelan instability… it felt, to Daniel, like the kind of place where Spider would thrive. He was in no doubt that this was the right lead to follow. He said nothing, not wanting to worry Sir Rory about his mental state. "I'll find out what I can," was all he left with, turning for the door again before Sir Rory could stop him a second time.

Before he left his flat with his bags packed for the airport, Daniel logged into the team's private channel from his new machine one last time. The group chat was a graveyard of unfinished conversations, snide comments, and half-hearted apologies.

He hesitated before typing.

Tonka*: We'll regroup. Eventually.*

But he didn't believe it. The team was shattered, and the web of trust they had built was beyond repair. How could he ever play alongside Underlord or Phantom again? How could Luna?

A notification popped up on his screen just as he was about to close and pack the laptop.

Luna: *You there?*

He hesitated, then typed back.

Tonka: *Yeah. What's up?*

Luna: *Just... wanted to check in. You seemed off last night.*

Daniel stared at the message, the cursor blinking in the reply box. Luna had always been the empathetic one, the glue that held the team together during difficult moments. But this time, even her presence hadn't been enough to stop the unravelling.

Tonka: *It's been a rough few days.*
Luna: *More than rough. You barely spoke. That's not like you. Did something happen?*

He hesitated. How much could he tell her? The truth was impossible, the channel was not secure enough. The deeper he got into investigating Spider, the more he felt like there wasn't a secure enough channel in the world. He had to say something that Luna would understand without speaking the truth. He hesitated and changed his mind three times before he finally said it.

Tonka: *I lost a friend this week.*
Luna: *Oh, god. Daniel. I'm so sorry.*

Daniel sighed, leaning back in his chair. Luna's persistence was both frustrating and comforting. She was someone who had known Nikita, even if only for a short moment in time. She would understand what brilliance had been lost from the world now that Nikita was gone.

But part of him, such a small but such a persistent part, couldn't help putting some of the blame on Luna for leading them to the trap of that warehouse in the first place.

Tonka: *And we lost the tournament.*

He had to bring it around to ‘normal’ conversation again. The kind of conversation someone would expect him to be having if they were monitoring his communications.

Luna: *I know. It sucked. We fell apart.*
Tonka: *It’s not just the loss. Today felt... different. Like everything’s changing, and I don’t know how to stop it.*
Luna: *We all felt it. The loss, the arguing... it’s not like us. I don’t know what’s happening either. But we can fix it. We always do.*
Tonka: *I hope you’re right.*
There was a long pause before Luna replied.
Luna: *You know, if you ever need to talk... like, really talk, I’m here.*

Daniel felt a pang of guilt. Luna’s kindness was genuine, but he couldn’t ever really talk to her now – not unless they were in person, where they could be more sure they weren’t being monitored. He doubted he’d ever be able to bring himself to get on a plane to Mexico again unless something incredibly drastic happened. The pain was too raw.

All too clearly, he saw a future in which Underlord was arrested, Phantom forced into the darkness as an agent for Spider, the others drifted away because they no longer had confidence in their abilities as a team, and he and Luna never spoke again.

They had shared some of the most intense moments of his life, but so easily, that could all go away.

Tonka: *Thanks. I appreciate that.*

Luna: *Just don't disappear on us, okay? We need you.*

Her words lingered on the screen, a plea for stability in a world that felt like it was falling apart. Did she mean the team, or was she relying on him to catch Spider and protect her and Eva?

Tonka: *I won't disappear. I promise.*

As Luna's status switched to offline, Daniel sat in the silence of his room. He had made a promise, but he knew it was one he might not be able to keep.

Daniel logged out, the weight of his next mission pressing heavily on his shoulders. The fractures within the team were deep, but his path was clear. Caracas awaited, and so did Spider.

This was no longer just a mission. It was personal.

"I'll find you, Spider," he whispered. "And I'll make you pay."

Chapter 34.

Cat and Mouse

Daniel's flight to Lisbon was uneventful, a rare reprieve in what had already become a labyrinthine operation. Disguised as a slightly dishevelled journalist, his round glasses and loose linen shirt gave him the air of someone perpetually chasing deadlines. Yet, beneath the facade, his mind raced, each mile in the air bringing him closer to the unknown.

In Lisbon, Daniel switched passports, becoming Peter Green, a Canadian journalist with just enough cover story to pass casual scrutiny. From there, his path veered into shadow. Arriving at El Dorado Airport in Bogotá, the pulse of the city buzzed faintly in the background, a mix of distant car horns and the rhythmic hum of a populace always in motion. But there was no time to linger.

Daniel boarded a bus heading south toward San Antonio del Táchira, dimly aware of several covert operatives moving around him, never acknowledging him or even meeting his eye. The journey was brutal, a gruelling twenty-seven-hour marathon across winding mountain roads and through bustling border towns. The bus was packed beyond capacity, with travellers wedged shoulder to shoulder. The air grew thick with the mingling scents of diesel, sweat, and the faint tang of unwashed clothes. Every checkpoint brought a fresh spike of tension.

Most of it flowed over him like water off a duck's back. There was simply no room for fear or doubt or discomfort with the grief that already filled his mind. Grief – and determination that Spider would not escape revenge.

Guards loomed at the roadside, their weapons slung carelessly, inspecting documents with the casual menace of people who knew their power. Daniel kept his head low, his heart pounding as his forged papers were scrutinized a moment too long. Each time, he held his breath in an attempt to avoid suspicious mannerisms until the guards waved him through, uninterested.

As the hours dragged on, Daniel was left alone with his thoughts. The bus rattled over potholes, the vibrations thrumming through his body like a drumbeat of unease. He stared out the dirt-smudged window at the sprawling countryside, the stark beauty of the Andes a sharp contrast to the inner turmoil tightening his chest.

What was he doing here? Every plan, every step forward seemed to pull him deeper into a web he barely understood. The weight of the mission, the delicate threads of deception, the risks of discovery, pressed down on him during the long stretches of silence.

By the time Daniel arrived in Caracas, he was hollowed out. The city's chaos greeted him with open arms, a cacophony of car horns, shouting vendors, and the hum of distant sirens. Faded murals of socialist leaders gazed down from crumbling walls, their idealistic visages cracked and weathered by time.

He checked into a modest hotel under his alias, the room a dim, claustrophobic box with a creaking ceiling fan that barely stirred the humid air. He paid in crisp U.S. dollars, the currency of trust in a nation riddled with uncertainty, and slumped onto the threadbare bed.

As he lay there, the scale of what he'd undertaken began to crystallise. He wasn't just a player in this game, he was a pawn being pushed toward the centre of the board. He had thrown himself right back into the very conspiracy that had resulted in Nikita's death. The realisation was chilling, but there was no turning back now. The spider's web was tightening, and Daniel was firmly ensnared.

That evening, he met Marisol Díaz at La Espiral. The gallery was a sanctuary of colour and light amidst the city's grit. Paintings of surreal landscapes and abstract figures adorned the walls, each one a riot of emotion.

"Peter Green," Marisol said with a knowing smile as she extended her hand. Her grip was firm, her demeanour cool and professional.

"Marisol," Daniel replied, matching her confidence as if the name had been his since birth.

They spoke in low tones, weaving their conversation between discussions of art sculpture. Marisol handed him a sculpture, a delicate metallic orb, and whispered, "The USB is inside. It contains the server locations Spider's been using. We'll talk more tomorrow."

Louder, she said: "You must take this gift as a reminder of your visit. If you like it, you can meet the artist next week. I'm sure he'd be happy to give you an interview."

Daniel took the orb with a smile, pretended to lift it up and admire it, and nodded as if he'd just been given a wonderful lead for his article. "I appreciate your help," he told her. "And any introductions you can manage for up-and-coming artists, too. The kind that no one else knows about yet."

Marisol's eyes glimmered with understanding at the cover he was building. If he was supposed to be meeting underground artists, it would explain away the fact that Marisol would need to introduce him to covert operatives and people who existed off the grid. People who weren't known to be part of the art world at all.

"I would be happy to find some names for you, Peter," she said smoothly. "I think we may be able to meet tomorrow evening at a café; I'll find someone who would be suitable for your research. Would that suit you?"

"Perfect," Daniel said. He'd already been informed by Sir Rory that Rafael would be meeting him and Marisol together, all of them using the cover of the art world to hide the fact that they worked for the same employer. "I'm going to spend the day looking for street artists. Do you have any local markets to recommend? Anywhere they sell locally-made art would be fantastic for my research."

Marisol nodded with a smile, writing him a quick list to go with his orb.

So far, so good.

But Daniel's skin itched with the need to go back to his motel, fire up his encrypted laptop, and see just what was on this USB stick – and where the evidence would lead him.

Chapter 35.

Rafael's Gambit

The next day, Daniel explored Caracas under the guise of researching local art. He visited markets and spoke to street artists, carefully dropping Marisol's name to establish credibility. That evening, he met her at a café in the Sabana Grande district.

"We believe that Spider has deep connections here in the government. We believe his network operates out of a tired-looking warehouse in the El Hatillo district," Marisol said, her voice barely audible over the clatter of dishes and the hum of conversation. "There's a server farm there, and the extreme energy levels it pulls could indicate cryptographic activity. Not only that, but it was a shell node first used by Cryptropolis before they sold up and moved somewhere better. It could make sense to operate out of the same space if you're trying to attack the company – maybe even find some people who used to work for them and still have insider knowledge. But it's heavily guarded. Venezuelan style. Shoot first, ask questions later. You'll need help."

A man was approaching them through the crowded street, his chin lifting as he caught Marisol's eye.

"Rafael!" she exclaimed, turning to Daniel in a much louder voice than she had previously used. "This is one of the artists I wanted you to meet."

Daniel met her eyes with a pasted-on smile and nodded. He tried not to show any recognition, to admit that he'd met Rafael before.

Rafael joined them at the table with an easy smile and quick eyes, playing loudly into their cover as artist and journalist. He was a wiry man in his mid-thirties, and his voice dropped quickly and easily through Spanish and English, his wit fast in both. Daniel knew from his last visit that he was former SEBIN, working for Venezuelan intelligence before he was turned to MI6's side.

"I'll get you close," Rafael said at last, on the tail end of a discussion about a 'gallery' that Peter just had to visit, his Spanish tinged with a local lilt. "But once you're in, you're on your own."

Daniel nodded. "I understand." He knew Rafael still had his own cover to maintain; if any of his contacts suspected that he was working for the UK government, he would find it almost impossible to continue doing his job.

After they finished their drink, Marisol left them. Rafael drove Daniel toward the warehouse in the gathering twilight. They entered a more salubrious area. Dogs roamed the empty streets, making Daniel jump when their rangy bodies appeared close to the car, their eyes fearless and empty.

Darkness shrouded them as they approached the warehouse at last, passing through battered and broken chain-link fencing that did nothing to keep anyone out. As the humid night air clung to Daniel's skin, they crouched behind a row of parked trucks that looked so battered, it wasn't clear they would ever be able to start again.

Another warehouse, Daniel thought to himself grimly. He was grateful that the location was different – the outskirts of a crumbling city, not the middle of an empty desert. If it had looked like the place he'd lost Nikita, he didn't know that he would have been able to go through with it.

As he raised his head to stake the place out, a shiver ran through him. Warehouses looked much like warehouses, no matter where they were. The shot rang out through his memory and he closed his eyes for a moment, tamping down the fear.

Nikita needed him to do this.

"The main entrance is a no-go," Rafael whispered. "There's a service door around the back."

Daniel nodded and slipped into the shadows, not allowing himself a single moment more to hesitate. The service door was locked, but a quick twist of a tension wrench and a pick had it open. Inside, the air was cool, the hum of servers filling the silence.

When he looked over his shoulder, Rafael was gone.

Daniel moved quickly, his heart pounding as he inserted the USB pen into the nearest terminal. The screen flickered to life, displaying lines of encrypted data. He began the extraction process, the seconds stretching into eternity. There was no one around, but he knew, too, that there was no Maria to help him here. If the surveillance was more sophisticated than it looked, he could be overpowered by armed guards within moments.

The files were vast and intricate – financial transactions, encrypted communications, and something that stood out: a series of digital transfers tied to an entity called "Ortega Holdings."

Alongside was a name: Sofía Ortega. He scanned what he could as the text streamed over the screen, trying to memorise anything he saw in case he had to leave without the USB for some reason.

Footsteps echoed in the corridor. Daniel's breath hitched as he yanked the USB out and ducked behind a stack of crates. Two guards passed, their conversation casual. Once they were gone, Daniel slipped out the way he came. He wasn't going to make the same mistake twice and consider wasting time looking for another server. It was too dangerous.

Nikita had taught him that.

***

Back at La Espiral, Daniel handed Marisol the USB. She plugged it into a secure laptop before Daniel could warn her about hidden eggs, her eyes scanning the data. Thankfully, this time, there was no encryption to sort through.

"Ortega Holdings," she murmured, her brows furrowing. "Sofía Ortega. That's a name I've heard before. She's probably tied to Spider's operations, likely laundering money for his network."

Daniel leaned over her shoulder, careful not to brush against her. His grief was too raw; even touching another woman by accident and with no further intentions would have felt like a betrayal of Nikita's memory. "Any idea where we find her?"

Marisol smirked. "She's a socialite. Always hangs out in exclusive circles from the magazines I read. But if we want to lure her out, we'll need bait."

"What kind of bait?" Daniel asked, noting a glint of mischief in Marisol's eye.

"You," Marisol replied. "She's known for her... interest in charming foreigners. We get you into her circle, and she'll come to you."

"And how do we do that?"

Marisol brought up a website on her phone, showing him the details of an upcoming event. "She'll be here," she said. "*Everyone* will be. A gala at the Gran Melia Hotel. It's exclusive, but Rafael can get you in. You just need to look the part."

"How do I do that?" Daniel asked. "I came with the wardrobe of a journalist, not a socialite."

Marisol scanned his frame for a moment, then smirked again. "It can be arranged," she said. "Come by tomorrow. My apartment is upstairs from the gallery. I'll meet you in the afternoon. But first, go by this boutique." She scribbled an address on a piece of paper and handed it to him.

Daniel took it with a growing sense of unease. He needed to become someone else yet again and do it convincingly, in front of the kind of people who sniffed out any sense of weakness or lack of belonging.

He thought of Nikita, how she had looked like a work of art with the setting sun streaming through the windows of their rental car as they drove through Mexican scenery, and clenched his hand around the note.

He would be whoever they needed him to be.

Chapter 36.

Sofia

Daniel walked up to Marisol's apartment in a tailored slim-fit dark navy suit that hugged his frame perfectly. The crisp white shirt and silk pocket square completed the look, complementing the single-breasted silhouette made from Italian wool. He caught Marisol's approving eye as she opened the door.

"Now," she said, "you look like someone who belongs at the Gran Melia."

Marisol's apartment was a blend of modern minimalism and artistic chaos. Paint-splattered canvases leaned against stark white walls, while a single vase of fresh lilies sat on an antique table. Daniel stood in front of a mirror, frowning at his reflection.

"This isn't going to work," he said, tugging at the sleeves. "I look like a librarian attending a wedding with a spy theme."

Marisol laughed, her melodic voice filling the room. "Patience, Peter Green. You're about to become the talk of Caracas; the man who walked into the Gran Melia and turned heads."

"Even if those heads are turning to wonder what a librarian is doing there?"

She stepped forward, adjusting his collar with practised ease. "You need something that screams confidence without being ostentatious. Sofía Ortega is clearly drawn to power, mystery, and elegance.

You have to embody all three. And if you look like a librarian, so much the better for your cover story of being an arts reporter."

A knock at the door signalled the arrival of Rafael; he was holding a cream-coloured envelope in his hand. Inside was an invitation on thick, luxurious cardstock, the name of the event embossed into it and Peter Green's name emblazoned in gold handwriting. Probably literally gold, Daniel thought, turning the card to catch the light across his false name.

"I used the cover you're already here under," Rafael explained. "We've got you listed as a correspondent for an arts publication, just like your travel papers say. It's niche enough not to draw scrutiny but credible enough to get you through the door. I didn't see any need to overcomplicate things."

"That makes sense," Daniel nodded. He knew Sir Rory would have done the work – right now, the arts publication in question likely had a raft of back-dated articles dotted across its website with Peter Green's byline. The cover would stack up under scrutiny. He felt more secure to stick with it than to make any changes. It felt, though, like Rafael was doing a little less work than usually expected.

Daniel wondered what the man had been doing all day, and why he'd had to beg off attending the boutique with Daniel if all he was doing was getting one single invitation.

Rafael handed Daniel a press pass with his photo and the name of the publication. "You'll need to pretend to interview a few people, I should think. These kinds of artists and society people can get a bit thin-skinned if they think they've been snubbed."

"What's my angle?" Daniel asked, slipping the forged credentials into his breast pocket where he could easily pull it out at the door.

Marisol chimed in. "You're writing about the influence of the elite on Venezuelan art. Focus on how their patronage keeps the cultural scene alive despite the country's economic challenges."

Rafael grinned. "Flatter them, make them feel important. That's all it takes."

***

The Gran Melia Hotel gleamed under the soft glow of crystal chandeliers. The ballroom was a sea of elegance, with tuxedos and gowns swirling in time to a live orchestra. Daniel entered with the confidence of a man who belonged, his tailored suit catching the light as he scanned the room.

Sofía Ortega was impossible to miss. She stood near the bar, a vision in emerald green, her dark hair cascading over one shoulder. Her laughter was light, but her eyes betrayed a sharp intellect that missed nothing.

Marisol had coached him on the approach: "Don't go straight for her. Work the room, make her notice you. Let her come to you."

Daniel followed the advice, chatting with a few guests, dropping hints about his 'article', and flashing his most charming smile. He caught Sofía glancing his way more than once.

When their eyes finally met, Daniel made his move.

Daniel walked over with a drink in hand, his smile disarming.

"Ms Ortega," he said, his voice smooth. "Peter Green. I'm writing about the interplay of power and art in Venezuela, and I'd be remiss not to speak with you."

"Why is that?" Sofia asked, tilting her head slightly. He thought perhaps she was testing him.

Thankfully, he'd read the research Rafael and Marisol had prepared for him.

"I heard about the extensive art collection you've built up through Ortega Holdings," he said. "I've heard a lot, too, about how connected you are. I'm sure this gala wouldn't be attended by anyone at all if you weren't invited, isn't that right?"

Sofía raised an eyebrow, intrigued. "You've done your homework, Mr Green."

"It's my job," Daniel replied with a playful shrug. "But it's rare to meet someone who bridges both worlds so seamlessly."

Sofía's lips curved into a smile. "Flattery will get you everywhere, Mr Green."

Their conversation flowed effortlessly, Daniel skilfully weaving questions about her work and interests into the dialogue. Sofía, flattered and curious, let her guard down just enough to reveal a sliver of her world.

"I have a villa outside the city," she said at one point, her tone casual but her eyes watching his reaction. "It's where I go to escape the noise and... work on my projects."

Daniel leaned in slightly, his interest feigned but convincing. "It sounds fascinating. I'd love to see how someone like you finds inspiration and also see your wonderful art collection."

Sofía's laughter was soft, almost conspiratorial. "Perhaps someday, Mr Green."

"Please, Ms Ortega," he said, "Call me Peter."

"Then you must call me Sofía," she replied with a leonine smile. "You see, we're on first-name terms already. You seem to be inching yourself closer to that villa invitation."

"Well, why not?" Daniel asked, trying to let his eyes sparkle with mirth – if that was even a thing. "It sounds a whole lot better than dinner alone at my hotel."

Sofía laughed at that. "Anything sounds better than dinner alone in a hotel," she agreed.

Daniel cast his eyes conspiratorially around the room. "Now," he said, lowering his voice; he didn't want to push too hard on the invite in case she got suspicious. "Would you do me the favour of walking around this room with me and telling me about who's who?"

Sofía linked her arm through his proffered elbow, shifting her clutch and champagne glass to the other hand. "I suppose I could share a little gossip here and there," she said, her laughter tinkling like crystalware clinking together. "Come, let's start over here."

And Daniel nodded along with everything she told him, even pretending to make notes a few times so that she would never suspect he was anything more than an overly flirtatious art critic.

She would never know he planned to betray her until the deed was done.

Chapter 37.

Sanctuary

Sofia Ortega's message arrived at the desk of Daniel's hotel room in Caracas, scrawled elegantly on the hotel's embossed stationery. The concierge handed it over with a knowing smile, as though an invitation from Sofia Ortega was a rare jewel bestowed upon only the most fortunate.

Mr. Green,
Join me for dinner this evening. I'd love to show you my collection and discuss my vision for Venezuela as the cultural capital of South America. My driver will pick you up at 8.
Sofia x

Daniel read the note twice, committing every curve of her handwriting to memory. Did she suspect him? Had she any idea that he wasn't really who he said he was?

The closer he got to the heart of Spider's operations, the more danger he knew he was in. There wasn't a single moment that Nikita's dying breath didn't remain at the top of his mind, filling his eyes and his ears, and he knew he could be walking into another trap that would see him join her in death.

Sofia was no ordinary opponent, either. She wasn't just a pawn in Spider's game. She was formidable in her own right: through her business, she had her hands in the pockets of the most important people in the country, from drug lords to politicians. She might have been an elegant socialite with an interest in art, but Daniel knew she was also ruthless enough to hand him over to a hit squad at any provocation – or maybe even do the deed herself.

He spent the day in nervous anticipation, not daring to go to Marisol or Rafael in case the invitation had prompted Sofia's people to keep an eye on him. They knew the plan, though, and Rafael would be out there somewhere, keeping an eye on him from afar.

At eight in the evening exactly, a sleek black Mercedes car arrived at the hotel. The driver, a young man with a practised air of deference but eyes that seemed to assess him fully at a glance, opened the door for him.

The journey to Sofia's villa was a study in contrasts. Caracas's streets, alive with the chaos of daily life, gradually gave way to an enclave of wealth. They passed the Caracas Country Club, where gated mansions rose from manicured gardens, guarded by high walls and security cameras. Sofia's villa stood apart, a palatial estate lit like a beacon against the night sky.

The villa's architecture was a blend of colonial opulence and modern extravagance. Expansive marble steps led to a pair of towering mahogany doors. The entrance hall was breathtaking, dominated by a crystal chandelier that cast a kaleidoscope of light onto the marble floor. A sweeping staircase coiled upward, flanked by walls adorned with art that spanned centuries—a stark juxtaposition to the economic reality faced by most Venezuelans.

Daniel did not have to stand there gazing around himself in wonder for long.

Sofia greeted him in a flowing emerald dress, her sharp features softened by the warm glow of the lighting. “Peter, welcome. I’m so glad you could join me.”

“Thank you for the invitation,” Daniel said, offering his most charming smile. “Your home is extraordinary.”

Sofia waved a hand, leading him into the dining room. “It’s a sanctuary for art as much as for myself. I’ll show you the collection after dinner.”

The dining room was equally lavish. A long mahogany table set for two was framed by floor-to-ceiling windows overlooking the illuminated gardens. Servants moved silently, pouring wine and serving a meal that could rival any Michelin-starred restaurant. The flavours were exquisite—fresh ceviche, slow-cooked lamb, and a dessert of dulce de leche tart.

As they dined, Sofia spoke passionately about her vision. “Venezuela has always been a country of rich culture, but the world only sees our politics and poverty. My dream is to make Caracas a hub for South American art. I want to showcase our talent to the world.”

“Ambitious,” Daniel remarked, genuinely impressed. “But it sounds like you’re the right person to make it happen.”

Sofia’s lips curved into a knowing smile. “Ambition is what separates visionaries from dreamers. Speaking of ambition, tell me about your recent travels. Surely your trip isn’t all work?”

Daniel's mind raced. He had to be careful not to reveal too much. There was no way, for example, he could mention his recent trip to Mexico; that hadn't been undertaken on Peter Green's passport. "When you love your work as much as I do, it's all the same. I'm here because there's a story worth telling."

"A story worth telling," Sofia repeated, her eyes narrowing slightly. Did she suspect he wasn't telling the truth? "Isn't that what every journalist says? And yet, often I see fluff pieces or hatchet jobs that don't do our art scene justice."

"I assure you, I'm here for a genuine look at the scene in Venezuela," Daniel replied smoothly, steering the conversation back to her collection. "I'd love to see the story you've built for yourself. Something tells me that your collection is going to be one of the most impressive I've seen."

The flattery seemed to do the job. Their conversation turned more pleasant for the rest of the dinner until Sofia stood and offered him her hand, promising that long-awaited tour.

Sofia led him through the villa, each room unveiling a new facet of her collection. Renaissance portraits hung alongside bold modernist works. A secluded gallery featured indigenous Venezuelan art, meticulously curated to showcase the country's heritage. Sofia's knowledge was encyclopaedic, and her passion was genuine. She was no mere collector; she was a custodian of culture.

Finally, they arrived at a private wing of the villa. Sofia paused at a heavy wooden door, turning to Daniel with a mischievous glint in her eye. "And this is where I keep my most precious treasures."

She stepped up to a panel on the wall, tapping it to produce a digital keypad. She typed in a quick code, then paused, stock-still, while a beam of red light scanned across her face. Both a code and a biometric scan were required to enter; that meant whatever was inside was valuable enough to keep safer even than all of the art on her walls.

Inside, the room was starkly different. Industrial, almost clinical, with steel walls and a temperature-controlled environment. The centrepiece was a series of servers encased in glass, humming softly. Sofia gestured toward them casually. "I'm also a patron of the digital arts. Everything here supports the cultural archives I've been building. The future of art is as much about preservation as it is about creation."

Daniel nodded, his gaze lingering on the servers. The setup was state-of-the-art, far beyond what he'd expected. He began immediately to formulate a plan. "Remarkable," he said. "The security measures are impressive. You've thought of everything."

Sofia's expression turned thoughtful. "In a country like ours, you have to. The more you build, the more there is to protect."

Daniel turned away from the view before she could become suspicious of how carefully he was noting every part of the room. "Well, I'm afraid computers are lost on me," he said, with a sheepish smile that he hoped befitted an old-fashioned art critic.

Sofia smiled back at him. "Of course," she said. "Shall we stroll back through the gallery? One last look?"

"I'd enjoy that very much," Daniel said, his smile deepening with the ever-present knowledge that avenging Nikita depended on how convincing he was.

The evening ended with Sofia walking him to the car. "Peter, this has been delightful. We must do it again soon."

"I'd like that," Daniel replied, holding her gaze for a moment longer than necessary to sell his cover deeper.

"Not tomorrow," she said thoughtfully, her eyes flicking upwards as though she was looking at a calendar in her mind. "I'm booked to attend an event in the city – very boring, nothing you'd be interested in, and I'm sure you have more people to talk to for your article. How long are you here?"

"Until at least the end of the week," Daniel said, not wanting to commit to a leaving date in case he needed to play a longer game here.

"Then perhaps we'll meet again the day after, or after that," Sofia said, fixing him with a mysterious smile. "I'll be in touch."

Daniel climbed into the car, his mind already working on the next step, but he kept his eye on her in the mirror as the driver whisked him away.

Back at the hotel, he briefed Marisol and Rafael. "She's out tomorrow evening. She mentioned it over dinner. That's our chance to access her villa, the servers."

Rafael frowned. "You're sure she won't suspect anything?"

"I'll make sure of it," Daniel said, his tone resolute.

Chapter 38.

Heist

The next evening, under the cover of darkness, Daniel and Rafael returned to the villa.

Daniel's earlier observations had served him well. All of the lights in the home were off. It looked as though there was no one around, but he knew there could be members of her security detail guarding the artwork; thankfully, he wasn't intending to come into contact with any of them.

Rafael had given him the equipment that he needed – climbing gear that was favoured by cat burglars, allowing him to scale the outer boundary wall almost soundlessly. From there, he navigated the grounds with precision, bypassing the security systems Sofia had unwittingly revealed during their tour. He knew that passing through the house would be impossible. But he didn't have to.

The hallway just before the server room was illuminated by a large window. It was sealed and the glass was so thick that he could never have cut through it before being caught. But he'd made an excuse while Sofia was closing up the door to the server room behind them; he'd tied his shoelace and at the same time, flicked the switch that locked the window in place at the bottom.

If no one had noticed…

It slid open on well-oiled hinges, opening only far enough that he would need to carefully squeeze through the gap – but carefully squeeze he did.

The industrial server room loomed ahead, its soft hum a beacon in the silence.

Now came the true test. Daniel had been able to glance up before he stood, watching Sofia's fingers fly over a numerical keypad that controlled door access. She hadn't bothered to hide her movements, believing that he was otherwise distracted. He thought he had the combination in mind: she'd started at the top left, moved down, then right and down again, before returning to the middle. 1 – 4 – 8 – 5. That was what it had to be.

He leaned to the side a little, trying to catch the moonlight shining off the keypad. It was polished and smooth, and perhaps he could see fingerprints on the surface – but no; there wasn't a sign. Either someone polished it regularly, or the material had been selected because it didn't bear smudges easily – making it a good choice for a security system.

If he was wrong, an alarm would likely blare through the building and give him away. He wouldn't be able to get out through the window again in time, and even if he did, they would be searching the grounds for him. If this was wrong, he was doomed.

Rafael had given him a device, one that would connect to this particular model and unlock it. It would take time, though, to brute force attack until it found the right combination. Or he could enter what he thought he knew were the right numbers and risk setting it off – but get inside quickly before there was any chance someone would come down the hall and find him.

How much did he trust himself and his own powers of observation?

Daniel took a deep breath to steady his nerves and punched the numbers in before he could second-guess himself. There was a moment that seemed to stretch forever in silence; then a red light stirred inside the device.

Quick as a cat, Daniel held up his phone to the light, making sure that it hit the correct part of the deepfake 3D projection he'd designed to match Sofia's face, using images and videos of her from social media. He'd even set it on a loop to blink, making it seem like a real, living person.

He held his breath as the light scanned from left to right and disappeared – until he heard a whirring sound and a click.

The door was open.

Inside, Daniel worked quickly, plugging a device into the main console. A login screen popped up, and he started running a brute-force dictionary attack to get past it. Time was his enemy, but Daniel's focus never wavered. He'd done this same action in much more intense situations. At least this wasn't a warehouse filled with prowling armed guards.

Within minutes, he had the data he needed.

Strangely, his heart pounded all the faster as he made his exit. He returned back the way he had come, almost falling through the window in his eagerness to get away. He fumbled his climb up the wall, almost falling – but as soon as he sailed down the other side, Rafael was there, grabbing him and pulling him towards the getaway vehicle where Marisol waited to drive them out of danger.

As they slipped back into the night, Daniel allowed himself a brief moment of satisfaction.

Sofia had been a formidable opponent, but he had played his role perfectly.

Now he just had to hope with everything he had that the data on the USB would help them find Spider, and Nikita could be avenged.

***

Daniel plugged the USB into his laptop with no small amount of trepidation. This was a lead in an investigation that was thin on leads, and if it didn't pan out, they were running out of time.

The launch of Veritian was getting closer and closer, and if he didn't have anything good on this USB, there was a high chance that they weren't going to be able to stop it.

Not to mention the growing fear that there would be yet another honeytrap here on this USB, giving Spider's team another chance to spy on him or infect his laptop.

He leaned forward on his elbows, his chin on his hands, watching with a frown as his decryption program worked on the data. It was a good encryption, but not *Spider* levels of good. This was something a little more standard, and that worried him.

It was likely that he'd stumbled across something that was related to Sophia alone, not Spider, and that thought sank like a stone in the pit of his stomach.

When the program had done its work, he opened the resulting file anxiously, his eyes scanning across the words as fast as he could.

But when he came to one of the lines, he stopped – and, surprising even himself, he laughed out loud.

He had it.

Spider would not escape him – not yet.

Chapter 39.

The Gibraltar Link

Sir Rory took Daniel's encrypted call in the heart of Vauxhall Cross, setting him up at the front of a room so that he could see everyone in it – and, with the camera on the phone, they could see him.

The debrief was exhaustive, an interrogation thinly veiled as a briefing. Sir Rory and the rest of the Joint Intelligence Committee wanted to know every detail about Caracas, the server heist, the parties, and, most importantly, the encrypted data they'd barely managed to exfiltrate before being discovered at the villa.

Daniel recounted the events methodically, masking the tremor in his voice. The room fell silent when he finished, the tension palpable as analysts pored over preliminary findings from the Caracas server.

"Spider's network is more extensive than we anticipated," one of the technicians muttered, scanning through a stream of decoded logs. "We're seeing data routed between Caracas, Gibraltar, and... Tulum?"

The mention of Tulum snapped Daniel out of his haze. "Tulum? Mexico?" he repeated.

Sir Rory nodded, the lines on his face deepening. "It's thin, but there's activity that matches the digital signature from Caracas. A series of data packets were routed through the server farm in Aldea Zama, Tulum. It's not conclusive, but it suggests coordination."

Daniel leaned back, his mind racing. Tulum. Sofia's name was tied to that region in the agency's fragmented records, and her recent movements had been elusive at best. Now Artem's fingerprints seemed to overlap with this location. This was the proof he needed, wasn't it, to prove that Spider was involved with Sofia's operations, or she with his? Why else would there be so much in common with their networks?

"We now view Artem Zheltonirvych as our prime suspect in placing the egg," Sir Rory said. "He went to ground after you left Mexico, and we haven't been able to trace him at all. But there was a private flight on a small plane, listed as carrying one passenger, from Tulum to an airfield just outside of Caracas. It's possible that he's there in the city with you now, so caution is advised."

"Are we saying Sofia and Artem are working together?" Daniel asked, his voice a mixture of incredulity and exhaustion. Hadn't Sir Rory read the chat logs? Artem didn't seem to know anything.

"We're not ruling it out," Rory replied. "And we have reason to believe Artem may be using Tulum as a relay hub for something bigger. With the way our traces are matching up, we think it increasingly likely that he could be Spider himself."

Daniel had his doubts. He believed Artem had been bait: a lure to draw himself and Nikita into a trap, making them travel to Mexico and almost costing both of their lives. Why else would he even mention Phantom? Just as a smokescreen? It didn't seem logical.

But he only had first-hand experience. He didn't have all of the information that Sir Rory did. Was it possible that he was missing something?

"How the hell did we miss this?" one analyst murmured, his hands trembling slightly as he pointed to an innocuous string of code buried in the blockchain's infrastructure. The attention of everyone in the room snapped to him.

Most of the code had looked ordinary when Daniel scanned through it, just ordinary hashes in the vast cryptographic latticework. He brought up that part of the file on his laptop and looked closer at the code, along with several others who gathered around the monitor in Vauxhall Cross, including Sir Rory. His expertise wasn't enough to pinpoint it himself, but the analyst put his finger right below the offending object – a line Daniel frustratingly couldn't see.

When he was directed to the right line number, he frowned. The subtle anomaly, a single additional character, hinted at something far more sinister than the innocuous line suggested.

"This isn't just encryption," another analyst said, her voice hushed. "It's adaptive. It mutates within the blockchain, hiding in plain sight."

The room fell silent as the implications sunk in. Alberto's egg wasn't just a dormant threat, it was a living, evolving weapon, capable of embedding itself deeper into the system with every transaction.

"This isn't just sabotage," the lead analyst concluded. "This is an economic weapon. If triggered, it could collapse the entire currency system."

"If?" Sir Rory asked. "Don't we mean, when?"

"This has to be done by human command," the analyst replied. "We've analysed previous attacks by Spider's eggs. In each instance, there has to be a kill command entered directly before the attack begins. Without that command, the eggs remain dormant – they could stay undetected for years. But once they're in the system, there's no getting them out."

Daniel's eyes narrowed as he followed the connections. Artem's communications patterns, linked to both Caracas and Tulum, were damning. Layered on top of that were Sofia's movements, her sudden trips to Venezuela and the Yucatán, raising more red flags. Spider was at the heart of this, yes, but Sofia and Artem could be the keys. Sofia seemed more of a backroom deal broker, but Artem… he had the coding skills to actually put things into action.

"Artem's our guy," Daniel said aloud to himself, though doubt lingered in the back of his mind. It wasn't just the evidence, it was how perfectly it all fit. Too perfectly.

The emotional weight of Caracas, Nikita's death, and the cryptic connections made Daniel's gut twist. But logic overruled instinct. Everything pointed to Artem.

"How do we turn it off, damn it all?" Sir Rory demanded, his voice rising. Daniel was startled out of his reverie, realising that the mood in the room had dropped considerably.

"We can't, sir," the head of the team said, wiping the back of his hand across his upper lip where sweat had beaded. "It's too sophisticated. It needs an encryption key and a password – and the only person who has that would be Spider himself.

There's just no way to brute force it, and he's too smart to leave clues where it really matters. The key will be something only he could ever guess. We can't stop this. It's a bomb we can't defuse."

Sir Rory, his face pale and grey, looked at Daniel.

"I can fix it," Daniel said, instinctively. His gut twisted at the expression on Sir Rory's face. He hated the idea of going back into the field, especially with Nikita's loss weighing heavily on him. He'd told himself that Caracas would be it, and he'd got through it. But this was important. So vitally, incredibly important.

It was the weight of millions of people who would suffer when the currency collapsed. It was the weight of Sir Rory's career, and behind it, his own. It was the weight of Nikita's last request to not let Spider win.

"Are you sure? We need that key," Sir Rory insisted. "If we don't, all of this has been for nothing. Spider wins. Either we have to pull the whole launch and both of our respective governments lose so much face they will likely also lose power; or we let it go live with a bomb hidden in the code and put everyone's personal data at risk. Daniel, we need to try before it's too late."

"We don't even know who Spider is," Daniel pointed out.

"We have two leads who do know," Sir Rory said grimly. "Artem, and Sofia Ortega. And there's one link between both of them."

Daniel knew what he was going to say before he said it.

"You, Daniel."

And he knew it was true.

Both of them trusted him, in at least a small way. He was the only one with the right connections to see this through.

In Nikita's name, he had to do this. He had to ensure her death was not in vain.

He had to find Spider and take him down – and once the code was safe, Daniel could ensure that vengeance, or justice, or whatever was on offer to him could be carried out.

The doubt gnawed at him, but there was no turning back. This was the path he'd chosen, and he would see it through, even if it cost him everything.

"That's what I'm trying to tell you," he said. "I can fix it. I know how to make Sofia tell us everything. There was something in those files that she will want to keep secret – so badly that I think she'll tell us everything."

"Then what are you waiting for?" Sir Rory asked with a raised eyebrow. "Find out where Spider is hiding – and do it fast."

Chapter 40.

Sofia's Weakness

This time around, Sofia didn't look quite so happy to see him.

"Peter," she said. "This is a *surprise.*" Her tone made it clear that she was really wondering how a thief had the gall to show his face back at the place he had robbed.

"I'm sure it is," Daniel said. He glanced around, looking inside the entrance of Sofia's palatial home. It was a pantomime, really, but it did confirm for his own information that no less than four armed guards were standing behind her, arms folded in front of themselves but no less ready to strike. "Are you holding or wearing any electronic devices, Sofia?"

"My phone," she said, frowning. This conversation wasn't going the way she had thought it might, Daniel could see. "Why?"

"I think it's a good idea if you leave that, and anything else, somewhere safe. Maybe on that table over there, for example." Daniel paused, eyeing the guards and cocking his head at the things he could see further inside the building: a smart thermostat, an electronic lock with a keypad, an alarm system. All things that could be hacked. "And it's probably best to walk around the grounds if we're going to talk."

Sofia scoffed. "*Are* we going to talk?" she asked. "Or am I going to have my men hold you here until we can decide on a legal recourse, Mr Warren?"

The use of his real name wasn't entirely unexpected, but it still turned Daniel's insides into jelly – more so than they already were at the task ahead of him. He couldn't let that show. He only blinked once and nodded in acceptance of the fact that they both knew a lot more about one another this morning than they had the night before.

"We are going to talk," he told her. "That is, unless you're perfectly happy to discuss Maracaibo right here, in front of your men and all of those wonderfully inventive devices with their microphones?"

Sofia blanched, her mouth twisting. It was abundantly clear that he'd hit a strong blow. She didn't want anyone to know what he had uncovered.

It was likely, given how lax her security was, that Spider already knew everything. But Daniel wasn't going to tell her that – not when it was the only thing standing between him and the information he needed. She could find out later.

The real reason he wanted her away from any possible eavesdroppers was because if Spider heard any of this, he'd be able to stop Daniel from following any information Sofia gave him – and they were far too close to the wire on this to let that happen.

Sofia tossed her blonde hair over her shoulder, spraying with it a scent of tropical flowers. "Gentlemen, I'm going for a walk," she said. "I'd appreciate it if you could monitor the grounds from a distance."

She turned and took Daniel's arm, as if they were just going for a gentle stroll around the grounds for fun – as if they were still back at the party, pretending they might be friends.

"Alright," she said, once they were suitably out of hearing distance of the house. They walked through a garden of vibrant flowers planted on either side of a pathway, leading them towards a bench set underneath a fragrant flowering tree. "You have me. What do you want?"

Daniel smiled. She was going to make this a pleasant kind of blackmail if she was this amenable all the way. "It's very simple," he said. "I want Spider."

"I don't know what you mean," Sofia said, her tone almost dead.

"I know you must be afraid," Daniel said. "Spider's a very powerful man. But I happen to work for a powerful man as well. This data that I uncovered about Maracaibo, well, it's already with the British government. In a few taps, I could also send it to the CIA. I also have contacts right here in Venezuela who would be interested to know about it."

Sofia's face was pale, but she walked with her chin held high. "So, if everyone already knows, what's the use in me complying?"

"I didn't say everybody knows *yet*," Daniel told her. "We're willing to keep the information under wraps and delete that part of our copy of the data. I'm part of a mission that is focused solely on Spider. We're not interested in whatever you get up to yourself. It's him we want."

Sofia took a long time to answer. Daniel was almost about to prompt her, but he knew she was still with him by the gentle pressure on his arm and the steady rhythm of her steps.

“Will your government protect me?” she asked, at length.

“From Spider?” Daniel asked. He considered the question. “We intend to arrest him. I suppose that’s about all the protection we can guarantee. If we were to give you more protection than you already have, someone would have to be told *why*.”

Sofia shuddered; he felt it through the connection of their arms. “Don’t tell anyone else,” she said. “Already having you know is bad enough.”

There was another pause.

"You’re hesitating," Daniel said, his voice low but firm. "That’s not like you."

Sofia didn’t answer right away. "I’m calculating. There’s a difference."

"And?"

She met his gaze. "And I don’t know if I want to lead you to him."

“Because you’re afraid?”

“Yes.” Sofia took a breath. “But the worst thing anyone could do to me is to reveal what happened in Maracaibo, and you’re already threatening that. So, if I do this, I might have at least half a chance of preventing my life from being ruined. I suppose that’s the best I can hope for.”

“It’s a raw deal, but you must have known Maracaibo would come back to haunt you eventually,” Daniel said mildly. He felt bad for her, in a way – but remembering what he had seen on that USB stick took care of any guilt he might have held. Sofia had dug her own grave, and she’d been living on borrowed time for years. He was only helping that time catch up with her.

"I know where he lives," Sofia said. The words took him off guard, said suddenly and with force. It was as though she'd had to force herself to get it out.

"How?" Daniel asked. The question he should have asked was *where*, but the admission startled him so much that he couldn't stop himself.

"I was there, at the beginning," Sofia said. Her voice grew distant. "When he founded Cryptropolis."

Daniel could swear he heard the sound of buildings collapsing, lives crashing into one another, in the far distance.

Cryptropolis… was Spider's?

It all started to slot together, the last pieces of a jigsaw puzzle that had never made sense before. The fact that only Cryptropolis was good enough to build security systems that kept Spider out until now. The way that Spider had managed to get into their servers and place an egg even though they were supposed to be unhackable.

The fact that Spider had been one step ahead of them, all the way.

Of course, he had. Sir Rory had been involved in briefings on the Veritian project with Alberto Lopez himself, the head of Cryptropolis, keeping them updated on their mission to stomp out the threat. But Alberto Lopez had been Spider all along.

"It's time, really," Sofia was saying. "It all went too far. It's time that someone stopped Alberto."

"Is it?" Daniel's tone sharpened. "You were part of Cryptropolis from the beginning. You helped him build it. And now, suddenly, you have regrets?"

She bristled. "I believed in the idea. We all did. Cryptropolis was meant to be a refuge from corrupt governments, from economic collapse. Do you know what it's like to watch your home country eat itself alive? To see people trading powdered milk for medicine because their currency is worthless? That's what Cryptropolis was meant to prevent."

Daniel studied her. "But it didn't stop there, did it?"

Sofia hesitated, then shook her head. "No. Alberto had other plans. Plans I wasn't meant to know about."

"You expect me to believe that you knew Spider had the kind of skills that could bring down governments, and you weren't worried?"

"Alberto never wanted to crash the system. He wanted it to confess."

What did that mean? Daniel pressed on, not willing to be dragged into cryptic riddles. "And yet you stayed. Why?"

Sofia stopped walking, turning to face him. "Because I owed him. And because I was afraid."

"And now?"

Sofia ducked her head. "Now, I'm more afraid of you."

Daniel didn't like the way that felt. But even as guilt coiled tightly around his gut, he remembered Nikita's face as she took her last breath.

Sofia might be afraid, but she wasn't dead. That made him still a whole lot better than Spider – than Alberto Lopez.

"I knew he needed to be stopped," she said. Her voice was low. "I tried. I did."

"How?" Daniel scoffed. As far as he could see from the records, Sofia had only lined her own pockets, getting richer and richer.

"I leaked the rumour."

For a second he didn't know what she meant – and then his eyes widened. "The rumour that Spider had hacked into the code and planted an egg?"

"Yes." She bit her lip. "Only, it wasn't the whole truth. The egg was in the code all along. He wrote it into the initial build, so there would be no stopping it. Even the backup version in the digital vault has the same egg."

Daniel's blood went cold at the thought. If Sir Rory hadn't believed the rumour, if Daniel didn't manage to find Spider in time, if the egg was deployed – not only would it destroy Veritian once, but twice, and as many times as they ever tried to use it. The project had been doomed from the start.

Not for the first time, Daniel thanked god that Sir Rory had the foresight to know a real threat when he heard it – even if he was the only one.

"Why didn't you just tell us everything?" Daniel asked. "You lied, told a half-truth. Were you trying to protect him?"

"To protect myself." Sofia took a deep breath, shuddering. "If I'd told someone about the flaw being built into the code itself, he would have known it was me. There are so few people who know the whole picture. I had to tell a little lie, to get you on the right track and keep myself safe at the same time."

Daniel looked at her and saw Nikita's blood spilt on the ground outside a Mexican warehouse.

So much work, so much loss. All because Sofia had been too much of a coward to just outright say it: Alberto Lopez had written a spider's egg right into the code of Veritian.

One simple sentence and Nikita would still be alive and well in London, and maybe one day he could have crossed paths with her by coincidence, on some other project or in a café outside Whitehall, and they could have had their lives together.

If only Sofia had been brave enough to risk herself.

Maybe she was right to be afraid of Daniel.

"His address," Daniel said, keeping his voice hard. "Is it the same we have on record? There's no hidden secret lair?"

Sofia laughed at this, but there was absolutely no humour in it. It was a desperate sound – the sound of a woman on the precipice. "He doesn't need to hide his address," she said. "He hides his true face instead. You'll find him exactly where you expect him to be. Just don't imagine you'll find anything without the help of the best computer experts in the world."

"I'm counting on it," Daniel said, turning to go. "And, Sofia? You're not going to warn him, are you?"

"No," she said, her mouth a firm line as she watched him walk away from her backwards, his hands in his pockets against the morning chill. "No, I suppose I don't want to face the consequences you would bring down on me if I did."

Daniel nodded and walked back to the gated entrance, imbued with new purpose.

Chapter 41.

Rafael's Choice

Daniel used his satellite phone in the privacy of his hotel room to send the extraction code Sir Rory had given him. The message came back within moments: *Wait for plan.*

So, he waited.

The instructions came a couple of hours later, before noon, the buzz waking him from an uneasy nap to make up for his lack of sleep the night before. *Sit at a table in the hotel's café. Matt will find you.*

Daniel wasn't sure he wanted to be out on public view, given that there was every chance Sofia would decide to have her men take him out before he left the country in search of Spider – or even that Spider himself was aware of his knowledge. If Sofia had gone behind his back and betrayed him the moment he left her home, Spider's hired killers could be hunting him down already.

Still, this was his way out.

He packed his suitcase, leaving behind the lovely suit Marisol had organised for him – she could get her money back, maybe, or give it to someone else, and he was sure she would easily find her way to the room once he was gone – and opened the door.

Immediately, he recoiled.

Rafael was framed in the doorway, and as soon as Daniel left an opening, he stepped inside –

shutting the door behind him with an ominous click of the lock.

"Rafael?" Daniel asked, but he already knew something was very, very wrong.

"I'm sorry, Daniel," Rafael said calmly. "I'm not going to be able to allow you to leave."

Daniel backed away slowly, letting go of his suitcase. It was useless to him if he couldn't get out, anyway. "Why?" he asked. Not only was it the only question that mattered right now, but he also needed to delay Rafael and get some grip on the situation.

Rafael's face was haunted. "I had no intention of betraying you," he said. "I was just here to keep an eye on you, make sure you didn't get too close. But you found that information on Sofia, and… I can't let you take what you know out of this country."

Daniel held his breath. Was it possible that Rafael really believed Daniel hadn't already shared the information? The truth was, he'd kept what he'd learned about Alberto Lopez to himself. Even with all the precautions they had taken, it was too risky to say it over the line to Sir Rory.

If Rafael had been tracking his communications, he would know that Daniel had kept quiet.

That had to be the only reason Daniel had even been allowed to finish the call.

"We need to go," Rafael said. He produced a gun from his belt and pointed it squarely at Daniel. "Leave your case and walk down the hall to the emergency exit staircase. We're going out of the back of the hotel into a car down there. I'll be right behind you. If you make a move to run or alert anybody, there'll be a new hole in the back of your head."

Daniel didn't doubt it. He nodded stiffly. He did exactly as he was told, even though getting into the car parked at the hotel's back entrance felt like putting himself into a cage – a cage he wasn't sure he would be able to get out of.

Rafael drove, keeping Daniel in the back with child-locked doors. The gun rested on his lap, a reminder that he wasn't going to let Daniel leave even if he was able to jump out of the moving vehicle.

They moved through the city, only stopping at red lights. Children hawking USB sticks loaded with pirated Hollywood movies crowded around the car until Rafael cursed and flicked his hands at them, yelling for them to go.

"What happened to you?" Daniel asked as they moved onto quieter roads again.

"Nothing happened to me," Rafael said. "I was Alberto's from the start. Me, him, Sofia – why do you think I could get you into that party so easily?"

"She knew as well?"

Rafael shook his head. "Your cover was real. I don't rock the boat unless I need to. Spider is good enough at covering his own tracks. But you're too close now, and I can't let you stop him."

They were driving deeper into the slums, past fallen-down buildings with dirty, thin teenagers huddled on the stoops, watching them pass by with suspiciously narrowed eyes. "You still believe in Alberto's mission?"

"I know what drives him," Rafael said darkly. "Unlike Sofia, I understand."

Daniel wanted to ask what it was that drove Spider, what it was that made him want to do something so catastrophic, but Rafael was stopping the car. They were outside a sight that was all too familiar to Daniel, at this point: the warehouse with the server farm.

It was clearly controlled by some shady group – Tren de Aragua? Cartel of the Suns? Collectivos? FARC? Did it even matter? – who were now back at their posts: the tattooed, scowling armed guards at the front of the building were joined by patrols all the way around the perimeter, and Daniel's heart jumped in his chest as he realised it wasn't luck alone that had allowed him in the first time.

"Why did you let me get the data?" he asked. "Surely you knew it would lead me to him?"

"Firstly, I do the work I'm paid for," Rafael grunted, getting out of the car. A second later, he was at Daniel's door, hauling him out by his arm. "And secondly, if you had been unable to decrypt it, you wouldn't have been a problem. I could have kept my standing with MI6, wouldn't have had to go dark. Now, you've forced my hand. You have to die, Daniel. Otherwise, you blow my cover."

Die?

Was this where it all ended?

Was this where he found out whether there was a place waiting for him after death, a place where Nikita waited too?

Did he care?

Yes – yes, because there was still more to do, and Nikita's last words would be lost and wasted if he didn't fulfil their promise.

"So, why aren't I dead?" Daniel asked.

Rafael nodded to the warehouse. "Because they'll do it for me."

He hauled Daniel in front of him and then pushed him forward, the muzzle of the gun cold against his spine. They walked into the building past the armed guards, who eyed Daniel with open hatred – though they had no way of knowing him. Inside, the air was cool, spurred by fans that prevented the servers from overheating.

Rafael muttered with more guards in the corner, and Daniel was shoved unceremoniously into a chair at the side of the room. Three men with assault rifles gathered around him, each of them wearing dark expressions under close-cropped dark hair. A certain kind of uniform. More muttering; communication that Daniel couldn't hear.

"You'll wait here," Rafael said, looking him over in a way that suggested it was to be the last time. "Someone's coming for you later. You'd do well to answer their questions. If you answer, it's quick and painless. If you don't…"

Daniel understood the implication.

He gritted his teeth, looking down at the ground, not willing to let Rafael see fear or tears in his eyes.

It had all come down to this.

All the effort he'd put in. The loss of Nikita. Walking into danger in two different countries. Hacking systems, decrypting data, all of the calls back and forth with Sir Rory, every briefing, every restless night.

It had all come down to this moment, and all of it was about to be wasted.

He glanced around as Rafael's footsteps departed, trying to get a measure of the room. This was a server farm, after all. This was his domain. If there was anything he could do, it would be here.

A shot ran out across the room.

Daniel's head snapped up, his body instantly curling in on itself, getting small. He heard more bullets whizzing through the air and he was there again, watching Nikita fall – only he wasn't there – he was here, seeing Rafael on the ground instead, a single small hole in his forehead starting to bleed, his eyes already vacant – and the guards around him disappeared, hefting their weapons and rushing forwards to meet the threat.

Daniel looked around wildly. They'd left him alone with the machines.

What could he do?

Even if he couldn't save his own life – even if the guards would be back soon to finish what they started – he could do something to hurt Spider.

He grabbed the terminal at the nearest server and woke it up, finding it still logged in – a touch of luck. If this was a node used by Spider, then he would have to function without it for a while.

Daniel's hands flew over the keyboard, executing commands – and creating his own makeshift kill switch.

The sound of gunfire petered out, but footsteps sounded further afield in the warehouse. There was hardly any time.

Daniel hit enter, and his switch flipped.

There was an ominous whirring from the servers all around him, and then they began, one by one, to shut down.

He'd done it.

He'd burned the Caracas node.

"Deal with that, Spider," he muttered under his breath, allowing himself one moment of victory before turning to meet his fate.

More armed men were emerging, moving across the warehouse. One of them pointed a rifle directly at him, squinting as if to make out his face. Daniel put his hands up automatically.

"Daniel Warren?" he barked, his accent heavy. Wasn't he familiar, somehow…?

"Yes," Daniel said because there was nothing left to lose at this point.

The man relaxed his grip on the rifle, letting it rest against his shoulder, pointing at the ceiling. "Come with us. Sofia Ortega sent us to retrieve you."

Daniel's eyes widened. Now he recognised the man: one of her guards, from her home.

"Me?" he spluttered, because he wasn't quite sure he could believe what was going on.

"*Si*," the man said. "Now, come with us. We'll get you back to your hotel – but we go quick before reinforcements arrive."

Daniel had never walked out of a place so fast in his life.

Chapter 42.

Extraction

Daniel's heart raced in his chest as he got out of the car, running up the stairs first to grab his things and then heading back down. Reaching the café, he took his seat near the window, picking up a local newspaper and pretending that he was reading it.

Sometimes, he even remembered to turn the pages rather than darting anxious looks out of the window every few seconds, his heart rate never slowing down.

Was the extraction still on? Or had Sir Rory's contact left, aborting the plan when Daniel hadn't turned up? Had he missed his chance to escape?

How long would it be before Spider sent another team after him?

Several people entered and sat, or finished their drinks and left, but it was not until a man in his late sixties sat at the neighbouring table that Daniel's attention perked up.

"Café con leche," he ordered, in clearly English-accented Spanish, and from that moment, Daniel's attention was trained on him as closely as it could be without daring to turn around and look.

The man took a sip of his coffee and then cleared his throat quietly. "Peter Green," he said at length, his voice low and pitched just for Daniel's ears.

"You must be Matt," Daniel replied. His relief was palpable in his voice. He hadn't been abandoned.

"Wait ten seconds and then get up and follow me," Matt said. "I'm taking you to the nearest harbour. We'll go by public transport for safety. They won't risk striking out at you so long as we stay surrounded by others, but you have to keep me in sight. Understood?"

"Understood," Daniel murmured.

"Good." Matt sipped the coffee, apparently finishing it off in short order, and stood, buttoning his jacket.

Then, he was gone.

Daniel watched him through the window, counting to ten – the slowest ten seconds of his life.

He got up then, clutching his suitcase, and hurried down the street in the direction Matt had taken. He wasn't hard to find again: he was tall, still straight-backed – perhaps a former military man? – and his silvery hair stood above most of the crowd.

Daniel followed him to a bus, where they sat several rows apart. The bus wound its way along a route that seemed infuriatingly labyrinthine; he was sure they doubled back on themselves several times, taking in side streets and wandering residential roads, before they finally came into view of the sea.

Matt got off the bus without so much as a backwards glance, and Daniel was quick to follow him. They walked together – one a short distance behind the other – out of the view of the busier areas, perhaps out of the seaside town completely, before Matt finally slowed to a stop in front of a boat pulled up on the shore.

"Get in," he said, nodding to the vessel – which seemed more like a pleasure craft than something suited to fleeing the cartels, but what did Daniel know – and before he'd even got himself settled properly on a seat, they were off, flying across the surf and heading out to more open water.

"Don't worry," Matt chuckled at his unease. "I've got a whole career of sailing experience behind me. You're in good hands!"

It was only when their point of departure had faded out of view that Daniel felt enough courage to speak.

"Where are we headed?" he asked.

"Georgetown, Guyana," Matt called over the roar of the boat's small engine and the hiss of the waves. "You've got an RAF jet waiting for you there. It's a nice way to travel!"

Daniel glanced around him. The water was choppy, and he was starting to feel a bit seasick. "Is this safe?" he asked.

Matt chuckled heartily. "They didn't send a retired Naval officer to pick you up for no reason," he shouted. "Don't worry. There's a British warship anchored about ten minutes from here. We'll get you on board there for the rougher part of the journey."

"Right," Daniel said faintly, clinging onto the side of the boat and hoping it wouldn't capsize before then.

***

The wheels of the RAF C-36 jet hit the tarmac at RAF Northolt with a jolt, pulling Daniel from a restless sleep. An arduous journey from Guyana, huddled up with lots of army personnel who had clearly been on jungle exercises in the Amazon, had not been conducive to rest.

His body ached in ways he hadn't realized were possible, his wounds, physical and emotional, still fresh. Nikita's death lingered, a raw and gaping wound that bled into every thought. He'd tried to compartmentalise it, to focus on what lay ahead, but the sound of the gunshot and her collapsing frame haunted him every time he closed his eyes.

Daniel rubbed his eyes, staring out of the small window at the muted grey sky above England. It matched his mood perfectly.

There was no time to rest – another flight directly to Gibraltar awaited him, and this time he wasn't alone. The private craft was already filled with members of the Project Maia team – including Sir Rory himself.

"Well done, Daniel," he said, clapping him on the shoulder as they settled into adjoining seats. "You've saved me on this one. Once we get access to Spider's private servers and find the proof of his egg, and get the man himself to disarm it, you'll have saved even more: the fate of our entire coalition's economies."

"Don't thank me yet," Daniel said grimly. "Thank me when we've got him."

Not, Daniel noted, that Sir Rory had explicitly thanked him in the first place.

***

The building was called Alees, and as Daniel arched his neck to look up at the white façade towering into the sky, it hit home just exactly whose apartment they were about to storm.

Alberto Lopez wasn't just one of the best coders, hackers, and all-around tech geniuses in the world; he was also very powerful and very, very rich. That much was evident from the home he'd chosen as his base. He apparently owned a whole floor of this behemoth, right in prime position, overlooking everything. Daniel gazed over his shoulder towards the coast and figured that Alberto could probably look over at Spain while he was having his morning coffee.

"What's the play, here?" Daniel asked Sir Rory, tension thrumming through his body. They weren't all arrayed in the open, yet. They were observing the building from afar, with various members of the team scattered around the neighbouring streets – including the members of the armed forces that had come along.

"You tell me," Sir Rory said. Daniel looked at him in surprise, and his mentor nodded approvingly. "This is your operation, from start to finish. You lead."

Daniel looked at the building again and squared his shoulders. He was already wearing a headset and an armoured vest. There was no time like the present to get started. The slower they were to start, the more likely it was that Alberto Lopez would spot something that tipped him off.

"Is everyone in position?" he asked, touching his earpiece to transmit his voice.

"Affirmative," the response crackled in his ear. "Waiting for your go."

Daniel cast his eyes up, counting the floors until he found the spot where Alberto would be waiting for them. There was no flicker of movement behind the windows.

"Go," he said, and walked forward himself, joining the flow of agents storming into the building.

The journey up was strenuous. They took the stairs, knowing that the lift had the potential to be compromised – having half their squad trapped in a decommissioned box in the air would not be a good idea. By the time they reached the right place, Daniel was out of breath and startled to find that the armed officers were not. They were used to a different level of training, clearly.

One of them stepped forward and attached an unassuming black device to the side of Alberto's electronic entry keypad. There was a flash of red light on the side, then a second red light – then all three lit up green, and with a click, the door opened.

They were inside.

Daniel's heart pounded wildly as he stood in the stairwell, letting the professionals go in ahead of him. He heard the various shouts of *clear* as they moved through the rooms and followed them, looking around.

The apartment was exactly as he had expected: sleek, modern, and full of shiny white surfaces. He was sure almost everything in here could be controlled with an app or voice commands, likely all linked to the most secure servers in the world for Alberto's protection.

But there was no time to marvel.

Up ahead, the open door showed him what he'd been looking for: a computer room.

He stepped inside, looking around in awe. Dozens of monitors crowded the wall, a huge window taking up the space just behind the array so that it all appeared to be framed by the sky. The low hum of the computers under the broad desk was accompanied by the shushing of fans, all of it state of the art.

The chair that sat behind the desk with its swooping black back, the white wall behind it bearing framed certifications in Alberto's name and news stories about Cryptropolis…

Daniel recognised it.

This was where Alberto had been sitting, every time they'd patched him into a meeting. This was where he'd controlled everything, reassuring the government on the one hand and deceiving them on the other. He sat here for online conferences, for presentations; everything Daniel had seen of him online that wasn't in-person photography. He'd been here.

One of the screens was still active, and eerily familiar. It was logged into the same encrypted chat system that Daniel used with the members of Liquid Tundra. He stepped closer, leaning forward to read the chat that had been left open.

His heart thudded in his chest, seeming to stop entirely, skipping a beat before it resumed.

It was the log of a conversation he recognised.

The last conversation between himself and the Liquid Tundra team.

Tonka: *This isn't working. We need to regroup.*

AranaNegra: *No time. Push mid.*

Underlord: *Great call, AranaNegra. Genius move.*

AranaNegra: *Shut up, Underlord. Maybe if you weren't feeding kills—*

Luna: *Enough! Both of you!*

AranaNegra: *Es la gota que colma el vaso*

Tonka: *Do you speak Spanish?*

AranaNegra: *It's something I picked up from a friend. Focus.*

Cogs were clicking into place inside his brain, churning, finally, everything making sense. The strange way that AranaNegra's comments had reminded him of the warehouse logs. The slip into Spanish in their last game. The fact that two of his teammates had been compromised – surely a high ratio for such a small and specific team. The way he tried to get Daniel – as Tonka – to talk about why he had missed those games, the ones after Nikita's death. He'd been fishing.

AranaNegra was Spider.

Spider was Alberto Lopez.

Lopez was AranaNegra.

All this time, he'd been treating the most notorious hacker in the world as his teammate.

All this time, he'd been giving AranaNegra access to his IP address – letting himself be tracked by the very person they were trying to hunt.

The metallic taste in his mouth could never sting as much as the revelation that he had been a fool since the start.

"All clear, sir," the commander of their group said, appearing at Daniel's elbow.

Daniel stared at him for a long moment, not comprehending at first. "Where is Alberto?"

The commander shook his head. "Looks like he cleared out. The bedroom's empty. His personal belongings are missing."

Daniel stared at the bank of monitors.

All of it was here at his fingertips, and yet he had no doubt at all that it was useless.

Only Spider could stop the egg.

Only Spider could get into these systems.

There was no one better than him.

Maybe, given time and a crack team, they could eventually get into his system and read his data. Maybe, given enough time and a good enough search algorithm, they could find a clue that would help them defuse the egg.

Maybe.

But that would require a lot of time they didn't have.

The egg would already be deployed before they even had a chance to stop him, and Spider was in the wind, off in the sunset, dropping off the face of the earth to become someone else.

Spider controlled computers, and this world was run on them. He could hack records to display his fake identity as a real one, make security cameras glitch when he walked by, create false trails all over the world to distract them. He could be anywhere in the world right now, and he could be anyone.

He might have left behind the riches and fame of Cryptropolis, but so what? He likely had offshore accounts under different names that he could access whenever he wanted to rebuild his life, and Spider was still as notorious as ever.

Daniel rested his knuckles on the edge of the desk, bowing his head and leaning his weight on them.

Spider was gone.

He'd failed.

"Sir?" the commander prompted. "What's our next action?"

"There isn't one," Daniel groaned, his eyes closed.

“Daniel,” Sir Rory said, disapprovingly. Daniel didn’t open his eyes to see his mentor joining them in the room.

“Secure the premises and start removing these computers,” Daniel said, which was actually the correct answer. “We need them back in London by tonight at the latest, so our experts can start working on them.”

And then he straightened up and walked out of the room, unable to bear staying there any longer.

“Daniel?” Sir Rory called after him.

“I need a minute,” Daniel said. His stomach was roiling, and he wondered vaguely whether he was going to be sick. Or cry. Or hurl himself off the top of the Rock.

They were back to square one, the launch of Veritian was imminent, and Nikita had died for nothing.

Spider had won.

Daniel’s movements were mechanical as he got into the lift and rode it down to the ground floor, no longer seeing the need to avoid it. Spider wasn’t around to stop him. He got out and walked out of the lobby, feeling cool air hit his face. For a split second, he hoped it would wake him up out of this nightmare.

It didn’t.

Spider was gone.

Had Sofia tipped him off, after all? It barely mattered. Either way, he was gone, and with him, the last hope of dismantling the egg before it exploded and corrupted the code.

Without access to the computer provided by Spider himself, it was highly unlikely that they would unlock it in time to provide evidence to any government that the egg was real. Alberto's absence could easily be explained by a trip to a server farm or work in the US to make sure everything was in place.

There was no way to stop this from happening.

He'd failed.

Daniel Warren had failed.

Nikita's face was all he could see in front of his eyes as he stumbled aimlessly through the streets away from Alees. Her last words.

"Don't let him win, Daniel..."

Well, he had. He'd let Spider win.

He'd let Nikita down.

And the world would suffer, all because he hadn't been good enough.

"Daniel."

The voice was so quiet that it almost did not touch Daniel through the rush of his despair. But he looked up when a figure stepped in front of him – and he stopped dead.

"We should talk," the man said, and Daniel didn't know whether to run screaming, calmly accept his offer of conversation, or punch him in the face.

"Alberto Lopez," he replied, his voice strangely detached and emotionless. "Spider."

"Hello, Daniel Warren, Tonka," Alberto said with a smile that reminded Daniel of a fanged snake. "Let's go somewhere we won't be disturbed."

Chapter 43.

Face to Face

Alberto led Daniel through the empty streets to a cable car without saying a word. He paid for both of them to ascend, then got in himself, waiting for Daniel to join him. They had the car to themselves, despite the capacity for many more passengers; Daniel suspected that had more to do with the bills Alberto had handed over for the tickets than the time of day.

"You found me," Alberto said, without turning around, facing steadfastly forward as the cable car climbed.

Daniel stood next to him, his pulse hammering. He wasn't interested in the view. His eyes were on Alberto. "Wasn't easy."

A moment of silence stretched between them. Old allies. Enemies now.

"You're here to stop me," Alberto finally said.

Daniel nodded. "I have to."

"Why?" Alberto finally turned to him, large brown eyes that seemed to take up too much of his face, that seemed to see into Daniel too easily. "Because of her?"

Daniel nodded again, wordlessly this time. He wouldn't sully Nikita's memory by discussing her with her killer. Alberto might not have pulled the trigger, but it was Spider who led them into the trap and gave the orders. He wasn't fit to say her name.

Alberto faced forward again. "You were a worthy adversary, Daniel. I had to meet you. You understand?"

"I think I do," Daniel conceded. No one else had ever been this close, had they? No one that Spider had not intentionally told of his real identity. "You want to know who it was that nearly beat you."

Alberto smiled, but it was bloodless and thin. "More than nearly," he said. "I liked my home, my company. I'll have to start again."

"That seems a small price to pay."

Alberto accepted the point with a gentle incline of his head. "Yes. But you're the only one who's ever made me pay it."

Daniel let that statement linger in the air for a moment before he spoke again. "Why are you doing this?" he asked. "Why destroy something that will have such catastrophic consequences?"

Alberto reached into the inside jacket pocket of the nondescript brown suit he was wearing. For a moment, Daniel tensed up, wondering if he was about to have a weapon drawn on him, his own fingers curling around the Hail Mary he carried in his pocket – but Alberto only took out a piece of paper.

On closer inspection, it was a photograph: faded, curling at the edges, marked with crease lines that cut through the image, splitting up the four people pictured in it. Alberto held it up for Daniel to see, not quite handing it over.

"This is why," he said.

Daniel looked at the photograph again, trying to understand. The photograph was obviously old, the real deal, a print taken maybe by a film camera or one of the old disposables people would carry on holiday. The people in the image wore old-fashioned clothing, though Daniel wasn't sure, for cultural reasons, what decade to place them in: the family were Black, the landscape behind them an arid one that wasn't familiar to him.

"Your family?" he asked, an educated guess. There were two young boys in the photograph, standing with a beaming mother and father.

"My mother, my father," Alberto said, pointing to them one by one. "Me. And my brother – Hassan."

"You never talked about your family," Daniel said. He was, of course, referring to their many conversations within the Liquid Tundra server. "Even when I spoke about my sister, when Luna told us she was living with her girlfriend, when Underlord told us about his family stuck behind in Ukraine. You never joined in."

"I had no family to speak about," Alberto replied, giving the photograph a long look. "They died a long time ago." He put the photograph back inside his pocket, keeping it safe, back where it clearly always sat. It was the one thing he had on his person, Daniel realised. He carried no bag, the lines of his suit were otherwise undisturbed. Wherever the rest of his belongings were, this was the one thing important enough to keep on him at all times.

"I don't understand the link," Daniel said. "You did this because they died?"

"Because of how they died," Alberto said. His tone was strangely emotionless, and Daniel tried to imagine how many years he'd spent cut off from this tragedy, acting as if that part of his past didn't exist, pretending to be someone who hadn't known loss. "It was an American strike on the airport. My parents were only staying in the hotel. The Americans killed them both."

"And your brother, too?" Daniel asked.

"No." Alberto's gaze went inwards, darker. "That happened later."

What could he even say to that? "You want to destroy the lives of Americans for revenge, then." There was a long pause, which Daniel took to mean agreement. "Even the innocent people? Even those in other countries, in developing nations, who take payments in dollars because they're worth more? You're willing to sacrifice them?"

Alberto said nothing, but his lips pressed tighter together, the tension in his face growing.

"Because *they* are who will suffer," Daniel went on, pressing the point home. "They are who will die. The rich? They might end up not being able to afford the private jet anymore. They might have to sell a holiday home or downsize to a smaller mansion. But they're not losing everything. It's the small people, the people who already have almost nothing, who will lose it all."

Alberto exhaled slowly. "Do you think it was ever going to end differently? This world? The systems that killed my family, that killed Nikita? You of all people should understand."

Daniel clenched his jaw. Alberto wasn't just a villain. He was a man who had lost everything. A man who had built the ultimate revenge weapon.

"*You* killed Nikita," Daniel said. It was the first time they had really acknowledged it, really spoken her name.

"Because the system forced my hand," Alberto said.

"Then don't let them win," Daniel said. "Don't become what they made you."

For the first time, something flickered in Alberto's eyes. Doubt.

Daniel had something here, he knew it. He just had to hold onto that thread, keep pulling, until he found his way to Alberto's core: his heart, his soul, whatever it was that made him tick.

The cable car clunked to a stop in its dock, and the swaying motion momentarily distracted Daniel. As the doors opened automatically, Alberto stepped out, gesturing for him to follow.

At first, they walked in silence. The path was steep and, in some spots, only wide enough for them to walk single file. There was no one else around.

Almost as if the cable car hadn't been letting anyone else come up here for some time.

Alberto had planned it all, Daniel realised.

He'd known Daniel would be coming for him, and he'd planned – or at least hoped – to be able to get him alone at some stage. The messages from AranaNegra on the screen – they had been bait. A signal just for him. No one else would have known the significance of Tonka or that particular conversation.

He had his phone in his pocket; a hacker as brilliant as Alberto wouldn't need to rely on luck to find him. He could just track the phone.

And he would have known, all along, throughout this whole process, exactly who Daniel was and where his phone was – because they'd told Alberto Lopez during the security briefings, thinking he was an ally.

Their path eventually came to the highest point of the Rock: a viewing platform, constructed to give visitors a panoramic vista all the way around them: Gibraltar below, Spain, the ocean, and further out, Morocco. It was breathtaking.

It was also not what Daniel needed to focus on right now.

It was difficult to turn your back on a three-sixty-degree view, but Daniel turned his head towards Alberto and didn't look away.

"What happened to your family was truly awful," he said. "I'm sorry for you."

"Thank you," Alberto said, and for a second Daniel thought he was talking to AranaNegra, his gaming friend and teammate, not a criminal mastermind bent on destroying entire economies.

He had to hold onto that.

"Where were you from, originally?" Daniel asked.

"Somalia," Alberto said. There was a distant look on his face, and Daniel had the feeling he wasn't really looking at the view, either. "I fled, paid a human smuggler to get me to Spain. Thankfully, my parents had taught me the language. I came over here to take advantage of the laxity here. No one asks what you do. You can get away with a lot, digitally, if you live in Gibraltar."

"Is that why you chose Venezuela and Mexico, too? The ability to operate outside of the law?"

Alberto's lips thinned into a curve devoid of humour. "Venezuela was more than just a base of operations," he said. "It was where the seed of this whole project was started. During the collapse. I saw it all. A government brought low, rendered powerless by its own currency, a nation shackled to its devaluation. Yet, amidst the chaos, people had found ways to survive. They turned to cryptocurrency, creating systems that defied borders, bypassed traditional banks, and rewrote the rules of economic exchange. Their resilience… fascinated me."

"It sounds inspiring," Daniel remarked. "Not for destruction, but for creation."

"It taught me that monetary systems, like governments, only have as much power as people allow them. If given an alternative—one that was faster, safer, and unregulated—people would abandon traditional systems in a heartbeat," Alberto said. He looked Daniel directly in the eye, and what Daniel saw there was an unwavering belief in his own actions. "I saw that I could exploit that by convincing governments to try to beat those systems at their own game, only to bring it down around their ears as soon as they were in my power."

"How did you build Cryptropolis?" Daniel asked. A theory was growing in his mind, and the more he stalled Alberto and got him to reveal more about himself, the closer he might get to figuring out a way to use it. "You came from nothing. How is it that you are one of the richest men in the world, now?"

Alberto laughed. "Not *one of*," he said, a casual statement that chilled Daniel to the bone. "Though there's not much in the official record. Anyway, money means nothing to me. It's a means to an end. If it was more than that, I could never destroy the dollar – it will cost me millions. As to your question: I started out with ransomware attacks."

"Oh," Daniel said, remembering the spate of high-profile attacks that had taken down hospitals, pharmaceutical companies, and their like. In order to get their systems operational again and continue saving lives, they had to pay huge amounts of Bitcoin to untraceable wallets. The money would never come back.

Had Alberto crossed that kind of line, even back then? Maybe Daniel was wrong in thinking he had a core that was good, that could be appealed to…

"I was only delivering consequences," Alberto said. His expression flickered darkly. "They were overcharging for insulin, refusing to treat low-income patients… I did what I could. Of course, it changed nothing. The corruption runs too deep."

"And you think you can dig out the corruption by doing… this?"

"Currencies are the pillars of governments," Alberto said. "You destabilize the currency, you destabilize the government. And when people lose trust in their leaders, they turn to whoever offers them stability. And then I thought, what if someone were to cause that financial collapse, rather than just waiting for it to happen?"

A moment of silence stretched between them. What could he say to that? Alberto's life, his circumstances, had created the man he was now. The things he had seen had painted a clear picture of the world for him and allowed him to build his own legacy, too.

Legacy… maybe there was something in that. Daniel still needed more time for it to marinate.

"My mother is Spanish, you know," he said instead, his tone conversational as he looked out over the sea. "That's why they chose me for this mission."

"I know," Alberto said. "I know everything about you, Daniel. I already knew who you were when we started playing together. I recruited every player in Liquid Tundra, one by one, putting you all together as a testing ground to see if any of you were worth hiring into my real mission. I took Phantom, and Underlord was a fantastic patsy. I had ruled you and Luna out, though she was close to my base of operations in Mexico and could have been useful to me; you were both too idealistic, too eager to defend the existing structures of power. I sent Underlord in Luna's place, and you, I left alone. Imagine how lucky I felt when I realised Sir Rory was sending you, someone I already had access to."

Daniel ducked his head. The thought that he was both the key to the mission and possibly the reason for its failure was a hard truth to swallow.

But he raised his head again. "Imagine how lucky *I* felt when I realised the man I was sent to stop was already a friend of mine, someone I knew and trusted."

Alberto's mouth twitched in response, almost a real smile. "You should never have trusted me, Daniel."

"Why not? You were always who you said you were, nothing more, nothing less. You've never lied to me, have you? You just chose not to answer if doing so would reveal that you were Alberto Lopez."

"Yash," he said faintly.

"Sorry?" Daniel frowned, wondering if he had heard correctly.

"My birth name," Alberto Lopez, Spider, said, "is Yash."

The idea was formed, at last, and Daniel knew he had to take this chance. If he didn't, if Alberto walked away, it was all over.

He looked up into the other man's eyes.

"I have a deal to propose," he said. "Would you like to hear it?"

Chapter 44.

The Rock

There were things Daniel – Tonka – knew irrefutably about AranaNegra.

The player had an amazing head for strategy. He liked to be in control, but if someone else had a better idea, he wasn't afraid to cede to them. He understood sense, reason, logic. The overall goal – of winning the game – was more important to him than ego.

That was what Daniel's plan counted on. That was what he rested on, now.

That – and the fact that AranaNegra had always talked about making Liquid Tundra the most successful, most lauded team of all time, even with most of the members using fake identities yet never getting caught.

His legacy as a player.

That was important to him, too – maybe as important to him as winning for winning's sake.

"I wonder if you know something off the top of your head," Daniel said because he had a feeling it was the kind of thing that a kid from Somalia with a plan to take down the US dollar *would* know. "How much does the entire continent of Africa, if you put all the countries together, owe the US in dollars?"

"About six hundred and eighty-six billion dollars," Alberto said promptly. "Though the number does shift over time."

Daniel tried not to smile at the fact that Alberto really *had* known. "And the amount of US dollars in existence across the whole world?"

"Twenty-one point two trillion dollars." Alberto smiled now. "Enough to make me a God-killer, don't you think?"

The figure owed collectively by Africa was about three per cent of the total amount of dollars in the world. Well. Daniel's plan had a chance of working, after all.

He was just going to have to go for it now and ask forgiveness from Sir Rory later.

"Why don't you just use your Spider eggs to destroy all records of the debt, instead of hurting all the innocent people in Africa and beyond who rely on the dollar to earn a living?"

Alberto blinked.

"The debt will be destroyed when the currency is," he said. "When the dollar's value falls to nothing, those countries will be able to pay it off immediately at very little cost."

"But the American people, the average man on the street – they aren't the ones who killed your family," Daniel pressed. "As for the UK, we had nothing to do with it at all. Why should people in my country suffer? Why should my parents lose their retirement? Why should my sister worry about how she's going to feed her kids?"

Alberto looked away from him, his neck bobbing as he swallowed. Clearly, Daniel was getting to him, though he didn't want to admit it.

Perhaps Alberto had been able to get this far simply by ignoring the unpleasant truth of what would happen to ordinary people as a result of his actions.

"Colonisers," he said, though his tone was less convincing this time. "Thieves. Have you visited the British Museum lately?"

"What do you think your legacy will be?" Daniel pressed. "You say God-killer – I say *child* killer. Life ruiner. Poverty maker. World ender."

Alberto's eyes snapped back to him with a flash of anger. "They'll see me as the person who ended the evil reign of capitalism."

"This won't end capitalism," Daniel shrugged. "It won't even end the US. The US has plenty of other things going on that are already making it suffer – why do you think they leapt at the end of creating a digital currency in the first place? The last President and his economic policies just about brought them to your knees without any help from you, and there are plenty of other countries happy to let capitalism continue."

"So long as the US falls –"

"But do you want that to be how people remember you?" Daniel pressed, not letting up now he'd found his angle. "They'll say you used ransomware to hold hospitals hostage and risk lives – they won't remember you were doing it to *save* lives in the long run. Not if you do this. You won't be Robin Hood. You won't even be David facing Goliath. You'll just be the biggest terrorist the world has ever seen. Bin Laden, Hussein, and Stalin all rolled up into one. The death toll caused by the collapse of a world-dominating currency? It could be higher than all of them combined."

Alberto's gaze was flat.

"Or," Daniel said. "You could destroy the egg. I know you built a backdoor into the code, one that allows you to erase it completely and make the currency safe. Why would you do that if you didn't want to use it, deep down? If you didn't know it was the right thing to do?"

"I..." Alberto said. He wanted to argue, Daniel could see that – but he couldn't answer. Perhaps this was the first time he'd ever had to interrogate his own decision in building a manual kill switch.

"You could be a hero," he said. "Nelson Mandela of our generation, only on a scale so big it's almost beyond comprehension. You could wipe out the debt of *every single country in Africa* without even blinking. Be benevolent, not malevolent. Give a gift, not a curse. You could be remembered as the man who liberated an entire continent from the shackles of American debt. *And* you'd hit the US government right where it hurts."

A flock of birds flew overhead, and Alberto looked up, tracking their flight for a long moment.

They were both silent. Daniel didn't want to push so hard that he lost his advantage.

"No," he said. "I won't do it. The egg remains."

Daniel looked down at the ground for a moment. "Is that your final decision?"

Alberto did not hesitate. "Yes."

Daniel, for one moment, *did* hesitate. His hand curled around the thing in his pocket.

Nikita's face was in front of his vision as clearly as if he had seen her only a moment ago. The blood draining from her body and paling her face. Her eyes fading until they were not eyes at all, except in a medical sense: totally empty of the thing that made them real and alive and a window to something deeper. The shutters closed.

"You've left me with no choice, then," Daniel said and pulled the gun he had in his pocket, pointing it at Alberto with his finger resting on the trigger.

Alberto raised an eyebrow. "You're not a violent man, Daniel."

"No," he agreed. "I never have been before. But if there is no way to convince you to do the right thing, then there's nothing to be gained from keeping you alive."

"And from ending my life?"

"Vengeance," Daniel said, the word not as strong as he wanted it to be, whipped away by a taste of wind across the rock. "For Nikita. A life for a life."

"And what will your life be worth, when you have taken one?" Alberto countered.

Daniel felt the ground move under him and knew it was just the way of his old teammate. AranaNegra had always been able to talk circles around all of them, convincing Maria that she was on board with his strategy even when it had been the exact opposite of the strategy she proposed.

He knew Alberto's ways. There was no way he could allow him to outmanoeuvre him yet again.

"I don't care," Daniel told him. "That's a problem I can deal with later."

"You aren't going to shoot me," Alberto said. "You haven't even taken the safety off."

"Thanks for the reminder." Daniel flicked the safety switch, disengaging the mechanism. He kept the gun pointed in Alberto's direction, never taking his eye off the other man. All that practice in the night when he couldn't sleep, when he was nervous about having to use it, had apparently paid off.

"Then do it," Alberto said. "Why haven't you shot me already, if you're going to do it?"

Daniel gritted his teeth. "Because you were my friend. Or, I thought you were, and that counts enough for me. Because I'm giving you a final chance. Because you could be a good person at last, and do something that makes a difference. It won't even matter if you don't. We'll just make sure that the Veritias system never goes live."

Alberto chuckled, baring chemically-whitened teeth. "It's already live," he said. "When I heard you were on the way to Gibraltar, I simply called my contacts in both governments and fast-tracked everything. If you look at your phone, you'll likely see a news alert about the release. People are setting up their accounts and connecting their money and their identities to it as we speak."

Daniel froze, panic and fear coursing through him in equal measure. *No*. It was done. The arm holding the gun wilted a little before he held it up again with renewed purpose.

"All the more reason to kill you. You won't be able to deploy the egg."

"I already have a timer in place that will detonate the egg if I am not there to stop it," Alberto said. His eyes were flat, almost dead, as if they were discussing nothing more than the weather. "I thought of everything, you see, Daniel. I calculated the right time to set it off and put everything in place. My *legacy* will continue, no matter what you do to me now."

If he killed Alberto, there would be no one to stop the egg from being deployed. If he called Sir Rory and the rest of the team to arrest Alberto, he wouldn't ever disarm it.

There were no paths forward that ended in a successful mission.

"Then I still have nothing to lose by shooting you," Daniel said. "Either way, the outcome is the same – but I get to avenge Nikita."

"Either way, the outcome is the same," Alberto parroted him. He had not raised his hands, not stepped back, not even flinched since Daniel pointed the gun into his face. "Kill me or not, I get what I want."

"This is what you want?" Daniel repeated incredulously. He gestured with his hands before remembering to keep the gun steady. "Really? To die for no reason other than stubbornness? You think this is what your parents would have wanted for you, your brother?"

At last, Alberto gave a sign: a twitch in the muscles of his face.

"You can't know what my parents or Hassan would want," he said. "No one can. They're dead."

"That's a cop-out. You know what they would have wanted."

Alberto's lower lip twisted, making his mouth into a sneer for just a moment. "They wanted me to make them proud. They can't be proud of anything, now."

Daniel took a deep, steadying breath. His arm was beginning to ache; he added the other, supporting his elbow with his left hand to keep it stable. "I'm giving you a way out of all this, Yash," he said quietly. "I wish you would take it."

"A way out?" Alberto shook his head. "You've given me nothing. I won't get what I want."

"You'll survive, and you'll have something better," Daniel argued. He was growing weary, the tension too much to carry. He wanted this to be over, but he wanted it to be over in the right way –

the way that caused the least loss of life. "The US will destroy itself – eat itself alive. You get to watch it happen. It's going to happen, sooner or later. And in the meantime, you get to help an entire continent get out from under crippling debt."

"The US government could simply reinstate the debt," Alberto said. "They might not catch absolutely all of it, but I'm sure someone out there has offline backups or printed documents. Expecting the debt to truly be forgiven would be naïve."

"Maybe not," Daniel said, seizing onto a renewed hope: if Alberto was arguing the points, that meant he was actually considering them. "Sir Rory works closely with the US Secretary of State. He's hosted a lot of other government officials in London, too. This is three per cent compared to one hundred per cent. I think they'll take that deal. Maybe even sign something to that effect. You could have it guaranteed. Sir Rory can make the moves to have that happen for you."

"And if they go back on their word?"

Daniel shrugged. "You're Spider," he said. "You just put another egg back in the code. Since when did not having access to something from the inside ever stop you from being able to hack it? Losing control of the project now wouldn't change anything if you really wanted to do it."

"And if I can't? If I have to spend another decade of my life building up a company just to get access to a program that can do this much damage? How will you pay me back the years I've lost?"

"I'll do it with you," Daniel said. His tone was serious. He meant what he was saying. "Me, Luna,

Underlord, Phantom – whoever else you have on your team."

Alberto's eyes went distant. "Underlord won't be joining us. On this or any other venture."

Daniel's mouth faltered for a moment, afraid to voice the question it wanted to ask. He cleared his throat and tried again. "Because he doesn't want to work with you again, or because he's…?"

Alberto didn't answer.

Daniel suddenly found he didn't want to know.

"Don't tell me," he said. "It doesn't change a thing. You can do good in this world, Alberto. Arana. Yash. You can live up to those names. You don't have to be Spider anymore. Or, rather – Spider doesn't have to be a force of vengeance. He can do good. He can build hope."

"You would work with me?" Alberto asked. "Even though I killed her? Even after everything I've done?"

Daniel looked into his own heart and answered honestly. "Yes. If you chose to do good, if you chose to help people instead of hurt them, yes. There's no one in the world that could do as much good as you. I'd stand by you." And let that be *Nikita's* legacy, he thought to himself: let her be the force that drove Daniel to do good as well.

There was a long pause, the longest Daniel had ever felt in his life. Alberto stared out, unmoving, his eyes tracing the line of the horizon. There was a weight in the air, the weight of history being made around their shoulders.

"I'll take the deal," he said. He turned and looked at Daniel, his expression as serious as the grave. "I'll deactivate the egg when I have the signed papers. I'm going into hiding, but I'll make it possible for you to reach me. Only you."

Daniel nodded, trying not to give away the sheer elation and relief he felt. He dropped the gun to his side, his arms aching with the effort of keeping it up. He didn't want to scare Alberto off by cheering or crying or approaching him closer, or any of the other ways he felt like reacting. He glanced towards the way they had come; he wanted to strike now while the iron was hot, before Alberto had a chance to change his mind.

"And, Daniel?" Alberto said, making Daniel hesitate and step back towards him. "After this is done, I'd like you to come and work for me, whichever way it all shakes out. I should have recruited you a long time ago. I underestimated you. I need someone who thinks the way you do, someone to keep me on the right side of history."

Daniel tilted his head, his throat too full of something for a moment to respond.

The answer should be no.

Alberto was responsible for Nikita's death, and probably, if he was honest with himself, Artem's too.

But Alberto was not just Spider. He contained multitudes. He was a brilliant businessman who had built the strongest digital security system in the world. He was Yash, that boy from Somalia who had lost everything, who just needed a family's love more than anything else. He was AranaNegra – Daniel's friend and caring teammate, who checked up on him when he didn't log in regularly, who called the best strategies, who saw things in such a purely strategic way that Daniel could believe he'd merely taken his eye off reality for a bit – seen the players as mere players and not real people with real lives to take.

"I'll think about it," he said, and walked away, back towards the cable car.

When he stepped in to travel back down the side of the Rock, he looked up one last time to see Alberto's silhouette against the sky, a miniature figure from so far away, his head still tilted up to watch the flight of birds overhead.

Chapter 45.

Cemetery

“The team have confirmed it.” Sir Rory put down the phone, beaming at Daniel in the close dimness of Spider’s abandoned lair. “The egg is gone. Someone hacked into the server remotely, deactivated an entire section of code, and then deleted it from the logs. They don’t know how, but after checking the digital vault, it appears *that* version has been cleansed as well.”

“It’s Spider,” Daniel said with a shrug. “I don’t think there’s such a thing as a vault, where he’s concerned.”

“It’s done,” Sir Rory said, finally sitting with a *whoomph* of relief on one of Spider’s white leather sofas. He was clearly exhausted; over two hours of tense negotiation, much of it shouted, across secure lines to both the UK and the US had taken it out of him.

But they’d done it.

Sir Rory had pitched it as his idea, a deal that only required the President to sign off on it before it could go into motion. In reality, Daniel knew Spider had already taken both the egg and the debt before anyone agreed to anything. Spider trusted Daniel, for better or for worse, and a deal was a deal.

Strangely, Daniel knew that out of any person in the world, Spider was the one he could trust the most when it came to a deal made.

"We've done it, my boy," Sir Rory said, full of exhausted joy. "There's a promotion in this. And don't you worry – I'll take you with me, as always. You've really proven yourself on this one."

Daniel nodded. "Thank you, sir," he said politely, not really sure he was emotionally or mentally connecting with the concept. So much had happened in such a short space of time. All he knew was that he wanted to go home and sleep in his own bed, and not have to look over his shoulder for cartel members or warehouse guards.

"Are you absolutely sure about this?" Sir Rory asked thoughtfully, his happiness wavering for a second. "You don't want any credit on the deal? I can still introduce you to some key players when we're back home."

Daniel shook his head. "No credit." He didn't want to meet key players. He didn't want to have his hand shaken by dignitaries or be offered roles in task forces or even watch all of them fawn over Sir Rory. He just wanted to go home and sleep.

Sir Rory beamed wider, a dazzling satisfaction that even managed to brighten the dingy room. With the curtains closed to prevent sniper shots and the view obscured, the house had lost some of its glamour.

"Well, I'd say you've earned a reward, Daniel," he said. "Just between you and me. What do you want?"

Daniel didn't have to think about it. "A break," he said and chose not to respond to the way Sir Rory's face fell.

***

At first, Daniel considered hanging around at the back, hiding amongst the gravestones and watching from under the canopy of rain, a mysterious mourner who never showed his face.

But the weather was uncharitably good, the sun shining, if weakly, from a clear sky; and when Daniel saw Nikita's father, a snapshot of her by half and grown to an age she would never reach, he found he had to go and stand with the others, after all.

He had never been introduced to her family. He didn't know the names of her friends. But Daniel sat through the service in the church in his black suit and then stood by the graveside, all the same, a handful of dirt that clung to his fingernails still after he'd thrown it down, joining a mound created by others.

So many people had loved her.

It was comforting, in a way, to know that he wasn't alone in that.

When the service was over and the coffin was lowered into the ground, Daniel didn't know what to do with himself. He lingered until it was only family left and it would have been awkward for them to talk to him, then backed off, taking up the position under a tree in the centre of the graveyard that he had been eyeing all along.

This was where Nikita would lie, forever. Her beautiful body gone to bone. Her brilliant mind turned to dust. It wasn't right.

It couldn't be real.

But it was.

Daniel memorised the position and placement of her gravestone, wanting to always be able to return here without losing her – not just in physical space, but in his mind. She deserved that. She deserved not to be forgotten.

He swallowed a dry mouth and tucked cold hands into his pockets, but didn't move until it began to grow dark. It was only then that he stirred, looked up at the sky, and began to walk.

First, and the first of many times, past her; then on, in the direction of his flat.

His sister, Rebecca, waited for him there, with a takeaway app and a bottle of wine and space for him to lay his head on her shoulder until he was ready to raise it again.

And then what?

It was a question he asked himself as he walked through London's twilight streets, preferring to take in the fresh air than shut himself up inside the Tube – far too coffin-like for what he had experienced today.

Sir Rory was keen to have him back in the office, to start him on the journey towards their next position – however lofty that might be.

But that was a path Daniel wasn't sure any longer he wanted to take.

Following Sir Rory had, ultimately, led him to the loss of Nikita, to danger, to a world he wasn't sure he wanted to belong to. How many ghosts would be haunting him if he continued on this road for ten years, twenty? How many were circling Sir Rory's head every time he tried to sleep at night?

And then there was the other option: Alberto, Yash, Spider – AranaNegra. Whatever name he would go by once he'd settled in his new life, away from the reach of those who would use evidence of the egg he'd planted in Veritian against him. Daniel had no doubt he was the kind of man who could make such charges go away, but it didn't matter. Too many agencies knew he was Spider, now. Alberto Lopez had to die and become someone else.

And he wanted Daniel alongside him.

Daniel, too, had considered that maybe it was the best place for him to be. Alberto had agreed to 'do good', but it was a vague promise – the kind that was easily broken. He'd appealed for Daniel to keep him on the straight and narrow, and the thought of the good that he could achieve at Alberto's side was dizzying. There was almost no corner of the globe he couldn't reach.

That kind of power needed checks and balances, and Alberto had none. There was no one to tell him to stop – like Sofia, anyone who knew who he really was grew too afraid to speak up. But not Daniel. He'd faced Alberto once and won. He felt confident he could do it again.

Still, it would be dangerous, not to mention covert. And it would require him to throw away his entire life, to give up everything he'd worked so hard for.

If he was ever going to make the move, now was the time – with no family of his own holding him back, no cushy high-up government job to tempt him further into staying.

But did he want to live that life, either? Outside of the law, always paranoid, dealing with shady characters, always trying to be the good spark in what could be an otherwise dark atmosphere?

He had the chance to serve at the right hand of two powerful men: one on the side of the law, and one against it.

Or was there a third option, a path where he was his own man and no one else's?

At his apartment building, he stopped to get his keys out of his pocket and find the fob that would let him past the electronic entry pad. A caw caught his attention, drawing his eyes up. A raven was sitting on the corner of his building, tilting its head to fix him with a steely gaze down the length of its grey-black beak.

Daniel unlocked the door and stepped inside, the weight of the day hanging on his mind like wet clothing, threatening to drag his head under the waves.

ABOUT THE AUTHOR

After thirty-five years in advertising, working at agencies including J. Walter Thompson and Havas, Pedro is now Executive Chairman of Bicycle London. Born in Spain to a Spanish mother and raised in South East London, he regularly travels between Gibraltar, Bilbao, and Estepona - locations that feature prominently in his debut thriller.

His inspiration for writing came from an unlikely source: boredom on a sun lounger in Torreguadiaro, combined with deep reflection on the hardships faced by those attempting to cross the Strait of Gibraltar. Having witnessed a major European cryptocurrency collapse first-hand and worked with Ukrainian gaming companies, he drew on these experiences to craft the digital conspiracy at the heart of his novel.

A trustee of Demelza Hospice and member of the London Writers' Forum, Pedro is passionate about proving that dyslexics who struggled with English can write compelling fiction. He credits Paul Theroux with inspiring his love of reading during his late teens on the train to Charing Cross, which eventually led to his own storytelling.

When not writing or running his agency, he enjoys travelling and photography. He attended London Business School at forty-five to reignite his creativity, proving it's never too late to learn something new - including, apparently, novel writing.

This is his first novel.

Printed in Dunstable, United Kingdom

65240412R00190